Saxon Slaughter

**Book 6 in the Wolf Brethren Series
By
Griff Hosker**

Saxon Slaughter

Published by Sword Books Ltd 2014
Copyright © Griff Hosker
The author has asserted their moral right under the Copyright, Designs and Patents Act, 1988, to be identified as the author of this work. All Rights reserved. No part of this publication may be reproduced, copied, stored in a retrieval system, or transmitted, in any form or by any means, without the prior written consent of the copyright holder, nor be otherwise circulated in any form of binding or cover other than that in which it is published and without a similar condition being imposed on the subsequent purchaser.
A CIP catalogue record for this title is available from the British Library.

Contents

Saxon Slaughter	1
Chapter 1	4
Chapter 2	15
Chapter 3	31
Chapter 4	44
Chapter 5	57
Chapter 6	68
Chapter 7	82
Chapter 8	94
Chapter 9	107
Chapter 10	114
Chapter 11	135
Chapter 12	148
Chapter 13	163
Chapter 14	173
Chapter 15	183
Chapter 16	190
Chapter 17	197
Chapter 18	205
Glossary	212
Historical note	215

Chapter 1

Wyddfa 617

Myrddyn and I visited the secret cave beneath Wyddfa's peak each Midsummer solstice. It had been an annual event since we came to the land of Cymri from the last British Kingdom of Rheged. We both dreamed in its dark halls with our torch's lights reflecting and dancing like fairies on the water which lay within. Sometimes the spirit of my mother came to speak with me and to advise me although lately, it had been the spirit of my sword, Saxon Slayer, which had done so. Myrddyn had told me that the sword had more time to talk since we had had peace. Myrddyn was closer to the spirit world than I was. I was a warrior.

There had been no major war for the past four years since King Iago Ap Beli had been killed in battle and his son, Cadfan Ap Iago had ascended the throne. The young king had sought sanctuary with me and had served with my warriors for some years. He was now a fine warrior and the best king his people had had for many years. The Saxons had been given a bloody nose but they now squatted at the Roman fort called Deva which they had now renamed Caestre. And it was true we had had peace. My warriors kept that peace with their shields and swords. My mounted men rode in plain sight and armed to warn the Saxons of Mercia and Northumbria that we would tolerate neither invasion nor attack. It was not cheap to maintain such men and weapons but the price was worth the peace as the land around the Holy Island of Mona prospered. We had a healthy trade with other parts of the world and the dispossessed of Rheged still came, in dribs and drabs to settle and farm on the lands I controlled.

Myrddyn had told me that Wyddfa smiled upon us for we kept the mountain safe and that was why the crops were so successful and why we had so many fine children born. It was true that we had never had such bounty before and I had never had four years of peace in the last forty years of my life. Yet lately I had been worried and I had looked forward to my visit to the cave even more than usual. We had, in the past, brought my former squire, Lann Aelle and my son Hogan. Both had been touched by the magic in the cave but this year I wanted the power of the mountain to work just for the two of us. I needed to know if the peace would last and I hoped for a glimpse of my future. Was I to be granted a peaceful old age?

We had, as usual, eaten and watched the firelight dancing on the ceiling of the cave. The followers of the White Christ liked, I am told, to build churches with high ceilings to show the majesty of their God. I had seen one such church when I visited Constantinopolis. For me, this cave was more magnificent. This was a natural church carved from the earth and it had more beauty than any man-made edifice. After we had eaten we lay in companionable silence watching the flames flicker from the water to the ceiling and off the sparkling walls. It felt as though the very rocks themselves were talking with us. I felt real peace. And then we slept.

The waters sparkled and then began to bubble. A grey figure slid from beneath the waters and began to swirl like morning mist in the valley bottoms. It began to wrap around me and lift me. I felt safe and comfortable as I was lifted up. The night sky was clear and filled with a myriad of stars. Beneath me, the land seemed, suddenly, further away. A voice spoke in my head and it was the voice of my mother. "This is the land that was Britannia and it is your land. Your work is not yet done. There are people who pray for your coming. There are people who need your coming. There are people who are dying while they wait. You must go back. The future is in the past. The past will have no future without you. Watch for a sign from the north. It will come and you must act. Trust your son. He is the future. He is Britannia." And then I fell; I found I was spinning and turning. I was dropping to the earth and I tried to scream but no sound came. I saw the waters of the cave beneath me and as they swallowed me up all went black.

"Wake Warlord. It is over."

Myrddyn stood over me. Myrddyn was a wizard and my adviser. He had walked the length of the land to serve me many years ago and was the only man, save my son, that I truly trusted. He held out his hand and I took it to rise. The light of the morning spilt like melted butter across the cave and made it somehow, warmer. The cave in daylight seemed like a sleeping giant as though it worked its magic while we slept.

"She came again."

"I know and she visited me." Myrddyn usually dreamed my dream. He always knew what was in my thoughts.

"She is becoming more like you on each visit Myrddyn. She talks in riddles."

He nodded, "And that is how it should be. You are now older and wiser than when she first visited you. You know how to use your mind as well as your sword. You will know what to do when the time comes."

"But she said nothing of peace."

"Perhaps that is because the time for peace is not yet here."

We exited the cave and found our horses waiting where we had left them. Even though we were far from any settlement we had not feared attack. We had brought no guards. Here, in the heart of the land, I ruled I was safe and Wyddfa would watch over me.

We mounted and began to make our way down the mountain to my fortress at its foot. "She told you what she told me?"

"I do not know Lord Lann."

I flashed him an angry glance. I hated lies and I hated being made a fool of. Myrddyn knew what I had dreamed. "Do not toy with me, wizard. Speak plainly. I grow tired of your riddles."

He smiled benignly. He never let my words get beneath his skin. His skin seemed like armour and protected him. He knew many things. Some of the things he knew were impossible and yet he knew them. It was said he could read minds but he maintained he merely used his mind as a weapon.

He shrugged, "I dream some of the things that you do Lord Lann but it is your mother who comes to us. I know that she wishes you to carry on the fight against the Saxons. I know that she wishes you to go back to Rheged but," he spread his arms, "I cannot see how we would do that yet. Perhaps there is something we do not know. I am intrigued by this messenger. The messenger may reveal the future."

"Perhaps." I had just had it confirmed that my wizard knew all that I knew.

We left the forest and saw the sea and the jewel that was Mona glistening ahead of us. We had lived at Caer Gybi for the first years of our time in this land but the raids of the Hibernians which had nearly ended the life of my wife and young children had made me move them here, to the most protected part of my land. Here Prince Pasgen, the last son of the king of Rheged had built a fort and, across the Narrows, I had built another. We had moved to the mainland as I could protect my land and my family better than on the edge of Britain where pirates and Saxons could raid.

Saxon Slaughter

The present King of Gwynedd was Cadfan. He had come to me as a young man when his father turned against him. I had trained him along with my son and we had helped him to defeat his father and gain his throne. He now ruled all the lands to the east of us as far as Mercia. He and the other kings of Cymri, Ceredigion and Dyfed acknowledged me as Warlord. Many of my people had wished me to take the title of king but that I would never do. I had been given my title by King Urien, the last king of Rheged and by the Byzantine Emperor. I needed no other, Warlord of Rheged sufficed.

"So wizard, what do you advise?"

He looked surprised at the question. He enjoyed being enigmatic. It made others fear him but I knew him better than any living man. "Advise? Do nothing. We have had no sign yet either from the north or any other direction. When the spirits speak they speak from another world not bound by our concept of time and place. The messenger may come today or next year. We just have to watch and wait."

I laughed, "You are becoming like Brother Oswald." Brother Oswald was a priest of the White Christ but he saw to the administration of my land and organised my armies. He was always speaking of mystical events. "You use these words to baffle the foolish. I am not weak-minded. I asked for advice, now give it to me."

Sometimes Myrddyn was alike a naughty child; he needed a good shaking.

He sighed, "In that case, I will give it to you. The Saxons to the east can be contained by King Cadfan; in fact, it will do him good to fight them without you as a crutch." I flashed another angry look at him. I did not like being called a crutch. He gave a half apologetic smile and continued, "To the north... well we have heard little for the last four years although our ships say that they have begun to colonise the island of Manau to the north." He shrugged, "Perhaps that is the sign but I do not think it is. My advice to you is to prepare to return to Rheged." He saw my face becoming angry and he held a hand up. "That is not as simplistic as you take it to mean. If you are not weak-minded, as you say, then you will know that you cannot leave your home and your people undefended. You will have to take a smaller army but one which can defeat the Saxons when they are found. Do you have such an army?"

I was silent for a moment. I was annoyed because he was right. Infuriatingly, he was nearly always right. We had warriors who could defend my forts and castles and keep my people safe but if we took them all north then the Saxons would flood in like a spring tide. "That is good, Myrddyn. You have advised me. I will judge if it is good advice later."

As we descended the lower slopes to the coastal road I had constructed I began to mentally plan what I would need to do. Despite my words with Myrddyn, I was looking forward to action again. After the last battle when I had lost some of my old friends and many comrades I was tired of fighting and the action which accompanied it. I yearned for peace and time with my family. I had had that peace for four years and seen Nanna, my daughter, grow into a precocious young woman who was forever sulky and Gawan, my younger son, become an active and boisterous boy who was close to manhood. Many his age and younger served me as despatch riders and slingers. I had spent the last three years listening to my wife, Myfanwy, complain about the home we had and the size of the rooms. Now I yearned for a different kind of peace; peace in the world of men. And, to be truthful, I craved action again.

I was a warrior. I had been a warrior since before I could shave. I had been killing Saxons for almost forty years and it was too late to stop now. I knew that my dream of a Britannia without Saxons was just that, a dream, but I clung to it. I had never been defeated by the Saxons and that kept me believing that one day the island would be free of the invidious Saxons.

I heard the sea to my left and that helped my thought process; it was a reassuring sound. It always calmed me. I had grown up far from the sea and it was one of the attractions of the land in which I now lived. The protection of the waters was mirrored by the protection of the mountain and the high passes. This was as safe a place to bring up a family as anywhere.

I was lucky in that I had great warriors and leaders close to me. My son Hogan and my former squire, Pol, had both studied military strategy in the court of the Byzantine Emperor. Their men were dressed and armed like the Cataphractoi of the Emperor's army. The Emperor had, in fact, supplied many of the shirts the men now wore. The equites or knights as they were sometimes called were few in number but had an effect on the battlefield way beyond their numbers. Lann Aelle, my nephew had also been my squire and he, too, had grown into a great leader. They were family. Prince Pasgen who was the last son of King Urien also commanded mounted and armoured horsemen but they merely had mail, swords and shields. Captain Tuanthal had been with me a long time and had been a young scout with me in Rheged. He led the rest of my horsemen. The Saxons did not use horses and we used that to our advantage. Aedh was the leader of my scouts and, although there were less than twenty of them, they were amongst the most valuable men in my army for they were our eyes and ears. I have lost count of the times they had saved me with their efforts. Finally, there was Daffydd ap Miach who led my archers. The Saxons were using more of them but none could compare with the bowmen of Daffydd.

We also had great warriors who could fight in a shield wall and behind wooden walls but I would not be taking them on my journey north. They would slow us down and weaken our defences at home. I glanced again at the sea and the island of Mona beyond. We had four ships and we could take an army north but we would be overcrowded. It was too risky and, besides, they brought great trade to us and therein lay our fortune. We were rich because we traded with other nations and we kept what we traded for our traders were also ships of war. The Hibernian pirates no long preyed on the ships of the Wolf Warrior. They had learned that we bit back!

We had improved my fort over the years. The wooden towers were now protected by cow hides and we had strengthened our walls with earthen walls protecting the bottom. The gatehouses were complex affairs and could not be negotiated easily but our greatest strength lay in the weapons of the Romans that we used. The Saxons still called us Romans and used the term as an insult. We took it as a compliment. We had machines which fired bolts and machines which hurled stones or fire, whatever we chose. Brother Oswald and Myrddyn studied the old Roman books for the designs and had improved upon them. Much of our trade with Byzantium was to acquire those pieces of machinery which we could not manufacture ourselves. We even had the secret of Greek Fire and that weapon frightened all who had to suffer its devastating effect.

I saw the signals from the towers and smiled to myself. The guards would be preparing Hogan Lann, my son; they would warn him of my imminent arrival. Perhaps I was a little strict with them all but it had kept us safe since I had fled Castle Perilous following the death of King Urien. The spirit of my mother was right; the job was not done and I would finish that job. That would be my legacy for the generations of Britons who followed me.

They saluted us as we rode through the gate and twisted right to reach the second. "So, Warlord, have you decided upon your plan yet?"

Saxon Slaughter

I laughed; I could see why people thought that Myrddyn could read minds. I knew his trick now; he knew people and could read people. Since I had spotted that trick I had begun to use it myself. I watched the way people looked and how they spoke. My people thought that I was becoming a wizard too. I did not put them straight. The mystery helped my reputation and I had learned that my reputation could be worth a hundred men on a battlefield.

We had enlarged the fortress by building a wall to reach from mountain to sea. It provided a barrier which would have to be reduced by war and it created a huge living space within. We had built barracks, halls and stables. We were very comfortable. They were not the halls we had used in the north or on Mona but had been built like the palaces of Rome with many different rooms in them. They all shared the same roof. In this way, my son and Prince Pasgen could have their own families separate from the men they commanded and yet still be close enough to participate in the training and exercises. The result was we never stopped working at being warriors. Even though we had not had a major battle for four years we had not lost that edge we once had used so effectively on the battlefield. Men were sent to the frontier forts to garrison them and raid Saxon lands. We went, not as they did, for slaves. We went to keep them under control and to take their weapons. Our blacksmiths could turn their crudely made weapons into magnificent tools of war. It strengthened us and weakened them.

There were a large number of men gathered in the main yard and I saw a warrior with a halter around his neck. I frowned. This was not the way we did things in my fortress. I rode up and they all bowed. "What is going on here?"

"My lord, we have captured a deserter. Prince Pasgen has ordered him thrown into the cellar until he decides what to do with him."

I did not like the sound of that. "In my fortress, I make those decisions. Did this man serve here?" The guard began to answer and I snapped at him. "He can speak for himself can he not?"

The guard quailed. I was not a man to be crossed, "Yes Warlord."

He took the halter from the man who fell to his knees. "My lord, my name is Kay and I served as a horseman in Rheged. I followed Prince Pasgen here and I became an equite. I fought for you on many occasions. I was a loyal and happy warrior but a trader who came to Caer Gybi last year told me that my brother and his family still lived in Rheged. I begged Prince Pasgen for permission to return home and find the truth but he refused. He said Rheged was now Saxon. It ate me up inside, Lord Lann, and I did desert but I have returned and I bring a message from the north."

My mouth almost fell open and I looked at Myrddyn who, true to his character, did not look at all surprised. He held his arms open and smiled knowingly at me. Had he known the messenger was already here as we travelled back from the mountain? He would never tell me. He enjoyed his secrets and his power.

"Give this man his clothes back and bring him to my hall." I glared at the two guards, "And treat him with respect. He is still a warrior of Rheged."

As they took him away I saw my son and Pol approaching. They had their bows with them and looked to have been hunting. They had heard the latter part of the conversation. "Trouble Warlord?"

"Not as such. If you please, bring all of my captains to the main hall."

Hogan knew better than to question me in public and he bowed and said, "It will be done."

I turned to Myrddyn. "You had better bring Oswald."

I dismounted and gave the reins of my horse to the stable boy who waited patiently. I strode towards my quarters. I would have time to speak with my wife and, if I was late, it would do them no harm to cool their heels and wonder why I had summoned them.

Gawan erupted from his room when he heard my boots on the floor. "Father, you are back! When can we practise with our swords?"

I smiled at the ball of energy as he threw himself into my arms. "First I will see my captains and then we will practise."

He looked disappointed, "Can I not come to watch?"

"When you learn to listen and not speak then I will allow you to attend." I held him at arm's length. "Do you think that you can do this now?"

I had taught all of my children the value of honesty and he shook his head. "But one day..."

"Aye, and one day you shall attend. Now, where is your mother?"

"Here, my husband."

Myfanwy had grown older, as we all had, but she had lost none of her beauty. She had fewer lines than the other women her age and her hair was not riven with white. I embraced her. "You look beautiful as ever."

"Get away you old flatterer." Her smile belied her words.

"I have to speak with my captains but it will not take long."

My wife knew me well and she looked at me carefully. "You dreamed?"

I nodded, "The spirit of Wyddfa came to me."

She smiled as she led Gawan away. She knew that the spirit was my dead mother. We had no secrets from each other. I removed my cloak but left Saxon Slayer, my sword on my belt. It was the unifying force at my table. Each man had sworn their allegiance on it and that was as sacred as the cross of the White Christ which Oswald kept about his neck.

My hall had a large oval table within it. It was a copy of the one I had on Mona. It could seat thirty and all could see each other. I had learned when in Constantinopolis, that men would conceal their thoughts and feelings. They kept secrets and I wanted nowhere for men to hide in my hall. I wanted all of us to see each other's faces and read the words in their eyes. I had detected traitors before by looking into our faces.

They were all seated around the table when I entered. I was no king and none stood when they saw me. Within this room, we were all equals. Once we went to war, then I was Warlord once more but here any could give his opinion.

Kay stood looking forlorn in the corner, still with his guard. Pasgen looked angry and sullen. I had known him since he was a child and I had helped to train him. I recognised that look. I also knew how to snap him back into the fold. Brother Oswald had brought pen and parchment as he always did. He kept a record of what was said. Brother Oswald had learned this from King Urien's priest, Brother Osric. We still used Osric's writings to guide us.

"Kay, come and take a seat. You guards can go."

Prince Pasgen stood and banged the table, "Warlord! I protest! This man is a deserter and should be flogged at the very least."

"Prince Pasgen, if you bang my table and shout like that again I am afraid it will be you who will be flogged." My calm quiet words had a threat within them. He sat down and reddened. I flashed a look at Myrddyn and Oswald who had shared a smile. "Although no man, as far as I know, has ever been flogged here; I think this would be a bad time to start such a practice." Many of my captains nodded their agreement.

Kay came forward and sat opposite me. There was no one for a number of seats on either side of him. I looked at the faces before me. There were just eight captains present. The rest were either on the border, in the forts, or at Caer Gybi. My brothers Raibeart and Aelle ruled Mona in my absence and I was confident that they could defend it against any attacker. They would not be needed for this venture.

"Kay, tell us your story." I turned to Pasgen who was seated just four seats from me. "And I would appreciate no interruptions until he has finished." I saw the confusion on some of the faces, not Hogan's, but some of the others. "Kay here, deserted because he received a message from Rheged that his brother was still alive but was refused permission to seek him out. He has now returned from the north with news which will be of interest to all of us. I will talk about the message later on. Pray, speak."

The mention of Rheged had made them all sit up and take notice.

"I sailed on a trader as far as Alt Cult where the Saxons had been thrown back. I had a little money and I bought a horse and travelled the back roads and secret ways into Rheged. I expected to see it populated by Saxons but I found very few and they were easy to avoid. They still squat in Carvetiorum but there are none in the land of the lakes and Lord Aelle's fortress has been burned to the ground. Nothing of it remains. I tell you this because I expected that they would have made it a fortress but they did not. I found my brother and his family. They were living close to the long lake which lies by the mountain called the Old Man. They have a good living but each year the Saxons come and take all that they have stored for the winter. Many die then. I travelled over the whole of Rheged and found the same story. These Saxons let the folk of Rheged do all the work and then they steal what they have done. They come each harvest time and take whatever they choose for there is no one to oppose them. Their girls are taken as slaves to work in their halls. Anyone who shows any sign of resisting is killed."

He paused and I signalled the servant who hovered nearby to give him a drink. He drank gratefully.

"I travelled as far as The Dunum and then to the Roman fort of Eboracum and found the same story. I crossed the mountain and arrived back here. I saw no Saxon armies on my journey but there were some at Eboracum and Mamucium. The message I bring back is simply this. Will the Warlord come and free his people?"

"Thank you, Kay."

I sat back and waited. The room erupted in many conversations. Oswald and Myrddyn sat quietly listening and Prince Pasgen no long fumed but looked embarrassed.

Saxon Slaughter

Eventually, the voices stilled and Hogan Lann said, "Warlord, you said that you would speak of this message from the north. Did you know of the message before you saw Kay?"

I was proud of Hogan Lann; he was my son in every way. I stood. "As you know Myrddyn and I were in the cave of Wyddfa for the solstice and I dreamed. The spirit of Wyddfa told me to heed the message from the north and said that my people needed me."

That brought smiles to their faces. I turned to Prince Pasgen. "Forgive me for my blunt words before, Prince Pasgen. Do you still wish to punish this man who risked his life to bring the message from our people back to us?"

Silence descended on the table and all eyes were on Prince Pasgen. He was amongst friends. All of these men had stood shoulder to shoulder with him in battles and he was the last King of Rheged. My words had given him a way out and I prayed that he took it and saved face.

"Warlord, forgive me. I acted and spoke hastily and I can now see that I should have allowed Kay to return home last year. My father made you Warlord and each day I thank him for that wise decision." He shook his head. "Every time I think that I can be as you are I come up short. I still have much to learn."

"Good and there is nothing to forgive. We are men and we have tempers. Better to let it out than let it fester. Now to business. Brother Oswald will you summon my council to meet me here in two days' time." He nodded. "Kay, would you like to rejoin Prince Pasgen's men or another company?"

There was silence again, "Prince Pasgen if he will have me."

The Prince strode over to him and embraced him. "Of course."

As the meeting broke up Myrddyn said, quietly, "You become more Byzantine each day."

I did not rise to the bait, "Perhaps I merely become more like a wizard each day although they are much the same thing anyway."

Chapter 2

While we waited for my captains and brothers to arrive I sent Aedh with Daffydd to gather as many of the hill ponies as they could. I wanted every man we took north to be mounted. I had no doubt that I would take my army north. No matter what my council said the idea had been planted in my head and nothing would shift it. It made perfect sense and the time was right. My horsemen and archers would never be better than they were at this moment. They were fit, well trained and eager to fight.

I went to the stables. I had three horses and I would only be taking one. I had three to choose: Nightstar was the biggest and the bravest warhorse I had. He was jet black with a white star blazoned on his forehead. He was fearless in battle. Then there was Silver Spirit; she was pure white and smaller than Nightstar. She moved smoothly and was quieter than any horse I had ever owned. Finally, there was Mona; she was gold in colour with an almost blond mane and two white socks. I had had her the longest and she was old. Not as big as Nightstar neither was she as swift as Silver Spirit but she had a heart bigger than any of my other horses. She would carry on to her last breath. I think I had decided to take her. First I needed to find out the condition of all my horses.

As I was talking with the stable captain, Hogan Lann came in. He knew me as well as any man save Myrddyn. I sent the stable captain away so that we could talk.

"Why do we go north, Warlord?"

"I have not heard the council's views yet."

He laughed, "As if that would make any difference at all. We are going north then?"

"And you think it is a bad thing?"

"I did not say that. I am merely trying to find out your reasoning. Here you keep the people of this land safe but in Rheged….are you doing this to make Prince Pasgen king?"

I had not thought of that. "I don't know. Would he want to be king?"

"You are the only man I know, save Myrddyn who would not be king so I think we can safely say that he would be king."

"That may not be a bad thing."

"True but why do you need to go?"

I narrowed my eyes; King Iago had feared his son might usurp his power and therefore had him imprisoned. Had I reason to fear my son? It was as though I had suddenly changed to become a monster. How could I even suspect my son of that kind of disloyalty?

"If you were Warlord what would you do?"

"Oh, I would go in a heartbeat." I had not expected such open frankness and I was taken aback. "My men and I are the best-trained warriors in this whole land and for four years we have chased bandits and sheep stealers. Our squires have had no opportunity to become equites. I would go now. I would go with just my men."

"So you would lead the army and leave me at home?"

He shuffled his feet. "Who else would you leave at home to guard your family and people?"

"My brothers."

"Oh." He seemed surprised at that. He nodded. "That makes sense."

"Why do you not wish me to go?" I held up my hand. "Let us be honest with each other, my son. I can read beneath your words that you do not wish me to go but I cannot read the reason."

"You are a symbol of our people. The army which goes north will be pitifully small and all of us will have a greater chance of dying. Our land can live without me and Pol, even Pasgen but it cannot live without you. You are the very heart and soul of this land." He pointed to Wyddfa. "You are like the mountain."

I was touched. "And that is the reason why I must go. My presence will bring forth all those old warriors and sons of old warriors who remember my name. I was never defeated and they will remember that. I spoke today after the meeting had dispersed with Kay and he told me the legends surrounding my name. The people say that I sleep under the mountains waiting to be called and save Rheged. Others believe that I passed over with King Urien and was sent back as a spirit of Rheged. The legends are just stories but they show that the people want me. Those legends mean that we can go there with small numbers and have a chance."

He put his arms around me. "Then I am convinced. You shall lead us and we will win."

"And your fears for Prince Pasgen?"

"I am not sure he would make a good king."

I nodded. "We will cross that bridge when we come to it. He may not be his brother either." His brother had sided with the Saxons against us.

He had been killed but the taste was still bitter in the mouths of many a Rheged warrior.

My brothers and my other captains all arrived well before the appointed time. They knew that I only called such council meetings when it was an important matter. Lann Aelle rarely saw his father; there was no discord, in fact, they were as close as Hogan Lann and I were, but Lann Aelle led his men well and was needed by them. They were often on patrol. I was pleased to see them greet each other so warmly. Raibeart and his son, Morcar, were also there. I had never taken to Morcar. That was probably because he was not a warrior like my son. He was pleasant enough but he enjoyed the comfortable life of a young noble who hunted and wenched. When Hogan Lann became Warlord he would have that particular problem to deal with.

The table was almost filled when they all took their places. The Bishop of St. Asaph was also present. I had known the saint when he had been bishop of the monastery and the monks were friends of ours. They helped us and we protected them. It was a symbiotic relationship. The bishop had learned that most of my men were not for conversion. We followed the old gods and the old ways. They were happy that we were moderate men and could be trusted.

I stood and the table went silent. I told them all Kay's story and of my dream. I hid my smile as the Bishop of St.Asaph shifted uncomfortably in his seat. If you had a profound dream then it should come from the White Christ or his mother, not a woman of Rheged who may have been a witch of some kind.

"I will take your advice now but you should know that I am of a mind to travel north." I noticed Hogan Lann and many of my other captains nodding. I knew that they were ready for war.

Raibeart stood, "We have had peace for four years now, brother. Do you deem it wise to stir up the hornets that have been quiet for the past four years?"

I was reading men even as they sat. Raibeart only used the term brother when he was trying to make me do something. He normally called me Warlord as they all did. It was an honourable title and a term of respect.

I said nothing but looked around the room. Aelle, my younger brother was before me and I caught his eye. He was a reflective and clever little brother. When he had lost his arm in King Urien's wars he had changed from a warrior to a planner; there was none better.

"What of King Cadfan? Would he be part of the quest?"

Again I merely nodded and waited for more comments. Finally, the bishop stood. "I feel that I agree with Lord Raibeart. The Saxons have been quiet of late and many of them are converting to Christianity."

The bishop should have known better. His call for leniency on religious grounds would fall on deaf ears. I had heard enough. I stood. "The fact that the captains have said nothing I take as approval." They all banged the table and said 'Aye', as one.

I held my hands out to silence them. I knew what they would say. "As for those who caution me," I looked at Aelle, "I will visit King Cadfan on the morrow. I would not expect him to travel with me and risk the men of Gwynedd." I looked at Raibeart, "It is not his people he is saving. And I would not leave if I thought that King Cadfan could not protect the Mercian border." Aelle nodded, satisfied. He would have made a great diplomat and I always felt it sad that he had not visited Constantinopolis. He would have gained even more than Myrddyn or I had.

"If the Saxons are followers of the White Christ then they will turn the other cheek and we will not have to fight them will we?" I knew that mocking the bishop was not honourable but I had had this argument over the years with Brother Oswald. The passive nature of the religion did not sit well with the warrior code.

"Finally, brother, why should we disturb the hornet's nest? Because, while those hornets leave us alone, they plague our people; the ones we deserted." I saw many of those around the table shift in their seats when I used the word deserted. "I swore an oath to the King of Rheged to be Warlord and protect the people of Rheged. Until Kay returned I thought that they had all perished. Now I know the truth and I tell you this, I would go alone to fulfil the oath I swore. I am no oath breaker."

There was a hubbub as voices were raised. Myrddyn stood next to me and said, quietly in my ear, "A masterly speech Warlord, you have learned well."

"Thank you Myrddyn although it gave me no pleasure to embarrass the bishop and my brother."

"You did not, you spoke the truth, and that is sometimes uncomfortable for people to hear."

I spoke privately with Raibeart and Aelle before I left to visit King Cadfan. Raibeart was disappointed in himself. I could see it in his face and hear it in his words. "I did not mean to challenge you. I would follow you to the edge of the world if you asked and you know that."

"I know and I did not take it as a challenge. I realise that you and Aelle had shunned the world of war and taken the road to peace. That is good. My people need leaders like you and one day they will no longer need a man of war to lead them. Until that day I must defend all the people who lived on this island before the Saxons came to steal what is ours."

Aelle, although the youngest, was in many ways the wisest of the three of us. "So brother, will you leave Hogan in your stead?"

"No Aelle, I have no need to. I have two brothers who can rule and protect my land and my home just as well as I can."

Raibeart seemed taken aback. "You would leave us in command?"

"You will have no need of war craft for each of my forts has a capable captain who will be more than able to defend our borders. I need men of vision who can provide food for our people and continue our trade with the far off places."

They both seemed happy about that. "When will you leave?"

"If we are to make gains before winter it will be in the next week or so. I do not intend to strip my forts of men. I will only be taking my horsemen and my archers. We will be mounted."

"But the Saxons are like the fleas on a dog. They have many warbands." Raibeart always looked on the pot as half empty rather than half full. He always saw the problems whereas I sought a solution.

I smiled, "And you think I do not know that? Do not worry Raibeart, I intend to return. I would ask that you visit my home as often as you can to give reassurance to, not only my family but Hogan's and Pasgen's. A man fights better knowing that his family is safe."

"I promise that we will do so."

I left the next morning for Cadfan's home at Wrecsam. I took just Aedh with me. The rest of my captains were busily preparing their men for the arduous journey ahead. I sent word that I wished to see Daffydd ap Gwynfor when I returned. I wanted to put in place a plan in case of disaster. The others might believe in my invincibility but I was a realist.

Cadfan had tried to build an army such as mine but he did not have the horsemen. My horsemen had been trained by the best in Rheged and we were like the old Roman army; those skills were passed on. Instead, he had made an army of spearmen and archers. He was content to hold the Mercians at bay. When he heard of internal strife inside Mercia then he took a little more of their territory and his forts, modelled on mine, withstood the attacks of the Saxons.

I needed no escort, as I rode up the Clwyd Valley. My forts guarded both ends and we had watchtowers along the Dee. Once I was in Gwynedd then my name alone was protection enough. King Cadfan's people had grown safe and prospered under my protection. I rode Silver Spirit that day. In my mind, I had decided to take Mona with me on the arduous journey north. Until then she could rest.

It was pleasant riding with Aedh. He had served me first as a slinger before progressing to captain of scouts. He chattered away as he always did. "When I look at this land Warlord, it seems like home and yet we were born many leagues hence. Will we even remember Rheged when we return?"

"You never forget your home Aedh." I patted Silver Spirit. "It is the same as it is with horses. I have not ridden Spirit here for many months but with a few steps, we are at one again. It will be the same with Rheged." I examined his face keenly. "You are worried that, as a scout, you might let me down."

His jaw dropped. "Warlord, are you becoming a wizard? How did you know the thoughts that were in my head?"

"I listened to the words you did not say and I know you well Aedh. Fear not. You will not let me down and you will soon remember the land you last saw as a child."

Wrecsam's defences had been improved since Iago's time and double ditches and watchtowers had been added all around it. King Cadfan had also taken a leaf out of my book and cleared the land to effective bow range. We were seen from a long distance away. My horse and my wolf banner were well known and King Cadfan's personal bodyguards rode out to meet us. He had ten bodyguards who rode as well as he did. Dai, his chief captain, was well known to me and it was he who rode at the head of the column and greeted us with a smile.

"What brings the Warlord to visit with us this day? "Hunting perhaps?"

"I would like nothing better than to go hunting with you Dai but I come to speak with your king."

"He is in the fort practising swordsmanship with Cadwallon."

Cadwallon was his son and was of an age with Gawan. "He is ready to train to be a warrior then?"

"He is, but I think that the king would keep him by him for a little longer. They are very close."

Saxon Slaughter

The guards at the gate saluted us and Dai ordered his men to care for our horses. "Come, I will lead you to the king." There was less mail and armour amongst Cadfan's men but they were doughty warriors and were well capable of holding their own against the Saxons. The king and Dai had moulded them into an effective army.

"How are the Mercians these days?"

"They occasionally flex their muscles and bring a warband to our forts but they have bled enough on our walls to know that they cannot remove us from our land."

"Good. That eases my mind."

Dai was a bright young man. I had fought alongside him and knew that he was not only brave but quick thinking too. "You are planning something then?"

I gave him what I hoped was an enigmatic smile. "If you are with us when I speak with the king then you will find out."

We went to the courtyard first where Cadfan and Cadwallon had wooden swords and were sparring. As soon as Cadwallon saw me he turned and ran to me, squealing his joy, "Warlord! Are you here to play?"

Aedh and Dai laughed at that. I normally came with Gawan and the two boys and I would play and rough house. "No, not today my little man. Are you ready to stand in my shield wall yet?"

His face became serious. "My father says that when I can beat him with a wooden sword then he will give me a real one and then Warlord, I will fight for you." I thought that if this were Gawan then I would have given him a real sword already. I was becoming a hypocrite. Gawan was the same age and I had yet to give him a real sword. We also only used wooden ones. I resolved to give him a real sword when we returned home.

Cadfan strode up to grasp my hand, "Good to see you, Warlord. Dai, take him to his mother and then meet us in my hall."

Looking disappointed Cadwallon followed Dai and walked off shouting, "I will see you later Warlord and show you how good a warrior I am."

"He is growing fast my friend."

"He is and his one wish is to fight alongside you."

"He had better hurry and grow up then for I fear my fighting days are coming to a close."

He stopped and stared at me. "You are yet a young man, Warlord."

"These grey hairs belie your words but I thank you."

Once in his hall, wine and meat were provided and we awaited the return of Dai. I nodded to the door. "If the door could be closed, what I have to say is for your ears only."

Dai shut the door and Cadfan said, "You have me intrigued, Warlord."

"Before I tell you of my plans what can you tell me of the Saxons? I have heard little of Aethelfrith."

"That is because he is no longer king. The new king is Edwin and he has taken over the land of Bernicia and Deira. It is a new kingdom called Northumbria." That explained why things had been so quiet of late. "He was supported by King Ceorl of Mercia." This also told me why King Cadfan had managed to gain so much territory at the expense of the Mercians. "I see from your face that you like the news so, pray, tell me what you are up to."

"I intend to wrest Rheged back from the Saxons. What you have just told me gives me hope that I can succeed. I came here because I would hope that you would protect the eastern borders of my lands."

"Of course. Are you taking all your men?"

"No, just my horsemen and archers."

"That would be an interesting army; mounted knights against the lumbering Saxon. But you would, of course, be outnumbered."

I laughed, "And when did that ever stop me."

He looked at me seriously, "You must take care, Warlord, you are our shield." He looked earnestly at me, "I have heard that the Saxons have taken Manau."

"Aye, I heard that. It was inevitable given that they tried to capture Mona so many times. It is a minor problem and I will deal with that once I have freed Rheged." I was not being totally truthful. I was not sure how to transport all the horses to the island. When I did attack the Saxons who were there it would need all of Myrddyn's guile.

Cadfan nodded and continued. "I am preparing my men for a winter of warfare. It seems this Edwin has the support of Raedwald, the King of the East Angles and he has married the daughter of King Ceorl. Take care. This is an ambitious man who has already forced Aethelfrith and his sons into exile."

I was beginning to see that. "I am pleased that I spoke with you, King Cadfan. You have shown me the dangers that I face. Perhaps this Edwin will try to complete his control over the whole country."

"It is rumoured that he sees himself as King of the whole of Britannia."

I snorted in derision. "The nearest we had to that title was King Urien and he was just King of Rheged."

"I know but it shows his dreams and you always taught me that men's dreams show their true intent. Take care Warlord."

"Farewell, King Cadfan."

Once I was back amongst my busy captains I spoke with Hogan and Myrddyn about this new set of events. It would not stop me from going; in fact, it made it even more urgent.

"I was going to avoid Deva or Caestre as the Saxons now call it and cross the Maeresea and Dee further east but if Edwin has just gained the land his eye may not be on this small fort. I think we should take it."

Hogan's face showed his disapproval. "We would lose valuable men taking it, Warlord. And it would let the Saxons know of our intent."

Before I could answer Myrddyn shook his head. "I think it will work, for the very reasons you gave yourself, Hogan Lann. If we take Deva then we can fortify it and protect our northern borders as well as give us an escape route back from Rheged should we need it. Edwin would not know of it for, with all the horsemen we are going to take none should escape. We can surround the Saxons. It will establish doubt in the king's mind. When he hears nought from them he will assume they are either disloyal or Aethelfrith is there. Either way, his eye will not be on the north and Rheged but the west and the Dee."

Myrddyn had a clever mind. I was already thinking along those lines but he got there quicker.

"What about the men we will lose taking it?"

"Firstly are you so lacking faith in our men that you think they will not be able to overcome the fort? Secondly, I do not intend to use horsemen to capture it. I will use the men we are leaving as garrisons. We have many more men now. The untried ones can be based here at this fort and the seasoned ones can go to the borders. The experienced warriors will form the garrison of the vital crossing of the Dee."

Hogan still looked doubtful. I shook my head and laughed, "Trust me, son. I hope not to lose any men in this attack. I hope to use subterfuge and deception."

"Magic you mean?"

"As Myrddyn will tell you that covers a multitude of sins."

After Hogan had gone, a little more optimistically than he had been earlier, I turned to Myrddyn. "So what is your plan to get inside Deva?"

He burst out laughing and that, in itself, was a rare thing, he rarely found himself surprised. "I thought you told Hogan that you would use deception."

"And I have begun already; I deceived him did I not? Come, old friend, let us put our minds together."

"Humph! When you call me 'old friend' then I know that you are trying to flatter me."

"All we need to do is get inside an old fortress. It is Roman. We have been in there ourselves and we know the layout. These are Saxons who have not been troubled since they captured it. They will be complacent and unsuspecting."

His eyes lit up and he nodded. "It is fortunate for you that I am so clever. I have the plan and you shall have your fortress."

After he left to create his plan I remembered what I had thought at Wrecsam and I sent for Gawan. Perhaps it was my imagination but he seemed older somehow. I had always seen him as a child but now I saw that he was almost the same age that Raibeart had been when we first fought the Saxons. He approached me nervously as though he had done something wrong. I suspected, from his look, that he probably had but this was not a time to tease him.

"How would you like to train as a warrior?"

The light in his face was as bright as the evening sun in the west. "I have dreamed to such a time. Am I ready?"

"To begin training? Aye. Let us go to the armoury."

We had our own smith; Hywel and he kept many weapons in his smithy. When we arrived he gave a slight bow. He saw Gawan and he grinned. "I am guessing Warlord, that it is time for a sword for this young man."

"It is Hywel. Have you one that would do?"

He went to the wall where various blades were hung. He looked down at them and then chose a seax; the short sword favoured by the Saxons. "This one will do for now but I will make him one fit for the son of a Warlord!" He handed the seax to Gawan. My son weighed it in his hand and then took a couple of exploratory swings with it. Hywel said, "Now the first lesson you will need is how to sharpen it. A dull sword is no use to a warrior." He took him to the wheel which was in the corner. He gestured to his assistant who began to turn the wheel. Hywel stood behind Gawan and showed him the precise angle he needed to achieve a sharp edge. "Now you sharpen your sword when it has seen action but not when you just practise with it."

"Thank you, Hywel."

"You are welcome and when you get your new sword keep this one as a spare eh?"

I took Gawan to old Artur who had once been a warrior in my shield wall. He now looked after the young men who needed sword skills. "Artur, while I am away I would like you to teach my son how to use a sword he would become a warrior."

Artur seemed genuinely pleased to have been given the task. "I will my lord and when you return you will have another warrior for your shield wall."

Gawan seemed quite touched by the gesture and he hugged me; it was something he had not done for years. I felt guilty for I knew I had neglected him. Even though I had been at home I had not given him as much attention as I had given to Hogan Lann. I would make up for my mistake when I returned from Rheged. I would be a better father than I had been.

It was a mighty host which left my fort at Rhuddlan. Hogan and Pol had fifty warriors armed as Cataphractoi; Prince Pasgen had fifty Equites in armour. Lann Aelle commanded the one hundred squires, each with a spare horse, which carried the armour of the equites. Tuanthal led the one hundred horsemen. Daffydd had his fifty archers and Aedh led but twenty scouts. It was not a huge army but it was mighty and it was powerful.

In addition, Bors, Mungo's son, led the fifty warriors who would help us to take Deva and then garrison it. We had said our goodbyes to our families at the Narrows and warriors never say farewell to each other. It is bad luck. If we die then we will greet each other in the Otherworld when we talk for an eternity about the old battles. None of us countenanced neither defeat nor death. Hogan led the bulk of our force and ten of Aedh's scouts to cross the Dee further upstream. Myrddyn, Aedh and I marched with Bors.

Bors was just like his father, a giant of a man. Yet he was the most gentle and funny warrior I had ever met. He could have me rolling on the floor laughing with his stories and his impressions of other warriors. Yet when he donned his leather armour and picked up his war hammer he was the most ferocious foe you could ever wish to meet. When we captured the fortress he would hold Deva, of that I was certain.

The fort had been fought over, taken and retaken more times than I cared to think about. King Iago had held it for years until Aethelfrith wrested it from him. The important fact was that neither Iago nor the Saxons had repaired much and they had never improved its defences. That was how we would take it. We knew, from our scouts, that the ditch had been used as a rubbish dump and contained no traps. They had not replaced the wrecked doors; they had repaired them, badly. It was a shadow of the fort built almost six hundred years earlier. We, however, would not risk either the ditch or the door to gain entry. Myrddyn and I had worked out a more subtle way.

We halted across the river. It was mid-afternoon and the day would be a long one. These were the summer days when the sun barely set. It suited us for it gave us light with which to work and yet our enemies would be tired. I expected that Hogan had encircled the fortress already with his ring of steel. No one would escape.

I took off my helmet and wolf cloak. We were going to pretend to be Saxons. Aedh could also speak Saxon and he came with us. Hogan had tried to dissuade me from accompanying the other two as he felt it was too risky, someone might recognise me. The men in the fortress might have fought me but they had never seen my face. I gave Saxon Slayer to Captain Bors for safekeeping as that would be recognised. I took an old Saxon sword we had captured.

We waited until an hour or so before sunset. Fifteen of Bors men had used the setting sun to cross the river and hide in the drainage ditch which was adjacent to the fort and the river. The three of us entered the water and floated across on a log. We had gained entry in a similar way once before but the last time we had tried it with a column of men. This time we were just playing three men. Another five of Bors' men accompanied us.

"Now remember you run back to the river once you are spotted. I want none of you hurt or killed in this madcap venture."

They grinned; Bors had chosen his men well. "No Warlord!"

Myrddyn looked at me, "Well Warlord, are you ready?"

"As ready as I shall ever be."

We stood and ran towards the eastern gate some two hundred paces away. We began yelling, "Open the gates! We are being pursued."

Bors had chosen men who could use bows and the five of them halted and loosed arrows at us. They came perilously close, as we had intended. They followed us, as we ran, and loosed more, my shield was behind my back and I felt one arrow thud into it. I was glad that it was stoutly made and that I was wearing my leather armour. Bors' men were playing their part well. I hoped it would convince the defenders that we were Saxon.

The last flurry of arrows must have done the trick for the gates suddenly opened. A dozen men charged out towards Bors' men. I hoped that they had their wits about them. We just kept on running until we were inside but I was happy when I heard the splashes of the men hurling themselves into the Dee.

As soon as we were inside we all affected a look of relief and joy. "Thank you brothers, the rest of our warband were slaughtered in the ambush." Myrddyn could be very convincing.

A warrior in mail with a full-face helmet and decorated with back metal raven's wings strode over to me. He did not take off his helmet and I had his measure straight away. He was trying to intimidate me.

"What warband? Who is your chief?"

Myrddyn began the story we had rehearsed. "We were sent by Edwin of Northumbria to reinforce your garrison. He had heard that King Cadfan is planning an attack in the autumn."

I saw the eyes narrow behind the mask. "King Edwin?"

It was as we had expected, they had not heard of the change of ruler. "Did you not know? Aethelfrith and his sons have fled and Edwin is the new king. He has the support of Ceorl of Mercia and Raedwald of East Anglia." We wanted to keep this commander on the back foot and so far it was working.

He took off his helmet which showed me that he was now less suspicious. "When did this happen?"

"At the end of last year. I know the new king sent messengers."

"Where did he send them from?"

I pointed to the east. "He was at his father in law's home in Mercia."

"That explains it then. The new king of Gwynedd is a better leader than his father was. He keeps us bottled up in here." He looked at each of us. "I am Lod, the garrison commander. Who did you say your chief was?"

Myrddyn jerked his head towards the gate, "He was Aelle son of Targh."

"Never heard of him."

"That is because we were in exile with King Edwin in East Anglia." Myrddyn thrust the hilt of his sword forwards. "Look, count the warrior bands. I have served King Edwin since he was a boy."

"All right calm down. I meant no offence but three of you are hardly going to stop King Cadfan are you?"

"The ones who weren't killed went back to Mercia. The king will send more men."

He seemed to notice that we were still dripping wet from the river. "You had better get by the fire and dry off. We don't have a warrior hall here but there are barracks. Just find one with a fire. There are spare beds. We only have thirty warriors here at the moment. The rest of the men have gone north raiding."

I hoped that my son had his wits about him. We went to the nearest barracks. Had the Saxons had any kind of wit they would have worked out how to make the hypocaust work and they would have had warm rooms throughout the fort. As it was they used open fires which filled the rooms with smoke and blackened everything. We left them discussing this change of king. We stood, steaming before the fire. A couple of warriors came in and fired questions at us. Myrddyn answered them all.

"When do you eat around here? We haven't eaten since this morning."

"We were hoping the warband would be back with food. You will have to make do with game soup and stale bread." He pointed to the door. "Should be ready about now."

"Aye, the soup has been watered down so much it is more like game water."

"I thought the Roman forts had bakeries. The one at Eboracum does."

"Lod can't be bothered. He would rather be raiding than sitting here on his arse."

The room was darkening which told us that the sun was setting. I stretched, "All that water makes me need a piss."

One of them gestured. "Outside, close to the south gate. The Romans built little channels under the walls. Me, I just piss anywhere."

His friend said, "They may not be barbarians like you."

The two of them set to arguing and the three of us left. We could see that most of the men were heading to the eating hall for food. I glanced up at the walls; there were just two sentries above the gate and one below. While Myrddyn went to begin the pretence of passing water, Aedh and I strode up to the guard on the gate. He looked as though he was ready to fall asleep.

"Been on duty long?"

"Too bloody long. They have no system here. No one else does his fair share."

He got no further. Aedh had rammed his knife into his unsuspecting throat. I had blocked the view of anyone in the fort and Aedh slid his body to the ground and then donned his cloak. Myrddyn and I lifted the bar on the gate but did not open it. We both went to the stairs to climb to the gate tower.

One of the sentries approached us. "What are you two doing here? Didn't you just come from the river?"

"Yes," I walked closer to him. His companion was joining us. "We have just arrived and your commander Lod said we had to earn our keep. He sent us to relieve you."

They relaxed and laughed. "That sounds like Lod." They came to walk past us. As they did Myrddyn and I grabbed them by the shoulders and pushing them tipped their bodies over the wall. They crashed to their deaths on the path beyond the ditch.

I yelled, "Now Aedh."

Myrddyn leaned over and shouted, "Now Bors!"

Myrddyn and I raced down the stairs as Bors and his men ran through the open gate. The remainder of his men flooded over the bridge. The Saxons were unprepared. Many were eating and none, save for the guards at the other gates, had armour on. I was unarmoured too but I didn't care. I joined Bors' men as we ran towards the eating hall where the confused Saxons were emerging from their paltry meal. I watched as Bors swung his war hammer to smash into the side of the head of the first warrior. I do not think they had ever seen that weapon and fear was in the eyes of the ones who followed.

A spear darted from behind the barracks to my left. It slid just before me. I grabbed the haft in my left hand and slashed sideways with my borrowed blade. The Saxon died without a murmur. The captain we had seen before had donned his armour and was trying to rally his men. He had eight men behind him trying to overlap their shields and form a shield wall. Bors' hammer smashed through a warrior's shield and bones to demolish the wall before it was even half-formed. Lod saw me and lunged at me with his sword. I wore leather gauntlets and I grabbed his blade and pulled him towards me. He slipped on the blood of one of his warriors. I thrust my sword into him and he gurgled his lifeblood away at my feet.

With their leader gone and his oathsworn too, the rest surrendered. They fell to their knees. "Spare us!"

There were just ten men left from the garrison. Bors and his men had been too fast for a formed resistance and none had managed to escape. I now had a dilemma. Should I put them to the sword? Give them a warrior's death? My head told me to do so but they had surrendered and I could not, in all conscience just kill them.

"Do you know who I am?"

They shook their heads and one man ventured, "No, my lord!"

"I am Lord Lann the Warlord of Rheged." They stopped looking at the ground to glimpse a glance at this man who had been terrifying Saxons for so many years. Many would have grown up with stories told by their mothers to make them behave. Saxon Slayer would come for them. The Wolf Warrior waited. I saw terror in their eyes. They still expected to die.

"I will spare you if you swear allegiance to me and my captain here, Bors son of Mungo." I turned to Aedh. "Fetch the sword." He raced off to our camp across the river. "Will you swear or do you wish the warrior's death?"

The man who had spoken earlier said, "We swore oaths to Aethelfrith and he has fled. For myself, I would swear my oath to you, Lord Lann." There was a chorus from the others, all desperate to swear loyalty.

"Very well. Captain Bors have your men secure the fortress."

"Aye Warlord." He grinned his approval at my decision.

Aedh arrived with Saxon Slayer in its magnificent scabbard. I drew it and held it before me. "This is Saxon Slayer; it was made in antiquity and is a magical weapon. Touch the blade with your hands and swear to be warriors of Rheged and to follow me and my captains."

They all swore eagerly.

"Give them back their weapons. I believe they will be loyal."

"Aye well if not you will know when you return for their heads will adorn the walls if they are oath breakers."

The first part of the task was completed and we had our first fortress in Saxon lands. My conquest could begin. Bors set his new men to work removing the rubbish from the ditch while he and his other warriors repaired the gate properly. I inspected the walls with Myrddyn while we awaited the arrival of Hogan Lann and the others. If the rest of the campaign went as well as this then we would have Rheged conquered by Yule.

Saxon Slaughter

Chapter 3

Hogan Lann and my horsemen had ambushed the war band which had been raiding without loss. It had been a successful start; in fact, it was hard to see how it could have gone better. The weapons and armour were left with Bors who now had a solid garrison and would be a rock upon which the Saxons would crash. As we left he smiled at me, "If I lose this fort, Warlord I will become a priest of the White Christ and you know how much I hate that idea!"

We spurned wagons and carried everything on spare horses. It kept us mobile. Aedh and his men ranged far ahead of us to find good campsites and to help us to avoid Saxons. As far as we knew there were no major Saxon settlements between the Sea and the land of the lakes.

Last year a Danish ship had put in for trade. They looked a little too warlike to be traders to me but they showed us no aggression and were happy to trade with us. They told us that their land was poor. I suspect had we made the offer they would have settled on Mona but we knew too little about them to take the risk. They were the ones who told us of the Saxons on Manau and about the empty land between the Maeresea and the land of the lakes. They had found fertile land but few people. Even before my mother's message, I was intrigued with the idea of resettling Rheged.

As we rode north I berated myself for my decision to leave Rheged all those years earlier. Had I clung on or even settled in this fertile land then who knows what might have happened. I thought of those who had died on the journey to Mona and on Mona itself. Could I have prevented that?

Myrddyn was riding next to me and saw my frown. He smiled and spoke quietly to me. "Warlord, you cannot go back. The decisions you took all those years ago were good ones. It was just *wyrd*."

Even as I heard his counsel and felt again how inadequate one felt next to him I felt anger too. "As I recall I was advised by you to go to Mona."

He was not discomfited by my aggression and attitude. "True but as I recall Brother Osric also thought it a good idea, not to mention you who thought of the idea when King Urien died. Besides we had to leave Castle Perilous. We were surrounded. Would your people have survived in the hills without walls around them? How many would have died of cold? Would Prince Pasgen have had a sanctuary? Would Mungo and his men have been rescued? No my lord. As much as one wishes to go back, it is impossible. You made the correct decision at the time. You are a man and so you live with that decision. You are now going to go back and who knows the effect that will have."

We rode in silence for a while. "But my decisions?"

"Were good decisions, both at the time and now, viewed through the tunnel of time. But you, Lord Lann, like all men, want a perfect world. We have to deal with life and its problems as they are handed to us. It is what makes us different from the animals. We change our world to suit us. Your fortress beneath Wyddfa is a good example."

He was right, of course, and my decision to come north was equally good. I turned in my saddle to look at the long column winding to the west of the ridge of hills which formed the backbone of Britannia. In Constantinopolis I had seen Ptolemy's maps of Britannia and I understood the land a little more than most men. The Saxons had come from the east and the hills were a natural barrier to their naturally avaricious nature. I could halt them this time but I would use nature to aid me. I had been younger when I had left but now I was older and wiser. I had gained knowledge in the court of the Byzantine Emperor. This new king, Edwin, would meet his match in me.

It was five days later when we saw the tops of the mountains, in the distance, marking the entrance to the land of the lakes. Aedh and his scouts had already reported that they had seen no sign of Saxons but there were villages ahead. On our last night before we reached our first target, I called a council of war with my captains.

"Our first task is to assess how many of our people there are remaining in this land. I will leave that to Prince Pasgen. I will leave Daffydd and his archers to help to rebuild my brother's fort. We need a base and a place in which to retreat if the need arises. I will take the rest of the men east and we will find the Saxons."

"Why are you leaving me here, Warlord?" Prince Pasgen must have been worried that he had offended me in some way for he added, hurriedly, "I merely wish to know your thinking, Warlord."

I smiled, "And it is a good question. I am becoming a grumpy old man. Expect me to be short and to snap. I mean nothing by it." I smiled to take the sting out of my words. "I need you to assess the situation because you are the last member of the Rheged Royal Family. I want the people to come to you and your banner. They will need someone to lead them and, I assume, that will be you?"

"Of course." He bowed his head, "Thank you, Warlord. I forget myself sometimes."

"We lost Rheged once because we underestimated the Saxons; let us not make the same mistake again. This time we will not rest on our laurels we will fight until the land is ours once more and a descendant of King Urien rules."

Myrddyn coughed and poked the fire a little. "With respect Warlord, King Urien made the mistake and not you. You warned him on many occasions of the danger as you did with Morcant Bulc. You have nothing to blame yourself for. But remember Warlord, look forward. The past merely gives us lessons about what we did wrong. The future is in our own hands."

The next day as we rode up the valley which marked the entrance to Wide Water I couldn't help remembering the men we had lost defending my brothers' wagons against the Saxons. As we saw the lake for the first time I could still make out the burnt-out bones of the boats we had used to flee down the lake. Their grave marked the place we had bought time with our blood. We headed up the western side of the lake. It was the one we were most familiar with. We were armed but, as yet, none of us was mailed our horses needed preserving for the long campaign ahead.

I turned to Hogan Lann and Lann Aelle. "Do you remember much of this place?"

Hogan Lann shook his head. "It is not even a memory."

Lann Aelle seemed to see the lake for the first time. "I remember when you came for us, Warlord. You were alone, save for Myrddyn and Aedh and I wondered if the wizard would fly us out of the trap."

Behind me, I heard Myrddyn snort. "I have never flown! Where do these legends come from?"

"Perhaps old friend," I reminded him, "it was the time you managed to escape unseen from Din Guardi."

He chuckled, "I thought that was the time they thought I had become invisible."

"Anyway," continued Lann Aelle, "that was the day I decided that I would be a warrior like you."

I glanced at the man who had so recently been a boy and my squire. There were three of them who had served me in the capacity and now they led men but it had been Lann Aelle who had been with me when I had come closest to death and we shared a special bond. His father had been a little resentful of our close relationship but Lann Aelle had spent long hours with him since that time and I think he understood. His father had been a warrior too, albeit briefly and had stood in a shield wall. He knew the magic of such brotherhood.

Aedh rode back. He had gone with Kay and they both looked happy. "The people are joyful at your return Warlord." Aedh came closer. "The headman believes that the Saxons will be coming for tribute soon. It has been a good summer thus far and there are many young cattle and lambs."

That meant my plans would have to change. We needed to be here when the Saxons came. I would not go to seek them out. "Prince Pasgen."

The prince brought his horse next to mine. "There is even more urgency to the wall building. The Saxons are coming."

His voice was resolute and his face grim as he said, "We will be ready."

Aelle's fort was marked by burnt-out timbers close to the water's edge. The people had moved their settlement further up the valley. I could see why for there was better grazing and pasture for their animals. It was however indefensible. I could now see how the Saxons had managed to extract tribute from them.

Kay's brother, Saelac, was pleased to see us and began with a flattering speech. I cut him short. I had no time for such niceties. "When the Saxons come, where do they come from?"

He looked confused and pointed to the east. "Over there."

I sighed with impatience. They were like sheep without either a shepherd or sheepdog. Their attention was on the ground only. "When they come do they arrive in the morning or afternoon and do they have horses with them? How many of them are there?"

He looked like a puppy eager to please his master. "They come in the afternoon but no horses. They come on foot." I could see he looked confused about the numbers

"Look at my warriors; compare them to us."

"As many as your men and sometimes more."

I reasoned that their sweep in autumn and late summer would give them food for the winter and they would need a large number to hold onto it. A warband the size of ours showed how much they needed the resources of this land. "And they camp here do they?"

"They use our homes."

"They take their goods and they head east again when they have taken all?"

He shook his head. "No, Warlord. They head up the valley to the other settlements." He pointed north.

I turned away from the headman and spoke with my captains and Myrddyn who were behind me. "They will be coming from the east and they will begin their tribute raid here."

Myrddyn adopted that superior look he always did when he was about to prove that he was cleverer than me. "You are assuming that, because they come in the afternoon they have walked from their homes and because they have no horses they have not camped."

"And you know different?"

"When I spied in their camps on the Dunum I noticed that most of them did not use tents as we do. They made shelters from wood and branches." He pointed to the bright blue sky of late summer. "They need no shelter. If you send your scouts a day's march east you may find where they camp for they will use the same place but I would guess that their home is beyond the hills. I think it would be closer to Stanwyck."

It was although an icicle had pierced my heart. Stanwyck had been my home and was the place my family and the rest of the village had been slaughtered.

I shook myself to remove the memory and smiled at Myrddyn. "Once again you have proved that you can see farther than any other man. Aedh, send your men out and find this camp."

I looked around the village. It could not cope with over three hundred horses. "Tuanthal, we will camp at the old fort." I smiled, "It means the men will not have far to travel to work!"

His scowl told me what he and the horsemen thought of building a fort. I could have asked the villagers to do the work but they would not have known what to do. They could watch us build this and then Pasgen could train them in the building of others.

Hogan Lann approached, "We cannot eat the villager's food, father. If we did then they would not have enough for themselves and they would not survive the winter."

"I know. Send twenty riders under a good captain to the coast. There is a small port we used called Alavna. Tell them to camp there and build a fire. Daffydd will find them. He has supplies."

He looked at me in surprise. "Daffydd is sailing here?" I nodded. "You planned this before we started?"

"You did not think I had all those meetings with my ship captains because I like the sound of my own voice, did you? I anticipated that we would need food and he has supplies for us. In the meantime why don't you and Pol take some men and go hunting? As I recall it is good deer and boar country around here." I pointed to the lake, "And I am guessing that there will be fish within the waters there."

"I have much to learn before I am Warlord."

"When I was your age I would not have thought that far ahead. You train your body, my son, so begin to train your mind."

"Myrddyn, Lann Aelle let us explore the land around here. I would familiarise myself with it."

We headed north. The mountains rose steeply to our right and there was a gentle ridge to our left. I remembered, as we rode, that this was the place with the two small lakes and the cave in the hills. We halted when I saw the small knoll and the wrecked remains of a tower. We dismounted and walked towards it.

"This is where the Saxons retreated and we attacked them. I do not remember a tower."

Myrddyn examined the remains. "That is because we were busy fighting and this tower is older than that. This is an old Roman signal tower." He stood and looked north and south. "It would be a good place to build one again." He pointed to the flat area between the knoll and the tree line. "Pasgen could have men stationed here. It would give early warning of an attack and would be a good place to control this valley."

As we mounted and continued to ride north I asked Lann Aelle, "Did your father not consider building a tower there or defending it?"

"It was a long time ago, Warlord, but as I recall we felt we had no need to defend there for the north was protected by King Urien and then King Ywain. Lord Raibeart also had a fort to the north. It was the south we feared."

That made sense. Prince Pasgen had much to do and I wondered if he would be up to the task. When he had tried to wrest his land from his treacherous brother and the Saxons he had been ineffective. Would he have changed? Would the years spent in my service have made him a better leader?

"Prince Pasgen has learned much from his time with you, Warlord. He now knows the strength of walls as well as the power of armour."

I hated it when he did that. "Do you have to read my mind the whole time?"

He laughed. "Like you, I was thinking of the lord who will have to rule this land once we have conquered it and I knew that you would be thinking the same."

We rode as far as the round hills to the north. We found many isolated settlements and they hid in their roundhouses when we entered. They were fearful until I spoke and the sound of their own language reassured them. The response was always the same; wonder and joy. The first village, which was nestled by the stream which bubbled into the grassy lake was typical. The headman came out and looked at our weapons and helmets. "So it is true. The Warlord has returned with Myrddyn the wizard."

"Aye we have returned and we will give you aid to fight the Saxons."

One old man came out of his hut limping. He had one arm. "It is good to see you, Lord Lann. I fought for your brother, Lord Aelle and lost this fighting the last time." He shook his head sadly, "Had you stayed then we would not have had to bury so many bairns who died of hunger."

The headman snapped, "Do not reproach the Warlord old one. He has returned has he not?"

"No the old man does right. I should have stayed but perhaps then the result would have been the same. I do not know. I know that we are now stronger." I pointed to Lann Aelle, "And this is Lann Aelle the son of Lord Aelle. Now he is a powerful warrior whom the Saxons fear. Perhaps our time away was well spent."

The other villages and their people had similar responses. We saw those who had been warriors and not fled with us and they told the same tale. The Saxons came like scavengers to take that which the villagers had garnered. The ones who died of the hunger which followed the raids were the old and the young. It was a sad tale. We did discover that many of the old soldiers had hidden their weapons and were eager to recover them and fight the Saxons once more. We would not have to find as many arms as I had expected. I was also pleased that there appeared to be many more men who could fight, once they were trained.

We returned in the afternoon. We were hungry. We had been offered food but I would not take it from a people who were so close to starvation. "Lann Aelle, you have been quiet. What is on your mind?"

"The people all hold my father in high esteem. They still respect him and yet he deserted them."

Myrddyn wagged an admonishing finger at the young warrior. "No, he did not. He gave all the people the chance to leave and these chose to stay. You cannot blame your father and you cannot blame the people. They made the decisions which were right for them and they have lived by those decisions."

He looked relieved, "Good for, when this land is made safe again I would, with the Warlord's permission, stay here. I would defend my father's people."

I looked at my nephew with new eyes. He had grown. "You would be my lord here?"

"I know that Prince Pasgen will rule for you but he will need lieutenants and I would be one."

"That is good. We will talk with the prince." This was *wyrd*. I had not planned this and yet it was a perfect solution. If Prince Pasgen ruled the north from Carvetiorum and Lann Aelle held the south then the land would be as safe as it could be. I wondered again about my mother's spirit. I knew that I would need to visit the waters at Carvetiorum where I had first heard my mother's voice. Her dreams were like a powerful drug; they became addictive. The more you knew the more you wanted to know. I had a thirst for knowledge.

Prince Pasgen and his men had worked hard in the time we had been away. There were shelters for us and the ditch had been cleared. Pol had had trees cut down for the walls ready to erect them the next day. We ate well for the hunters had been lucky and skilful. We even had more than enough to share with the villagers. As we ate Kay came to me, apologetically. "I am sorry about my brother. He is hard working but no one could ever accuse him of being clever. I fear it is why the Saxons have put upon them so much. Had I been here I would have ensured we could defend our homes."

"And that is why you left with Prince Pasgen for you bow your neck to no man. We need men like your brother just as we need warriors like you. Tell me this, will your brother stand in a shield wall?"

"Aye and the others too. So long as someone tells him what to do he will do it but do not ask him to think for himself. Animals and farming are what he knows."

Prince Pasgen would have his work cut out to make these farmers into warriors. I began to work out a system which would help Pasgen. I summoned Myrddyn. "Do you have Osric's maps still?"

"Yes, Warlord. I'll fetch them."

He returned with the pieces of parchment painstakingly created by King Urien's priest, Brother Osric. I began to peer at them. The names of the places were in Latin and bore little resemblance to the names used by the villagers we had met.

"What do you look for Warlord?"

"I am trying to work out where we went today. I need a picture, in my mind, of the settlements."

"Ah, in that case…" he pointed to one red dot on the map. "We are here. This is the village by the grassy lake…" he went through all of the villages we had visited. "And here is Carvetiorum."

"Excellent."

"You have me intrigued Warlord. I know you well enough to realise that these are not idle questions and yet I cannot fathom your purpose."

I smiled. "So you do not read my mind the whole time. That is reassuring. I am trying to work out a system to enable Prince Pasgen to defend his land when we finally make it secure."

"Ah. You are working out how to utilise the farmers as warriors."

"Exactly. Now if we take the villages close to here as typical then they could all send, say ten men from each village to be trained here by Prince Pasgen. If they needed to be called to war then those would be the ten who would go. Each one would have a natural leader."

"And those ten could train others. Interesting."

"I counted before when we first came here, and there are eighteen men and boys. There would be more than enough to provide warriors to defend this place."

"The village by the lake had twenty men and boys. I would calculate that the villages and farms around here could provide Prince Pasgen with seventy men. It would be a workable system. He would need to communicate with them."

"Let us reinstate the boy riders we used. There are still hill ponies and that is how Aedh began."

"It is and that reminds me, Warlord. Where is our scout? I expected him some time ago. Even though the days are long it is now turning to night."

Hogan, Lann Aelle and Pol joined us. Hogan looked to the eastern sky which was now growing ever darker. "Are you worried about Aedh too, Warlord?"

"Yes, this tardiness is not like him."

"Shall we take the rest of the scouts to look for him?"

"No, we wait for morning. We have too few men to risk losing any."

We stood in silence, each of us peering east. "I will make sure we have sentries well-positioned this night."

Hogan Lann had learned caution and I was pleased. If Aedh had been captured or killed then it was possible that his men may have been tortured to tell what they knew about us. Our only advantage lay in the fact that the Saxons did not know our numbers or where we were. If Aedh and his men were captured then we could end up being trapped and ambushed by the Saxons. I would not underestimate them.

I retired to my hard bed but I could not sleep. Partly that was discomfort. I was no longer used to campaigning. But mainly I worried about Aedh. He had served me since he was a boy as a dispatch rider and then as a captain of scouts. He too had been, briefly, my squire and I would wish no harm to come to him. I was aware that I was now in unknown territory. I might know the land but I had no idea, any longer where my enemies were. Back at Wyddfa I knew every track, trail and pass a Saxon might use to launch an attack on us. Here? I was in the dark.

I was not asleep when Aedh and his scouts returned. I was on my feet almost as soon as I heard him ride into the camp. I was wide awake in an instant and I counted his scouts. They were all there. Aedh dismounted and, even in the glow from the fire, looked tired. "Trouble?"

He grinned and still looked like the despatch rider of all those years ago. "No, Warlord. It was my fault. We found their camp really quickly." He pointed to the east. "It's just twenty miles or so that way." Hogan, who had also woken at the noise, gave him a beaker of ale. "Thanks. I decided to push on and see if I could find where their forts are. I crossed the Dunum and found some Saxon settlements." He paused. "They have fortified Dunelm."

That was a major blow. Dunelm was a steep rock on an island in the middle of a powerful river. I could not take it with my horsemen. It would take a Roman Army complete with artillery and many foot soldiers to capture that. I knew for we had defended it against a mighty Saxon army. I would have to rethink our strategy.

"Thank you Aedh, as usual, you have done all that I asked and more. Now you and your men get some sleep." Hogan Lann and Myrddyn joined me.

Myrddyn gave me one of his enigmatic smiles. "Instead of having the beaker half empty make it half full, Warlord."

"What?"

"Instead of worrying about Dunelm being fortified, rejoice for we have found their camp and that means that we have the initiative. We can catch them before they have even begun to raid our people and, best of all, they will have no idea. They will go to their usual camp in high spirits knowing that they are but a day's march from the chickens they intend to pluck. The wolves will feast upon them."

"But Dunelm?"

"It is many miles hence and they cannot reach us quickly. If you wish to reduce it there may be a way but if your avowed intent was to recover Rheged then why should Dunelm worry you?"

"I don't know." I did. I wanted to rid the land of every Saxon. Until we had reached Rheged I had thought we would be fighting battle after battle just to get here and now I saw that they had not even colonised my land. I had begun to dream that I could drive them back into the sea.

"Yes, you do. Remember when we were in Constantinopolis?" I nodded. "In the library, I read a book about a Greek idea called Hubris. It is where the pride of someone makes them lose touch with reality. The reality is, Warlord, that at the moment you can neither take Dunelm nor rid this island of the Saxons. The sooner you come to realise that then the easier all our lives will become."

Hogan Lann had become silent and the guards looked fearfully at Myrddyn who had dared to berate the Warlord. He was right of course and he knew it. "One day, wizard you will go too far."

He laughed and I felt Hogan Lann relax. "Not as long as I speak the truth."

I went to bed and found that I could sleep much easier. It had been the fact that Aedh was missing which had made me restless. Myrddyn was right. We now knew what to do and we would strike the first blow. I was not sure it would be the only blow we would need to take but only time would tell.

I rode with Aedh, his scouts, Myrddyn and Hogan Lann to see for myself the Saxon camp. I recognised the lake as one we had fought down all those years ago. It was a long lake in a very narrow valley. It was not far from our camp. The problem we had was that it did not suit horses. Hogan Lann summed it up as soon as he saw it. "We will have to hit them before they reach this valley. Once in the valley, we will have to attack on foot and that does not suit us."

Aedh took us along the valley. When we emerged at the head we saw the round moors rising to the north and west. The land flattened and widened quite considerably and we could see a long way toward the hard spine of the country. Myrddyn pointed to the ridge which ran to the north of the road. "The archers could wait there and your horsemen could sweep along their flank when they retaliated."

Hogan Lann nodded. "We will need to keep a watch here. We will be able to see a warband approaching from a long distance. Aedh, you rode this road to Dunelm. How long will it take them to reach here?"

"We took one day but we almost killed our horses. I would say two or three days. They know the area they are using and so will probably get here towards late afternoon."

I could see it now. "They will be tired and they will see what they expect to see; the land that they know so well. They will not expect to be attacked. But I think you need your advance scouts over to the east; where the high peaks are. The Saxons will be easy to see because of the size of the warband and we will need to be in position before they reach here."

"Then Warlord we need another camp, up there where we can wait."

I could see his mind at work already. "See into the future wizard and tell me when they will come."

"Not in the next seven days."

Hogan could not resist the question. "How do you know?"

"Many of the sheep are still on the fells. They will want as many in the villages as possible. It is a month before the weather turns but it will take them at least ten days to visit all the villages and collect all their tribute and the journey back will take at least six days with the animals."

I did not ask the question because I knew he would have worked it all out. We had a week to finish our defences.

The men who had been to the coast returned three days later with a string of hill ponies. "Brother Oswald thought we might need them and Captain Daffydd said he would return in one month with more supplies."

Hogan Lann laughed, "Brother Oswald has a mind which is so organised."

"Aye my lord and he sent a dozen Saxon swords which had not been melted down and made into armour yet."

I was pleased, that meant we could begin to arm the people of the village. I summoned Prince Pasgen and explained to him my ideas for a force of ten men in each village. "It is like the Roman system and will enable you to use the men effectively."

As usual, he affected a frown which was a sure sign he was trying to work out what it all meant. I sighed and began to make it clearer. "When we leave Prince Pasgen, I assume that you will remain and rule your father's land."

"It is my dearest wish."

"You and your horsemen can ensure that the whole of Rheged is patrolled but you will need your men in the villages to be able to withstand an attack until you can deal with the threat. By having your men in tens you can gather them together quickly under one man; a leader of fifty or a hundred." I saw enlightenment dawn. We need the first of those leaders and I have one in mind, Kay."

Prince Pasgen nodded. "I think that would be a good decision, Warlord."

I bit back the snappy reply which was in my mouth and was ready to leap out. Kay had proved that he had a brain in his head and knew how to deal with people. The Prince did not. I turned to Lann Aelle, "Summon Kay."

When he arrived he had the nervous look of someone who thinks he has done something wrong. I smiled to put him at his ease. "Kay, we have a task for you. You can refuse but I hope you will not."

He bowed, "I owe you my life Warlord, whatever you wish I will do."

"Good," I explained my idea and his face told me that he approved of the promotion. "So you would be based here." I pointed to the ten swords. "You would train ten of your brother's men as warriors. They would be armed with these swords. You would appoint someone to be in command of the ten and then you would move on to the next village. By then we should have more weapons. When the army returns to Mona after we have secured this land you and the Prince should have a hundred men in the villages who can be your defenders. With stout walls, you should be able to withstand the Saxons for this land fights for you as does ours."

He glanced in Prince Pasgen's direction. The prince had the good grace to smile and nod and Kay gave a slight bow. "I accept and I will fight to protect this land and these people."

I was genuinely pleased. I now had two leaders, here in Rheged, whom I could rely upon. I needed more but they would reveal themselves in time. Of that, I had no doubt.

Chapter 4

We left a day later to make a leisurely journey of it; we needed to protect our horses as much as we could. Aedh and his scouts were already to the east of the high hills and we would have ample warning of the arrival of the Saxon band. Hogan Lann was full of questions as we headed east. "How do you know that they will use this route again?"

"There are three main routes east to west. This is the most southerly. There is one which runs along the old Roman Wall and another which is further north in the land of the Picts. Had I been the Saxons I would have used the route by the Roman Wall for the road is good but there is less shelter along the way. When we have dealt with this warband we will ride further north and see what we can do there."

"What of Castle Perilous?"

"That lies not far away on this route. It would be a good barrier to further incursions but it needs a good commander."

Myrddyn sniffed imperiously, "It had one as I recall."

"What was it you called it, Myrddyn? Ah yes, Hubris. I will not make that mistake again."

The valley we rode up was dark and threatening despite the fact that it was summer. The valley sides rose up steeply on each side making the journey seem ominous. I was pleased when we emerged on the open ridge which overlooked the old Roman Road. My captains set the men to building a camp using branches and trees while I rode with Myrddyn to the high hills to the north. These were totally unlike the hills around Wide Water and nothing like Wyddfa. It was as though the gods had made a pudding and inverted the bowl. There were few trees and they afforded a fine panorama. I looked east.

When we reached the top we saw the mountains which surrounded the land of the lakes to the south and the land rolling away north to Carvetiorum. We could even glimpse the sea, far away to the west. But it was to the east we focussed our attention. To the northeast, hidden by the hills before us, lay Castle Perilous. It was my old home and was not far away. We could have been there and back in the time it took to cook a leg of venison I wondered how it had fared. The Saxons would pass by its shattered and burnt walls. There were so many memories there. It had been the castle entrusted to me by King Urien. I had been Rheged's doorkeeper and I felt proud that it had been the last place to fall to the Saxons.

"I keep telling you Warlord; do not dwell on the past."

"Wizard I am doing what you told me to do. I am looking at my mistakes so that I do not repeat them." I pointed to the northeast. "Castle Perilous was a good idea but it was too isolated. We need to make this whole route riddled with barriers to the Saxons so that we slow them down. The hills help us and they may tire of trying to raid our people."

He smiled, "Good. Now you are thinking like a wizard. Remember when we were in Constantinopolis?" I nodded. "The Emperor kept few guards in the city. The rest were dotted around the Empire ready to aid each other when attacked."

"They had many more men than we have Myrddyn."

"How do you know? We have merely seen those within a few miles of Wide Water and already you have seen the potential for seventy men who can defend that land. We have all of Rheged to visit. Let us not judge until we have seen all."

I turned Mona to descend the hill again. "And let us not speculate until we have rid ourselves of this particular problem." I pointed towards the road from the east and there was a rider galloping down it. "If I am not mistaken, that is one of Aedh's men and it means the Saxons are coming."

When we reached the camp the scout was talking with my captains. They stopped when we returned. Hogan Lann pointed east. "Aedh has his men about ten miles away. There are over two hundred of them."

I nodded and asked the scout, "Are there many in mail?"

"Yes, Warlord. The ones at the front all wore mail. I would guess that there were thirty of them at least wearing a mail shirt."

Then this was a powerful leader and not just a collection of robbers intent on pillaging an area. Most Saxons had a shield and a helmet. Some had swords while others had spears but few, save the richest and most powerful, would have a mail shirt. It was the same with my men. Only Hogan Lann and Prince Pasgen's men wore mail. Many of my men had some mail protecting their necks or upper arms and most had leather armour as some of the Romans had. But mail byrnies were rare.

"So we need to ensure that those at the front are the ones we kill first." That was not as easy as it sounded. Our plan had been to rain arrows on them but if they wore mail then that would not be as effective. Prince Pasgen and Hogan Lann take your equites to the west and hide yourselves there. Tuanthal, take your men to the south and hide in the undergrowth. I will stay with Daffydd, Lann Aelle and the squires. We will ambush the column and when they see how few we are, they will attack. Once they are committed to the attack then your horsemen can attack their flanks and their rear."

"That sounds risky, Warlord."

"Hogan Lann, all life is a risk. I will have the Roman horn sounded when you are to attack." I could see that his face was riddled with doubt. "I will have Myrddyn with me." I turned to him. "Have you dreamed of my death yet?"

He grinned, "Not yet."

"Then I will survive the day."

Lann Aelle prepared the squires. Their horses were taken to the rear and tethered with two men to guard them. He had the ninety-eight remaining men form a wall of spears and shields in front of the archers. Daffydd had brought plenty of arrows. We had left many more at the new camp. Then we waited. I had Myrddyn go to the road to see if we could be seen. When he returned he said, "I knew where you were but I had to look really closely to see you. They should be unsuspecting."

"What we need is to make sure that are looking down the road." I smiled. "Like a magician uses one hand to hide what he is doing with the other."

Just then Aedh and his scouts galloped up. They appeared from behind us. "We did not take the road. We did not want them to see us." He pointed east. "They are two miles away. Those Roman mile markers come in handy."

"Aedh take one of your scouts and position yourself down there on the road. I want the Saxons to see you. Pretend you are examining your horse's leg. Be incompetent and do not see them until they are within bow range and then flee west as though you fear them."

He laughed, "That is a hard task Warlord but we shall manage it." He and his chosen man dismounted and led their horses to the road.

Myrddyn nodded his approval. "This way we shall know when the Saxons are close for Aedh will ride away."

I took the compliment and nodded. My strategy skills had improved since we had returned from the court of the Emperor. I had learned to think a little more. I knew that someday my skills with the sword would not be enough and there would be better swordsmen. I would then need to use my mind more than I had had to when I was younger.

Saxon Slaughter

It is hard to wait patiently; it was many years since I had faced a shield wall. I began to slide Saxon Slayer in and out of its scabbard. Myrddyn smiled at my nervousness. He was busily watching a pair of blackbirds arguing about a tree. The fact that they were doing so showed that we were well hidden and were not disturbing the wildlife.

Suddenly Aedh and his men tried to mount their horses and struggled to do so. It was a masterly performance. We heard a roar as the warband hurtled towards them and then the two riders were gone. We needed no words and Daffydd raised his arm. We waited until the mailed warriors were past us and then he lowered it. Lann Aelle and his men stood up as fifty arrows soared into the air followed, a heartbeat later, by the second flight. The warband had had no time to raise their shields from this hidden enemy and many fell. The third and fourth flights cleared the men on the road.

Lann Aelle's men locked shields and held their spears before them. An enemy would have to face the long weapons before they could close with the warriors holding them.

The mailed Saxons stood before their dead and dying comrades and formed a shield wall. I peered through the undergrowth to see their leader. He would be the one we had to kill quickly. He was a broad warrior with a full-face helmet, a broad axe and a shield with a red boar's head painted upon it. His oathsworn had similar designs and were gathered around him. They began to advance in a boar's snout formation. This was like a double wedge. The men behind held their shields up to protect those at the front from the arrows and they advanced steadily confident in their ability to deal with lightly armed spearmen and archers.

Daffydd and his archers now had fewer targets and he slowed down the number of arrows they were loosing. They only needed to keep the shields of the Saxons raised. The warriors at the front hacked away the undergrowth and closed with the squires. This was the first test of the squires as warriors but I knew they were eager to prove themselves. When an equite fell in battle the best squire would join that elite group and all were keen to impress Lann Aelle and me.

I turned to the squire who was next to me and held the Roman buccina. "Sound the horn."

The Saxons were committed now and it was time for my horsemen to do their worst. The warriors slowed and looked at each other when they heard the horn. Their leader shouted, "On! Charge! There is just a handful of them!"

Saxon Slaughter

They hurled themselves at our line and I saw the shield and body of a young squire severed as the war axe smashed down on his head. The line was being forced back. I knew that it would. However, the extended line and the boar's snout formation meant that our flanks lapped around theirs and then I heard the wail of the dragon standard as Prince Pasgen and my son charged their left flank. I stepped forwards to join the line of spearmen. We had to hold them to allow the horsemen to begin to thin them out. As I slid Saxon Slayer from my scabbard I saw the line of horsemen led by Tuanthal. Although without mail they all held three javelins.

The squire before me fell and I stepped into the line and faced a mailed warrior with a plaited beard. He had an open helmet and I could see that he anticipated another simple victory. His sword smashed onto my shield and stopped as it jarred against a metal stud. I had metal and leather covering the oak shield and it would not be destroyed easily. I saw the look of surprise on his face and I swung Saxon Slayer overhand towards his head. He held his shield up and the force of the blow cracked the shield and forced it down onto this helm. He was shaken and before he could strike a blow in retaliation I swung it again and his shield shivered and a crack appeared. As he swung his sword I punched with the boss of my shield and he reeled from the blow. He was now no longer in control and he panicked. I lifted my sword and he swung his shield in anticipation. I twisted the blade in the air and stabbed him in his throat.

I saw that Tuanthal and his men had now joined the fray and the pressure on the squires had lessened. There were now many gaps which showed that they had stood their ground and died. I glanced to the left and saw Hogan Lann laying about him with his mace. I could see the lances protruding from the dead oathsworn of the leader of the warband. Even as I watched, Pol smashed his mace into the head of a mailed warrior who briefly stood, like a statue, and then fell to the ground. That was the effective end of the battle for the best of their warriors had died and it was now a slaughter. Daffydd and his archers picked their targets and, one by one, the last of the warband died.

As the last warrior died my men let out a huge cheer and began chanting, "Wolf Warrior". I had not fought beneath my wolf banner as I did not want my enemies to know I was back in Rheged. As none of the warband had survived my men could indulge themselves and they had

Saxon Slaughter

earned a famous victory. The squires who had survived could look forward to becoming equites soon.

My men were soon stripping the bodies of weapons and armour. We could begin to arm the men of Rheged once more. "Myrddyn, find out the cost."

When he returned he had a grim face. "The Saxons fought well, Warlord. The equites lost four knights and the squires lost fifteen men. Captain Tuanthal only suffered five casualties.

While the losses were heavier than I had wished they would not hurt our ability to hit the enemy with our heavy horses for four squires would now replace the dead equites. Next time I would have to be more careful with how I used them. Now I had to order my men to perform a grisly but necessary task.

"I want the heads taken from every Saxon." I waved Aedh over. "Find enough shattered spears and javelins. Take the heads back to Castle Perilous. I want the heads mounting atop the spears and leaving as a warning to the Saxons that we are back. Captain Tuanthal, have your men help Aedh."

Lann Aelle said, "This is not like you, uncle."

"It cannot hurt the dead and if I can intimidate the Saxons then so much the better. We need them to fear us and this will cause them to be nervous next time we fight them."

"It may make them keen for revenge."

I smiled, "Even better for a hothead does not think clearly."

We headed back to Wide Water with the equites and squires carrying our booty. Hogan Lann rode next to me. "The squires did well."

"Aye but I hope we do not have to keep using them in this way. They are too valuable for us to throw away. I hope that we have bought enough time to train up some of the men of Rheged."

Myrddyn coughed, "It will take them the better part of a month for the Saxons to realise there is a problem. By the time they send men to investigate it will be autumn and travelling will be harder."

I nodded. Hogan Lann said, "And what are our plans?"

My son knew me almost as well as Myrddyn. "We will not sit back and wait. We will take the war to them. Before the month is out I want to hit them."

"At Dunelm?"

"No that is a nut which is too hard to crack with horsemen. We shall do as they do and strike at their outlying settlements and make them go on the defensive. Myrddyn is correct. It will be spring before they try to wrest this land from us."

"Perhaps they will not try at all. Maybe they will just hold what they have."

"I pray for that but I do not think it will be. Their new king, Edwin, cannot afford to show weakness. Aethelfrith and his sons would return and recover their kingdom. No, he will fight and then we shall see the measure of this new king."

I left Hogan Lann with the archers, squires and the wounded at Wide Water while Price Pasgen and I headed north to Carvetiorum. I had no idea what I would find there but Kay had told me that the Saxons had only occupied it for a brief time. It was deserted. I had no idea why; had I been the Saxons I would have made that my base for it was a soundly built castle and, unlike Deva, had not been abandoned after the Romans had left. It had been maintained and looked after by King Urien and the kings who preceded him.

I promised Hogan Lann that we would retreat if we felt we were in any danger. I had to smile to myself as we headed north. My son was worried about his father. Perhaps he was fooled by the white in my beard and hair. I was a little slower than I had been but the grey did not impair my thoughts. Aedh and his scouts rode with us. I could see that he was desperate to be off the leash. He liked the freedom scouting brought. After we had left the land of the lakes the land became gentler leading to the fort which had been Luguvalium in Roman times. I could see that there were still people living close to the river but the fortress itself looked to be abandoned. I wondered if the smaller fort, the Petriana which was further north, was also abandoned.

I could see the distress on Prince Pasgen's face. This had been his home and when he had been a boy the thought of a derelict and deserted fortress would have seemed impossible. Myrddyn spoke quietly so that just the prince and I could hear. "It can be made good again Prince Pasgen. The walls have not been breached. Remember Deva; that was in much worse condition than this is. The good news is that we do not have to bleed men to recapture it. This is a gift from the gods."

The villagers from Civitas Carvetiorum hid in their homes when we rode in. It was only when they recognised the dragon standard of Prince Pasgen that they came out, fearfully at first. Then one of my old soldiers recognised me and rushed over, one arm hanging uselessly by his side. "It is true! The Warlord has returned. The prophecy was true!"

That was the signal for the whole settlement to rush out and greet us. Myrddyn gave me a wry smile and a little shake of the head. He knew that he was as much responsible for the legend that was the Wolf Warrior as I was. We had created a monster. The one-armed man came to my side. "Do you remember me, my lord? My name is Aidan. I served you at Castle Perilous."

I took his good hand. "Of course I do and I remember the spear which took your arm. I am glad to see that you live still."

"It has been hard, my lord. The Saxons come each year and take what little we have saved. There are too few of us to stand and fight and we have no weapons." He looked fearfully to the east as though expecting the imminent arrival of a warband. "They are due soon. We dread this time of year."

"They will not be coming this year, Aidan. We have slaughtered them and we will be bringing weapons for you to use. Prince Pasgen is coming back to this land."

I had thought that would have pleased Aidan but he came closer to me. "His brother King Ywain invited the Saxons to our land. The people will fight for you, Warlord. They know you will not let them down."

It was like a dagger to my heart. I had let them down and I had deserted them. I resolved to do better this time. "Prince Pasgen is not his brother and he has been with me and my warriors fighting the Saxons since he left Rheged. This time we will defeat them." I could see the other villagers speaking with men they recognised amongst my retinue. "Aidan, who is the head man here?"

"That would be me."

"Good. We are beginning to raise an army of Rheged to defend the land from the Saxons. We are raising companies of ten men under a leader and we need men who can train them. I know you have but one good arm yet I know that you have the head and the ability to train men. Will you be my leader of a hundred for this land?"

His face lit up. "I would deem it an honour Warlord. And I will learn to fight with my left hand."

"You need not Aidan for it is you as a leader that I need. We will talk more. If you will visit with me in the morning and let me know your thoughts on the men you will train."

Myrddyn and Tuanthal had been listening to me. Prince Pasgen had been busy acknowledging the crowds who gathered around him and his magnificently attired equites.

"I fear we have much work to do with Prince Pasgen Warlord."

I knew that Myrddyn was right. "We will make sure that he is as well trained as the people he will lead before we return home."

We dragged the reluctant prince into the fortress. The doors were just open. It was as though the garrison had walked out one day and never returned. The ditch had not been cleaned and required work but it was not beyond repair. It was both sad and exciting to ride into the building once more. This was where I had learned to be a warrior and I glanced over at the Praetorium building where Brother Osric had toiled away. It was normally the first place I visited.

"Captain Tuanthal, put the horses in the stable and allocate the men to their barracks. Find men who can cook. We will be in the king's quarters."

I could not help myself and I strode towards Brother Osric's cell. I just had to inspect it. As soon as I entered I felt the presence of that tiny man. I could almost see him there. The room was empty but it was as though a shadow remained. I could see that animals had been ferreting in there and birds had nested but no one had disturbed it and that was as it should be. I closed the door as I left.

The rest of the king's residence showed the same traces of animals although all the other rooms had had anything of value or use taken. If Prince Pasgen was going to live there then he would have to begin afresh. None of us spoke as we examined every room. We all had our own thoughts as we each remembered the past.

"It is sad to see it thus, Warlord."

I turned at the sound of Tuanthal's voice. I was about to speak when Myrddyn said, "Visiting the past is always difficult but at least we can have a new start." He looked at me and then nodded towards Prince Pasgen. This had been his home. His mother and father were buried just beyond its walls.

"Prince Pasgen, would you live here again?"

He seemed wrapped up in his memories and I was about to repeat the question when he said, "Until I re-entered this room I did not think so but now I know. I shall bring my wife and my daughter here. She can furnish this home and make it a palace once more."

That pleased me. The house of King Urien would live again. "Good and I have spoken with the headman, Aidan. Tomorrow he will meet with us and give us his assessment of how many men the town can provide." I swept a hand around the great hall in which we stood. "This will need guards who are not your equites and you will need an income."

I could see from his face that he had not thought about how he would pay for his new home. Myrddyn obviously had for he said, "This year the people of Rheged will need to enjoy the fruits of their labour but next year you must tax them for the defence of the realm. Until then," he grinned, "I think that the Saxons should pay."

We spent the next five days visiting the surrounding area and creating the defenders of Rheged. I am not a vain man but had I been then the flattery and praise I received might have gone to my head. It did not and that was partly due to Myrddyn's sharp tongue which brought me down to earth each time I forgot myself. We left Prince Pasgen to organise his land. "Bring your horsemen to Castle Perilous in five days' time. We march to Northumbria. I will send the weapons for your men."

Already Aidan had organised sentries and guards for the fortress. It would be easier once winter arrived and there was less for the men to do around their farms. He had begun to train them and by mid-winter, they would be able to defend the walls of the castle. It would take time but Rheged would have an army once more.

The fort at Wide Water was completed by the time we returned. Kay had his ten men who took it in turns to guard the new stronghold. He smiled at me and looked ten years younger when I reached his walls. "My brother and his people are happier now, Warlord. Even if we leave them again they feel that they have somewhere they can defend themselves and be safe."

The comment, although innocent enough, was like a barb. The people had been abandoned. Would I have to abandon them again? I thought of my family safely sheltered beneath Wyddfa and I wanted to go back. I probably would abandon them again and I hated myself for that. I had sworn an oath and the Wolf Warrior was in danger of breaking that oath. I did not sleep well that night.

We left the next day for Castle Perilous. I was a truly grumpy old man as we rode along a similar road to my old home. Only Myrddyn understood my humour. The younger ones, Lann Aelle, Pol and Hogan Lann all kept their distance. I think that Tuanthal and Aedh as well as Daffydd saw me differently; I was Warlord and not like other men.

The fort was a blackened scar on the landscape. The fire which I had started to cover our escape had raged through the wooden walls and buildings. The stones which had been white were black with soot. It was where Hogan's mother and his sister were buried and, when he saw the remains, he too, became more morose. I wanted to see if we could build a fort there again. As I trudged the ruins I knew I could not. There were too many memories. We would have to build another site. We had already passed a suitable site close to the ford at the river. We had seen a small village there called Penrhyd. There was a hill overlooking the ford and it still defended the road to our heartland. It would make a good place for a fort.

We made a camp by the river and waited for Prince Pasgen. Aedh and his scouts were sent east to find our next target. Soon it would be autumn but we needed to both hurt the Saxons and provide the means to make Prince Pasgen's army a force to be reckoned with. His people needed more food and weapons.

We headed east as soon as Prince Pasgen arrived. The road we followed was still the ancient Roman one. Having destroyed the warband I was not worried about meeting any Saxon warriors. The road would bring us, if we followed it to its end, to the old Roman road of Dere Street which transfixed Northumbria. The Dunum was the lifeblood of the southern half of Northumbria. It would be a good place to begin.

Aedh found us on the high pass of Stanmore. Even though it was still late summer the winds blew from the cold east and chilled us to the bone. Those of my warriors who had their own wolf cloak were grateful for its warmth as the east wind whistled. "There are more villages than when we were here last, Warlord. They have begun to build forts too. The villages close to the Dunum plain look to be the better targets. They have many sheep and cattle."

"Then that is where we will go."

Hogan Lann had been quiet for some time. "You are silent my son. What troubles you?"

"This raiding of the Saxon villagers does not sit well with me."

"Nor with me and I will tell you this, I would not harm any of the people but we need to provide for our own. The villages we will raid have benefited from the Saxon depredations in Rheged which is why there are more of them. We are redressing the balance."

He still looked doubtful. "What if they fight?"

I laughed and pointed to the column of men who followed us. "If you were a Saxon and saw this mighty host what would you do? Fight or run?"

He smiled, "Run as fast as I could."

Saxon Slaughter

"We will take their animals and any crops they have gathered. We will not burn their homes and we will not take their lives. They will have a hard winter but the Dunum is a fertile river; they will survive."

Myrddyn's voice came from behind us. "And that will sting the Saxons into action and they will send warriors west. We can defeat them on our ground for we will have time to prepare. It is a necessary evil Hogan Lann. When you are Warlord then you too will have these difficult decisions to make."

Myrddyn was right and I had a duty to begin the training of the warrior who would take over when I ceased to be Warlord. He needed to be as ruthless as I had become or Rheged would wither and die.

As soon as we dropped down the other side of the pass we noticed the change in the climate. It became warmer once more. We also saw flocks of sheep gathered on the hillsides. The cattle were in the pastures lower down. Here there were many isolated farms and we began our work.

"Lann Aelle, we will use the squires to gather the sheep and the cattle. Detail twenty to take these sheep and cattle back to Wide Water."

"They will not like it, Warlord. They want to fight."

I could have snapped a reply but Lann Aelle was my nephew and he was speaking the truth. "Hopefully we will not have to fight at all, Lann Aelle. Tell them that."

Our numbers dwindled as we headed east. When we found animals the people fled and we sent the captured animals back to Rheged. By the time we reached Gainford the squires had all left us. We would use the horsemen of Tuanthal for the next sweep. Aedh pointed east as we gathered by the river. "This is a good base. There is a deserted village to the south of the ford which we can use and then carry onto the coast."

Aedh was not only a good scout, but he also had a sound military mind. With the squires gone we needed somewhere to store the spare horses and the armour of the equites. "Good. Prince Pasgen, take your equites north of the ford and gather what you can. Hogan Lann, head to the coast and Tuanthal we will head south. Daffydd, guard the camp." I smiled, "I grew up around here and there is fine hunting to be had in the woods."

The land to the south of the river was familiar to me. I had grown up there. We rode towards Stanwyck. The remains of my village lay like the bones of a long-dead animal. It had been picked over like a carcass by carrion. The Saxons had not occupied the site and it felt like a graveyard as we rode through its banks and ditches. I kicked Mona on and we descended towards the fertile plain which bordered the next hills. The villages and villagers soon hid when they heard the thunder of our approach and we managed to collect twenty cattle which we drove back to Gainford. We were the first to return.

Aedh and his scouts were divided between Prince Pasgen and Hogan Lann's equites. The lighter, more nimble horses of the scouts would give them the speed the equites lacked. Hogan Lann and his men had a flock of sheep to show for their troubles but I could see that his equites were less than happy about being shepherds. We wondered where Prince Pasgen had got to when two of Aedh's scouts galloped in.

"My Lord, Prince Pasgen and his men have been ambushed by a Saxon warband."

Chapter 5

"We were heading back with twenty sheep and a few goats. The horses of the equites were being led. We were close to the old deserted Roman fort when the warband fell upon us. They outnumbered us and the prince have taken refuge in the fort. He is surrounded. We were ahead and we rode here."

"Hogan Lann, have your men don their armour. Daffydd, leave half of your men here to guard the animals and bring the rest. Tuanthal, we will ride now. Follow as soon as you can, my son."

Prince Pasgen's men had not been armoured and were vulnerable to an attack from Saxons. I cursed myself for my arrogance. I had assumed too much. It had been so easy I thought there were no Saxon warriors. I had been wrong. The fort I knew well and it was less than three miles away along the river. As we rode I questioned the scouts again. "How many Saxons were there?"

"There looked to be over a hundred my lord but they attacked from the woods and it was hard to count."

I could not blame the scouts. They had managed to bring us the news of the disastrous attack. "Have your swords ready. With the Prince's men and ours, we should outnumber them. Daffydd, dismount your men when we are close."

"Aye my lord." There were only twenty archers with us but they could prove to be the difference.

We could hear the clash of arms as we approached the fort on the river. The Saxons were pressing the walls. There was no gate and I could see Prince Pasgen and some of his men fighting valiantly.

"Rheged!" Tuanthal's men roared our war cry as we crashed into their rear ranks. I hacked at the head of a Saxon who turned at our approach. Mona cleverly sidestepped a second Saxon who swung his sword at her head. I kicked at him as I passed. I threw myself from my horse and swung my shield around. Two warriors headed directly for me. I did not wait for them to close and I ran at them. I punched at one with my shield while I hacked at the second with my sword. Saxon Slayer is a powerful blade and the force of it shattered the shield of the warrior. He looked in surprise as the two halves fell at his feet. I brought the sword around in a sideways slice and laid him open. The man I had punched with my shield stabbed at me and I felt his sword slide along my side. I had decided not to wear armour and I felt the blood begin to trickle down my leg. When he saw the blood on his blade his face showed that he anticipated victory. It was premature. As he raised his sword for the killing blow I brought Saxon Slayer overarm to cleave his helmet and skull in two.

I looked around for there were no enemies before me. Behind me, I could see Tuanthal's horsemen fighting desperately to reach the walls. Then I heard the Roman horn and my son and his equites thundered in. There were only fifty of them but they had lances and armour. They washed over the Saxons like a wave on the beach. The Saxons fled. Hogan Lann and Pol pursued them north as they ran.

Myrddyn ran to me. "Warlord you are wounded."

"It is nothing." I put my hand down to my side and it came away covered in blood.

"I think it is." He cut away the cloth and there was a gash as long as a man's hand. He gave me a wad of cloth. "Here hold this to the wound." One of Aedh's scouts was nearby and Myrddyn grabbed him. "Help the Warlord while I get my pack." Myrddyn kept his potions and medicines with him at all time.

The scout looked in horror at the blood. He helped me to keep tight pressure on the cloth. I began to feel a little light-headed and I swayed. "Warlord, lie down before you fall."

I took the scout's advice and he helped me to sit on the ground. When Myrddyn returned he poured water on the wound and then took out some catgut. He began to sew the wound. He did not use neat stitches. I could see that he was just trying to stop the bleeding. I was just about to ask him how Prince Pasgen was when it all went black.

I opened my eyes and saw Hogan Lann looking down at me with concern on his face. I could smell burning. "What happened?"

Myrddyn's voice came from behind me. "You passed out. The wound is too big for stitches. We will have to use fire. Hogan Lann, Pol, hold his arms." I saw that Myrddyn had Saxon Slayer in the fire he had started. He smiled at me. "I believe we will use the magic of your sword to heal you. This will hurt Warlord but it will save your life." I watched as he brought the glowing weapon toward me. I could feel the heat as it passed close to me and then I smelled the burning of the flesh. The pain was excruciating and, had I not had my son and Pol holding me I would have wrenched myself free. I heard Myrddyn sigh. "There it is done and the bleeding has stopped. Lie there for a while. I have others who are wounded."

I looked up at my son and saw the worry on his face. He shook his head sadly. "I think we should have brought armour father. The Prince has lost ten equites and you nearly died."

"I know my son. We can return west now. We have enough for the winter and we have bloodied the Saxon's nose. Did you lose any men?"

"No Warlord. We had armour But Captain Tuanthal lost eight more men and he has others who are wounded."

"The Prince?"

"He lives. Now lie back. We will wake you when we are ready to leave."

Later as we rode the two miles back to our camp I reflected that we had been lucky. Had the prince been further from our camp then he would have died along with all his men. We had, in addition, gained weapons and armour from the eighty Saxons we had slain. I knew that they would pursue us but the Saxons did not use horses and I hoped we could reach Wide Water with our animals before they did so.

I slept fitfully for the wound, although sealed, still hurt. Myrddyn gave me a draught of something which numbed the pain but I feared the ride home. Hogan Lann was there when I rose. "Warlord, until you are healed I will command."

I was taken aback. His face showed that he would brook no argument. "Why? It is only a slight wound."

"It is not. Myrddyn is worried. You should just concentrate on getting home. Let me worry about protecting the animals and the men." He swept his arm around. "You have them all worried. They do not want to lose their Warlord and I do not wish to lose my father. Let me take the burden of command."

And so, for the first time, I allowed someone else to lead my men. Had it not been Hogan I would not have agreed but he was my son and I knew he had the ability. I had had a close encounter with death and it had made me think. Over the next three days, as we headed back west through increasingly cold weather, I wondered if the gods were sending me a sign. It felt like it to me.

Kay had not only trained his men while we were away he had had a warrior hall built for us. It made a difference for the autumn had begun on the way west and the wind wildly whipped us home. Myrddyn was concerned about my wound and made me undress completely when we were in the hall. "It is a little redder than it should be. We will have to watch it." He shook his head. "If we were close to Wyddfa I would have you bathe in its waters; they have healing powers."

"There is water close by which has that power."

Myrddyn said scornfully, "You mean the Wide Water? I think not."

"No Myrddyn. Before you came to us my mother's spirit came to me in Civitas Carvetiorum and told me to throw the sword in the lake by the fort. I did so and the sword came when I called for it."

I could see that he was dubious but the mention of my mother's spirit swayed him. "If your mother's spirit is associated with this water then perhaps there may be something in it. We will try it anyway."

We returned with Prince Pasgen and his men. The dead equites had been replaced by squires and the prince would need to begin to mould his new men into an effective fighting force. The journey north allowed us to talk.

"You have now seen the problems of fighting without armour. I fear this means that we will not be able to enlarge Rheged. We will have to hold what we have."

"I know Warlord. The new fort we will build at Penrhyd will have to be the eastern border."

Myrddyn said, "You forget, Prince Pasgen, that your fortress at Civitas Carvetiorum is also on the eastern edge of Rheged now. You too will be at the border. It is the land to the west which you will protect."

"It seems that Rheged will just be an island holding against a sea of Saxons."

I smiled, "Much as we have on Mona but we succeeded there Prince Pasgen. I have hopes that you too will prevail."

Myrddyn pointed to the sea. "You need trade, my prince, you need to use your ports and create trade. You know how well it worked for the Warlord."

"And perhaps Alt Cult may rise from the ashes and resist the Saxon oppressor."

"You both sound hopeful."

"It is the only way to be. Doubt is a savage enemy and weakens worse than war."

Like Kay in the south Aidan had not been idle and the fortress had an air of power once more. There were only two or three guards on the walls but the gate was closed and Prince Pasgen's dragon banner flew proudly from the tower. After the horses were stabled Myrddyn and I went to the lake. It was not large but it was deep. When Myrddyn saw it he nodded. "This would have been built by the Romans to provide fish for their fort. It may well have a link to your sword. Take Saxon Slayer with you."

I undressed and stepped into the icy water clutching my blade. As soon as the water touched the wound it seemed to numb it and it did not ache as much. I closed my eyes and let the water ebb around me. I wondered how long I should stay but I was in no hurry to leave. I felt at peace. Eventually, Myrddyn said, "The water has had time enough. Come and I will examine the wound."

He was pleased with the effect. "It is less red and angry. How does it feel?"

"It feels less painful and I can move a little easier."

The wizard looked at the water. "I will have to think about this lake. There may be power here." He looked around. "And yet I can see no reason for its magic."

"Perhaps there are older forces at work here Myrddyn."

Myrddyn was never afraid to admit to his failings and he nodded. "You are right. I suspect Osric and King Urien might have been able to shed some light on this phenomenon." Sadly they were in the Otherworld and we would never know from whence the waters derived their powers but they had worked. My wound healed well from that day and I was just left with another scar.

We spent autumn travelling around Rheged and using the weapons we had captured to arm the men in each area. Prince Pasgen had used the ambush in a positive way. He threw himself into the raising of the army. As for me, I took the opportunity to allow Hogan Lann to organise my forces. It was he who supervised the patrols to the east as well as the building of the fort at Penrhyd. I was healing but it was slower than I would have liked. Myrddyn saw my problem and counselled me. "Warlord you have lived longer than most men. You are now of an age with King Urien, probably older than he was. Your days in the shield wall are gone and soon you will have to relinquish the power you hold."

"But I am Warlord and the people expect me to lead."

He looked at me with a world-weary look. "It is a title. Could not Hogan Lann fulfil the same title?"

It was then that I saw what was stopping me. It was not the title, it was the sword. Saxon Slayer was part of the Warlord; how could I give it up. I knew that it would go to my son but I felt that if I gave up the sword I was saying that I was no longer a leader. If I did that then what would I do? Would I spend the days bouncing Hogan Lann's children on my knee? I could not give up the title for I was not finished yet. I had a promise to keep.

I had forgotten how harsh the winters were in Rheged. The island of Mona was washed by balmy winds and seas, even in winter. The only time we saw snow was on the top of Wyddfa but here the land was buried by snow. The one consolation we had was that it prevented the Saxons from avenging our attacks and we could continue to train and arm the men.

Hogan Lann and Prince Pasgen came to me after the first snow. "Warlord, we think you should return to Mona for the winter. You are serving no purpose here and we can carry on your work. Return again in the spring."

It was blunt and I was taken aback. "You do not need me?"

"We did not say that. We said that you could return and be with Myfanwy, Nanna and Gawan."

I looked to Myrddyn for help. He smiled enigmatically. "It was my idea, Warlord and I will return with you. Daffydd is due at Alavna in the next week we can return with him and your wound will heal faster closer to Wyddfa."

I looked at my captains in turn and they all nodded. "It seems you all conspire against me. I will do as you wish but reluctantly."

Hogan Lann laughed. "So long as you do as we wish I care not." He came and embraced me. "Take this as a sign of the love we have for you, father. We nearly lost you and we would have you lead us for some time to come."

"You do not wish to take over from me?"

He shook his head. "I will always follow you wherever you lead for as long as you wish to lead us."

I left with Myrddyn the next day. Aedh and his scouts escorted us and we took the road over the high pass to Alavna. It seemed the weather was also against us for we had to travel through the snow which came up to our horse's withers but Aedh and his scouts made a path for us and soon we dropped down to the warmer coastline and the snow disappeared. I did not envy Aedh his journey back but he did not complain. They waited with me for the ship which arrived a day later.

We took the opportunity of starting a defence force for the port as well as creating a headman to begin trading with other places. They were keen on the change. Fishing was an erratic business and trade would make them all rich. As I waved farewell to Alavna and Aedh I wondered if I would return and what changes I would see. My wound had changed my life, of that I was certain.

The voyage home was a stormy one in more ways than one. The fierce winds from the east which had battered us in our fort now forced us further west than we wished to go. The two horses were terrified as the winds buffeted and smashed into us driving us well off course. We struggled all afternoon and well into the night to control the bucking ship. When dawn broke we saw, alarmingly to the west, land. That could only be Hibernia. I knew that the Hibernians would dearly love to get their hands on me. I had bested them every time I fought them. I had sailed into their heartland and killed one of their kings. We had to sail as far away from that place as possible. Daffydd headed east.

When we saw the land appear to the east Daffydd looked worried, "I am afraid, Warlord, that we have sailed from one danger and into another. This is the island the Saxons call Man. They now control it. We will have to sail around the coast of this dangerous place and hope that they have no ships to chase us."

I knew what he meant. The Saxons used oared ships and, as we were sailing into the wind, they could easily catch us. I nodded to Myrddyn. "Let us man a bolt thrower. It seems we are not meant to have a leisurely journey to our home."

Daffydd looked genuinely upset, "I am sorry Warlord."

Myrddyn answered for me, "It is *wyrd*, captain. We can do nothing about it but just the best that we can. Do not worry, the Warlord and I have faced dangers like this before. We will survive."

Myrddyn had an optimism I did not share. We had just four warriors on board and only two bolt throwers. If more than one ship came to capture this valuable prize then we would be dead men. I felt better as we took the canvas from the bolt throwers and prepared them for action. It gave me something to do and I felt useful once more. As we checked the tension on the war machines I glanced over to the hump of an island which rose menacingly to our right. I could see smoke from their fires and, as we passed the northern tip, I saw fishing boats in the small bay. Perhaps we would have some luck and it would just be fishing ships that we saw.

Our progress was slow as the wind was coming from the east and Daffydd was fighting both wind and tide. I was glad when the island became slightly smaller as it showed me that we were moving away from the danger. I saw a larger village and, with a sinking feeling, I saw the two larger ships. There were Saxons there. Perhaps they would not have noticed us or would not be able to man the ship in time. Myrddyn and I stood and stared. Myrddyn shrugged as he said, "They are coming. It would be best to put your mail on Warlord."

He was right, of course. It was unlikely that it would make much difference but at least with mail I might survive long enough to give the others on the ship a chance. We were tantalizingly close to the sanctuary of Caer Gybi. I could see, just on the horizon, the white tipped top of Wyddfa. It might as well have been on the other side of the world for the Saxon ships were being rowed hard to catch the prize that was my ship.

When I had armed and donned both cloak and helmet I stood again at the stern with Myrddyn and the captain. I could see that the two ships were closing rapidly and we were barely moving. I looked at Daffydd. He had been my captain since he had been a young man and he was a good seaman. "Well Daffydd, if you have any tricks up your sleeves now would be a good time to try them."

He smiled and looked up at the pennant on the masthead. "We could gain some speed if we sailed with the wind on our quarter but that would mean heading back to their island for a short time. Once we were beyond the southern tip we would have sea room." He pointed at the ships, "They cannot keep this speed up for long but they will catch us soon unless we do something."

Myrddyn rubbed his hands together. "Then turn the ship and we will try the bolt thrower. The gods help those who help themselves."

It was a move the Saxons were not expecting. I tried to picture what they would see. Instead of our stern, heading fearfully away they would see us beam on. They would think we had panicked. As the ship heeled over and the wind suddenly caught us we had to hold onto the bolt thrower to keep our balance. Myrddyn aimed the bolt thrower as one of the Saxon ships shifted course to try to intercept us.

"Have another bolt ready Warlord."

I knelt down to pick up another of the deadly missiles. Myrddyn released the bolt. It flew across the water and smashed through the rail at the bow. I heard screams as splinters of wood struck the rowers and then saw the boat yaw as the bolt embedded itself in one of the men steering the ship. It slowed, not by much but enough to allow me to load the Roman weapon again. The second boat increased the rate at which the oars struck the water and it followed our turn. It was safe from our bolts so long as it stayed there.

Myrddyn changed the trajectory of the second bolt and we struck the Saxon ship just below the waterline. As I loaded again I watched. There appeared to be no effect at all and then, suddenly, they stopped rowing. I saw the bows of the ship dip as the crew fought to seal the breach our bolt had created.

"Warlord, let us get to the other bolt thrower." There were two on each side. Had the ship been fully crewed for war there would have been extra men on board to man them. Daffydd had not expected trouble and was travelling lighter.

I could see that we had passed the southern tip of the island and Myrddyn shouted to the captain, "Put her hard over captain."

Everyone on board knew how clever Myrddyn was and yet it seemed to go against common sense. We would be heading into the wind and we would be almost stopped. I nodded to Daffydd who put the tiller hard over. We ran to the other side. The machine was ready to send its deadly missile across the water. The Saxon ship was going at full speed and was slicing through the sea. As we turned the bow of our ship raised and then dipped as we stopped. It was bizarre; we were in the path of the Saxon ship. Their captain had a quick decision to make. Did he ram us and risk sinking the ship with whatever cargo we carried? He chose the alternative and turned slightly. It was the opportunity Myrddyn had been waiting for and he loosed the bolt. Without waiting to see the effect he ran to the second thrower as I reloaded the first. I watched as the bolt crashed through the sides and the rowers. The mast shivered on the Saxon ship as the bolt smashed into it. The second bolt hit the ship at the stern. The tiller shattered and the Saxon ship was dead in the water. Myrddyn reached me as I had just readied the first bolt thrower and he sent the last bolt into the ship's bowels. It began to take on water.

Daffydd's men cheered and we resumed our course. I could see the Saxons as they began to bail out their ship. The two ships would survive but they would take some repairing. I saw the captain of the second ship staring across the water. I took off my helmet and stared back. He would know the prize he had missed. Any Saxon would sacrifice two ships to get their hands on Lord Lann, Warlord of Rheged and Wolf Warrior. They had come close again but failed.

We headed for the landing stage close to my home. Wyddfa looked welcoming despite the snow on the top of its craggy peak. As we gently bumped into the wooden jetty I said, "I think that, from now on, we will man our ships fully, no matter what the journey. I would not have us lose a ship. Until today I had not thought that the Saxons were so close. We will need to watch them."

"Aye Warlord. I have already increased the number of bolt throwers at Caer Gybi. I wish to discourage any attacks from the west."

We rode the short way to the gates of the fortress. No one knew we were coming but my horse and my armour were recognised. Myfanwy's face showed her concern and was echoed by her words. "Why have you returned my love?"

I briefly thought of lying but I knew that when she found the truth there would be a bigger price to pay. "I was slightly wounded and my son thought that it would do me good to recover here." She nodded and held my hand. "Besides it will do him good to lead men."

She led me indoors. Myrddyn called, "I will speak with you later Warlord. I have much to do." We had spent some of the journey working out better ways to protect our men and to fight our foes. Myrddyn and Brother Oswald would put their heads together and provide solutions. That I knew.

Once we were in our quarters she said, "Show me the wound."

I had learned, over the years, not to argue with Myfanwy. I could get away with many things but this was not one of them. She frowned as she saw the cauterised wound. "Is it sore?"

I shook my head. "The sea voyage hardened it up a little."

She ran her fingers over the wound. "Why did the wizard not stitch the wound?"

"It was too big."

"And I assume you were not wearing your mail?"

"No, but we were not expecting to fight." I saw her opening her mouth and her eyes widening. I held my finger to her lips. "I have promised Hogan that I will wear my mail at all times from now on."

She snorted, "A little late for that. Anyway, you had better bathe. King Cadfan visits on the morrow. I did not know you were coming home so it will be a surprise for him too."

I could hear the reproach in her voice. "Perhaps I should have stayed away then."

She put her hands on her hips and cocked her head to one side. "Listen to me Warlord, I am pleased to see you home and I would like you to stay. Let us leave it at that."

I grabbed her and kissed her. "The bath can wait."

"And what about the wound?"

"I am a warrior!"

Later when I had bathed and dressed I felt much better. The sea voyage was long forgotten. It was quiet around the table that night. Nanna and her mother had been arguing and there was a frosty silence. Gawan was keen to hear about the battles but his mother forbade such talk at mealtimes. I winked and said quietly to him, "Later, I will tell you." That satisfied him and I ate a hot meal in a comfortable room. I was getting too old for campaigning.

After the meal, I told Gawan of the raids and the skirmishes. I realised that soon he would need to begin his training in earnest. He would have the skills with a sword soon but a warrior needed more than a sword. I would have to find a good warrior to help me. There had been a time when I would have relished the role but I had too many responsibilities. Even Hogan and Pol had too much to do. Perhaps Lann Aelle would be the best choice, but he was in Rheged.

After the children had retired Myfanwy asked me how I thought Rheged would be ruled. "Prince Pasgen can be the head of the land but he will need help."

"You?" I could hear the doubt in her voice.

"I do not think so. It is no longer my land. I am content to be here. I missed this, you and the children. I am getting too old to sleep in fields."

"Nonsense, you love it."

I shook my head. I do not mind leading men in battle it is all the other elements I do not like."

She took that in and then went on. "And Princess Pasgen, what of her and his daughter, Riemmelth."

"I think he will want them with him. You would wish to accompany me too would you not?"

"I would but I am made of sterner stuff than the Princess Pasgen. "

"Carvetiorum is a comfortable palace. She will be happy."

"In a land of warriors? What will she do without female company? Here she has other women to speak with."

I was confused. She had her husband; what more did she require? Pasgen's warriors will marry eventually."

"Pah! Men! I will have to come up with something."

I had no doubt that she would come up with something. She was a very resourceful woman.

Chapter 6

King Cadfan came with just his family and his bodyguard. I made sure that we gave him the honour guard he merited but Cadfan had served as a squire with many of the men who now bowed a knee to him. His power had not gone to his head. His father had allowed the crown to give him delusions of grandeur. Cadfan was a more thoughtful king. I noticed how much Cadwallon had grown. Gawan was keen to see him and they ran off to rough house in the stables. We retired to my hall where Myrddyn awaited.

"You have returned early then Warlord?"

"I was not needed. We bloodied the Saxons and took many sheep and cattle. The land does not suit winter warfare but I will return in the springtime. And you King Cadfan?"

Myfanwy stood and held out her hand to the Queen. "Come your majesty, let us leave them to talk of war we will go and find the other ladies of the court."

I smiled at her as she left. She was already plotting and planning. Cadfan visibly relaxed as they left us alone with Myrddyn. "I am pleased we are alone. I always feel guilty talking of war and plots in front of the ladies."

"I know what you mean. Cadwallon is growing up quickly is he not?"

"Yes, Warlord and I would ask a boon of you."

"If it is in my power then I will do it."

"I would like you to train Cadwallon as you trained me."

I was taken aback. I had thought that the king would wish to mould his son himself. Then I saw the hand of *wyrd* in all of this. My son Gawan was ready to be a warrior too. The two of them could be trained together. I just needed a warrior to help me. "If you are sure then I will accede. How does his mother feel about this?"

He smiled ruefully, "I think he is a little boisterous for his mother. She hopes that the next child will be a girl."

"That is women all over for you but she should be careful what she wishes for. Nanna and Myfanwy butt heads more times than mountain goats." I looked at the door. "And I pray that you do not tell my wife the inappropriate image I just used."

Both Myrddyn and the king laughed, "It is good to see that something scares the Warlord." The king became more serious. "How did it go in Rheged?" I told him and I saw the relief on his face. "I know that it is selfish but I am pleased. It means King Edwin and his Mercian allies will be looking north and I can encroach a little more into Mercian territory."

Myrddyn went to the table in the corner and brought out the map he and Oswald kept updating. It had begun life as Brother Osric's pet project and it was now a comprehensive picture of the lands around Rheged and Gwynedd. "Can you give me any more details of places further east?"

The eastern side of the map had more empty spaces than the west and the north. We had a good picture of the land north of the Roman Fort of Eboracum but further south we just had the Roman Road and the main Roman towns. We spent the next hour adding detail. "Thank you King Cadfan. I will have Brother Oswald make you a copy."

Myfanwy had arranged a feast. Princess Pasgen as well as my daughter in law and the other captains and their ladies were present. She always handled feasts well and was like Niamh who had been the wife of King Urien. She always ensured that everyone, children included, was catered for. When Gawan and Cadwallon were told that I would be training them they were delighted. They were less happy when I told them that Brother Oswald and Myrddyn would also be part of their education.

Poor Cadwallon's face fell. "I thought I would just be learning how to use a sword."

"If you were just to be warrior then that would be enough but you will lead your people, both of you and you will need other skills."

"But father you have Hogan to lead the armies. Can I not be like Lann Aelle and just be a warrior?"

"Lann Aelle also learned much from Myrddyn and Brother Oswald." My son did not yet know of my plans for my nephew. Perhaps when he did he would understand better.

Myrddyn shook his head and pretended to be offended, "I do not know if I wish to teach such ingrates, Warlord. Perhaps my magic is not for them."

Gawan suddenly became interested. "Magic? You would teach us magic?"

"I might it depends upon the respect that I receive."

"Oh, I am sorry Myrddyn. I meant nothing by that. Forget my comments. I just thought it would be book learning. Brother Oswald is a kind man but he is dull."

Myfanwy was shocked, "Gawan! Do not be rude. Brother Oswald is a good teacher."

The two boys realised that they had said too much and they scurried out of the room as quickly as they could. "Their real training for war will have to wait until we have made them stronger and Lann Aelle returns. Tell me, would you wish your son to come with to Rheged."

Myfanwy looked appalled, "You cannot take them to war. They are too young."

"I had already killed men when I was younger than they are. However, if you do not wish them to go then they can stay here."

"Oh no, husband for then I would be the wicked one. But you will have to watch out for them." My wife had a mind like a bear trap and she knew of the problems she would have with Gawan if he had to stay at home. Life with Nanna was hard enough.

I sighed. "As if I wouldn't."

She was right however, I would have to be more careful when I took the boys north with me in the spring.

The next few months were busy ones for me. I had another ship to commission and I had to increase the trade with Rheged. The two boys saw more of Brother Oswald and Myrddyn than they did of me. I still had not found someone to train the boys. Perhaps Wyddfa felt my dilemma for a visitor arrived who would change our lives and prove a more valuable warrior than I could have wished for.

He was Einar the Dane. He had journeyed from Hibernia to serve me. He arrived not long after we returned from Rheged. A small trader brought him to the island and he crossed the island of Mona to serve me. My warriors were a little worried at first for he looked a little like a Saxon but he was much bigger. He was a blond giant. The young warrior told me that he wished to serve me. He had heard the tales of Lord Lann and Myrddyn and he had left his home in Hibernia and sailed to Mona to see if the legends were true. We were always looking for good warriors but we rarely looked beyond our own people. There was something about Einar which made me break my own unwritten rule. He swore on my sword and became my oathsworn.

My other warriors soon told me how good he was with a sword. He deigned mail, probably because he could not afford any and his sword was not of the highest quality but he bested all of the warriors in my fortress. He was not just a good warrior he was a great warrior. His people liked individual combat and he excelled at that. That was why he would not make a good warrior for my shield wall. He did not have the discipline to stand with locked shields. That meant he was perfect as a mentor. He would be able to make the two young men stronger. He was a fine teacher and they enjoyed all of their lessons. I think the variety kept them occupied although they found it physically draining even with two young men with energy to spare. I also worked out with Einar. He helped me to recover from my wound. He knew how to build muscle to help protect a warrior's body. He had proved a godsend and I wondered how he had ended up in my land; it was *wyrd*.

 The days were getting longer when we journeyed back north. I had decided to take Einar with me. Not only would he be able to keep an eye on the boys, but he would also be like a bodyguard for me. We took my new ship and two others when we headed north. I had many more weapons for Prince Pasgen. Myfanwy had also mentioned to Princess Pasgen about her eventual home in the north and we carried many items of furniture which my wife had assured me would make life more bearable in the far north.

 As we sailed through the icy grey waters off the coast of Man I noticed Einar looking west. Myrddyn and I joined him. "Do you miss Hibernia?"

 "No Warlord. I went there seeking my fortune but they are just pirates and backstabbers. They have no honour."

 I was puzzled, "Then why did you come to me? None of my men has fortunes."

 He looked uncomfortable. "I had heard the stories of how you and the wizard fought against the Saxons and then vanished. I wished that I could have met you. Then one night, when I was in my home, I was visited by a spirit. She came to me through the fog and she told me that I should travel west to the golden island. The men in my village said that at one time that had been the island of Britannia but since the Saxons came it was a dark place and they said the spirit must have meant Hibernia. They were wrong. When I found out how wrong they were I went on a journey and I found steps made by a giant. I travelled along those steps and I saw an island in the east and the sun was coming up behind it. It looked golden. On my way back I found a cave on the hillside and I entered. There was a lake and it was restful to lie there. I fell asleep and the spirit came again to me. This time I saw her as a woman and not just a fog with a woman's voice. She said, "Seek the wolf warrior, seek the Warlord." When I awoke I went to ask the men in the village of the Wolf Warrior. They told me it was you, Lord Lann. I knew then that I was meant to serve you and so I left Hibernia as soon as I could."

Myrddyn and I shared a look. Einar said, "You do not look surprised."

"No Einar for that spirit has visited both Myrddyn and me often. It is the spirit of my mother. You were meant to come to my home. There will be a task for you although I cannot see it yet myself."

The young warrior appeared genuinely moved. "I have already sworn an oath on your sword, Warlord but now it means even more. I shall serve you faithfully for I believe our destinies are entwined."

"He is right Warlord. His coming is part of something we cannot see yet."

The two boys adored the Danish giant. He knew ships and he took them around the boat as we headed north. Our journey was less eventful than the one south but the spring seas made it unpleasant and we were glad to see Alavna hove into view.

The headman had done as I had asked and there were now a few armed men around the village. The increased trade had made all of his people better off and we were greeted as though I was King Urien himself. I never liked that kind of attention and it amused Myrddyn but Einar and the boys were impressed. We had to unload the ponies we had brought to take the new supplies to Wide Water. I had hoped that someone would have sent men to help us but there were none.

The headman was visibly upset, "You will need men to lead the animals, Warlord."

I laughed, "If the five of us cannot lead twenty ponies a few miles then it is time I retired. We will be fine."

The boys took the task to heart and each led his five ponies as though they contained all the gold of Byzantium. Myrddyn and I smiled as they peered behind every rock and bush for an ambush. They slid their small swords in and out of their scabbards so often it almost made a tune. It showed me that they were serious about their duties and would perform them well.

We had left the furniture for Prince Pasgen's home at Alavna. I did not mind leading ponies but not heavy wagons. The ponies would be there to use for the young despatch riders. We had had many volunteers before I had returned to my home and now they would be able to use the ponies and take messages across Rheged. That would be a load off my mind.

Saxon Slaughter

Communication was vital. Prince Pasgen would have to learn how to administrate his land and I wondered about asking the monks at St.Asaph for a clerk. The monks of the White Christ were quite useful when they weren't trying to convert my men.

"Have you been to this land before Einar?"

"No, Warlord. I have never seen such high mountains before. Wyddfa is high but here the mountains seem to roll north forever. They must have been fashioned by the gods themselves. My land is flat."He shifted uncomfortably on his horse, "and I am not used to riding on a horse."

I laughed, "You will get used to it. My son, Hogan, is almost part horse. I ride when I have to."

Aedh's scouts found us close to the cave above the lake. "We wondered when you would return Warlord."

"It was very pleasant to be in a castle with fires but I was persuaded." They laughed. "How goes it?"

"Quiet, my lord. The snows closed the high passes until recently and we have not seen any Saxons. The roads are open now."

Myrddyn nodded, "Then we came at the right time."

The stronghold at Wide Water was finished. There were barrack blocks with fires and the double ditches would withstand a Saxon assault. My captains were glad to see me. "Aedh, send a rider to Prince Pasgen and tell him that his wife has sent furnishings for their home. They are at Alavna."

"This is Einar; he will help Lann Aelle train Prince Cadwallon and my son to become warriors." I was pleased with Lann Aelle's reaction, he seemed genuinely happy.

Hogan Lann laughed, "Well little brother, you will soon learn what it is like to be a warrior."

"Lann Aelle, take the boys and Einar and get them settled in and I will speak with Hogan Lann, Daffydd and Tuanthal." After they had gone I sat in one of the seats the warriors had made over the winter. "I see you have finished the fort."

"Aye, and the one at Penrhyd. There are local men who man it but the weapons you have brought will make me happier."

"How goes the training of the archers?"

"Slowly Warlord but we both know that the best archers have to be trained from a young age. The older ones will be able to loose arrows but they will not have the range we have. I am more hopeful with the younger boys."

"And the Saxons?"

"Dangerously quiet. We have never fought this Edwin. If he was clever enough to outwit Aethelfrith then we should be worried."

"I agree." Aethelfrith had been a clever opponent who was able to come up with many strategies to try to defeat us. He had forged alliances with strange bedfellows and come close on a number of occasions. "Tuanthal, split your men into two groups. Let Pol lead one of them. We will do the same with the squires. With Prince Pasgen's men that gives us five flying columns who can range far ahead to give us early warning."

I saw Myrddyn nodding his approval but Hogan Lann seemed less convinced. "Is our strategy to watch and wait then?"

"We do not have enough men to attack. I would rather ambush. Let him extend his supply lines." I pointed east. "We will let the ridge of hills which splits the land in two be our defence. There are few places there where he can build forts. He will have to try to bring us to battle." I waved my hand at Myrddyn who took out a copy of the map we had used in my fortress. "There are two main routes he can take. Both of them have a Roman Road. In the north, at the Roman Wall, we can keep men and use the Roman defences for shelter. Captain Tuanthal, that will be your area. Here we will have to operate out of Penrhyd. That will be your role, Hogan Lann. I will keep the squires here with me and I will support you, Hogan Lann. Daffydd, I want your archers split between Penrhyd and Carvetiorum. I assume you have two lieutenants you can use."

"Aye my lord."

"You will build up a force of forty archers. Travel around the settlements and train them there. If we had time I would build bolt throwers but we lack the expertise for the time being. Prince Pasgen will have to improvise."

Hogan Lann was still to be convinced about this defensive strategy. "We wait until they come?" I nodded, "And then?"

"And then we use Aedh and his scouts to bring all of our forces together so that we can ambush them. They will go for one of our forts. There are three of them, which is why I want one of you based at each one. If you are trapped they will, at least, have a leader upon whom I can depend."

"My equites are wasted inside a fort."

"They are only wasted if we use them needlessly." I sighed. I had to be patient with my son. He was becoming better but he still only thought about those men he personally commanded and seemed incapable of seeing the whole picture. "Edwin must replace the animals we took. He has to come for them. No matter how many men he brings the sight of a force of horsemen will stop him. Horsemen can evade the slower warriors until help is at hand. When we have all of our men in place then we can use your equites to smash our way into their shield wall. Edwin may have heard of your men but he will have no idea of their power on the battlefield. Our army relies on all three elements; horses, equites and archers. That is why we can defeat their superior numbers." He smiled showing me that he was in agreement. "We will leave and return home when Pasgen is secure. If you wish to return to your wife for a while I will understand."

His face fell, "No, Warlord. Forgive my questions. It is just that my men itch for battle."

Myrddyn shook his head. "That is what makes us different from animals. They have to scratch an itch. Man can control his feelings."

Pasgen nodded and then brightened, "Trade has already started Warlord. Some traders came from the islands to the north and we acquired some seal oil."

"Excellent, that is a start. Begin by sending some to each of your forts. It makes an excellent oil for lights."

That pleased me more than anything. Trade would be the making of Rheged. It would give it security in addition to its walls and men.

I made sure that Lann Aelle and Einar were happy about the training regime and then Myrddyn and I headed for Carvetiorum. We took an escort of squires. All of my captains were now worried about my mortality and insisted that I be well protected. The Prince looked concerned when we arrived. He hurried Myrddyn and me into a small room away from his men. I was worried and my first thought was that he had suffered some sort of defeat.

"Warlord, I have had an emissary."

"Who from?"

"King Edwin. A messenger arrived in midwinter."

"He travelled across country in winter?"

"No, he came by ship." That was a worrying thought. The Saxons could defeat my strategy if they arrived by boat. "He said the king wanted an alliance."

"As I recall the same thing happened with your brother and Aethelfrith."

"That is what is worrying me."

"What did you tell him?"

"I told him that I needed no alliance with Saxons."

I was relieved but Myrddyn said, "Perhaps you should not have been so hasty."

I was shocked, "You would condone an alliance with the Saxons?"

"Of course not, Warlord. Remember the Emperor? He would play one enemy against another."

"As I recall that involved lying."

"Not necessarily. If the prince had said he would think about it then it would have delayed an attack. This way King Edwin knows that we are belligerent."

"You are right Myrddyn. We use any means possible. If they try it again then tell them you are thinking about it. You need time to build up your armies. How is the training of your levies coming along?"

"They are better than they were."

"Daffydd will provide archers for you." I then explained my ideas for patrolling the main routes. "I would also suggest you use your equites to lead the men of your villages. They are all good leaders."

"I will. Thank you for bringing my furniture with you."

"My wife is worried about the lack of ladies at your court. Perhaps you need to think about how you would make your wife feel comfortable here."

"I will." He hesitated, "I do appreciate all that you have done for my family Warlord, past and present. I do not know what we would have done if you had not been here."

"I gave my word but you realise that eventually, I will have to split my time between Rheged and Mona."

"I know. I hope that the Saxons give us time to build up our strength." That was my fervent wish too. I did not think that they would oblige. As Myrddyn and I rode south I wondered how long King Edwin would give us.

He did not give us long. We had been back for a mere month when Aedh's scouts reported a warband heading west from Dunelm. He estimated it to be three hundred strong with many mailed warriors. He had chosen his moment well. Many of Pasgen's farmers would be busy with their fields and their animals. We would have barely enough men to man the forts and there would be no levy to give us numbers on the field of battle. We would have to lure him into a trap.

I had given Einar an old mail shirt. He had not wanted one but, as I told him, "You are the bodyguard of a prince. I need you to protect the two squires."

Gawan and Cadwallon were adamant that they did not need protection but I brushed aside their objections. "So long as the two of you are my squires you will do as I say or I will put you both on a ship back to Mona."

We gathered our mounted army and headed east to meet them. Aedh kept us aware of the position of this King Edwin. I was surprised at his numbers until Aedh reported that there were Mercian banners amongst the force. It explained why this was such a powerfully armed war band. He had not brought any lightly armed men; all of them would be seasoned warriors.

I halted the army at Castle Perilous. We had a fort at the ford of Penrhyd. That would be where we would hold him but I needed him to be drawn onto the teeth of our defence. Prince Pasgen, the squires and Hogan Lann's equites were sent to the north. All that I wanted King Edwin to see was my eighty horseman and my archers. Hogan Lann tried to dissuade me from being present.

"Let Tuanthal lead the men. Why does it need to be you?"

"Because he will want to fight the Warlord and I can make him reckless."

"You do not know the man. He may not rise to anger quickly."

"I will have Myrddyn the wizard with me. I am sure that he will come up with something." I smiled to soften the harshness of my words. "Your heavy horses are powerful but we have to protect them. Tuanthal and Daffydd can flee quickly away from King Edwin and I can still ride a horse as well as any."

We camped among the ruins of my old home and Myrddyn entertained the boys and Einar with the stories of our times there. I was pleased that Gawan took such an interest in Myrddyn. He could learn much from the wise man. Hogan had always liked to have a weapon in his hand. Myrddyn would teach Gawan that a mind was a powerful weapon too.

The two of them armed for war before dawn the next day. Both had short mail shirts which were more than suitable for wearing on a horse. They each had a small shield and carried a spear as well as a sword. Lann Aelle taught them how to use the spear well and Einar was a superb swordsman. I just hoped that they would not need to test those skills in this encounter. Einar was not happy about fighting on the back of a horse.

"Einar, I do not want you fighting. You and Lann Aelle are here to make sure my son and Prince Cadwallon escape the battle alive. Hopefully, we will not have any fighting today."

I had Lann Aelle carrying my Wolf Banner. He always enjoyed that honour. Myrddyn rode on my right while Einar and the boys waited behind. We sat before my horsemen and archers at the bridge over the river. Aedh was still shadowing the Saxons and it was his scouts who would ensure that we knew what the enemy was up to. One of his riders rode in. "My lord. They are five miles down the road."

"Good, then we can dismount and save our poor horses' backs."

The two boys' faces showed their disappointment. Lann Aelle wagged a finger at them. "Your horses need all their energy to take us to and from battle. They do not need to stand there bearing your weight when you have two good legs."

"Sorry, Lann Aelle."

Einar hid a smile. Lann Aelle had learned his trade from Pol and Hogan Lann. They too had been strict teachers. "Will he fight Myrddyn?"

"He may not, Warlord. If he fights then he must win. He will know that Aethelfrith found you a tough nut to crack. He might try deception or negotiation. If he sent word to Prince Pasgen then that may be his way. Do not forget his marriage was an alliance with Mercia. He sought refuge with the East Angles. I am guessing that King Edwin is a cleverer man than Aethelfrith. He finds other ways to get what he wants; he does not have to rely on bloodletting."

"And he was clever enough for me." I turned to the boys. "Listen to this wise man. Sometimes you tiptoe to war and do not rush in."

It was Aedh who brought us the news. "I have left two men watching them but they are a mile away. They are marching in a column ten men wide."

He left to take his place at the side of us. As we mounted Prince Cadwallon said. "What does it mean a column ten men wide?"

"It means that he can form a wedge, a boar's snout or a line easily. He has not yet decided what to do."

We saw the warband in the distance. There were five riders at the front and I assumed that they would be King Edwin and his leaders. I was

Saxon Slaughter

ready to give the order to release arrows but I would wait to see what he did. I took off my helmet. I wanted him to see my face.

They halted half a mile away. It was brave of the king for my archers could, from the hill behind me, cause casualties amongst them. Perhaps he had never met my famed archers but I was sure that there would be Saxons amongst his men who had fought me. They spread out a little but still had a front sixty men wide. It was a defensive formation. Even horsemen would struggle to break a line eight men deep. The front rank had locked shields and it bristled with spears.

A rider detached himself and rode towards us. He had his right hand held up as the sign for a truce. They wanted to talk.

The white-bearded warrior reined up in front of me. I could see that he did not sit comfortably in the saddle. The axe which hung from his pommel told me that he would be happier in a shield wall. Horses and axes did not mix. It was too easy to take off your own horse's head.

"I am Aella of Dunelm. King Edwin, king of this land would speak with you."

He sounded scornful and I decided to show him we did not fear him. "This land? This is Rheged and we have never had a Saxon upstart as king; even if he is married to the Mercian Royal family."

The warrior was not put out by my words. "You would stop us with this handful of warriors? I could take you all with just my oathsworn."

"Then you must wish to see the Otherworld desperately to risk fighting the Wolf Warrior." I touched the hilt of my sword, "This is Saxon Slayer and he has taken the lives of more cockerels than I can remember." I smiled as I did so.

I had irritated him. I could see it in his face. He had no reply to that. "Will you talk or will you fight?"

"I never mind fighting Saxons but we will talk. Come to the middle of the bridge." As he rode away I said to Einar. "Watch the boys."

"Can't we come?"

Lann Aelle snapped, "You will be cleaning the armour of your brother's equites if you do not obey orders instantly."

We rode down the hill towards the old Roman Bridge. It was just wide enough for four men and so our three horses would effectively block it. I did not yet know this king. I would not trust him until I knew his ways.

He was young; not much older than Hogan Lann. He did not have the physique of a warrior and, as we approached I began to deduce that he was less of a fighter and more of a player. He would try to trick me with words. I did not think that he would stand in a shield wall. His sword, when I had a closer look at it, had the warrior bands around it but there were not as many as had been on Aethelfrith's. I knew that he would be appraising me too.

He rode with his other four riders. It was a breach of the truce agreement. You normally brought the same number of men to the meeting. I had three and he had five. I was not worried. Lann Aelle and Myrddyn were more than capable of watching my back if I should need it. In addition, I had the insurance of Daffydd and his best bowman who already had the bridge in their sights.

I did not speak but I smiled. The scars on my face made my smile somehow threatening. At least that was what others had told me. He did not seem intimidated and he smiled back. "So you are the Warlord. You are the man who raided my lands and stole from my people."

I nodded, "I am the Warlord but you were wrong when you say that I stole your animals. Those animals had been taken from Rheged. I was merely returning them to their rightful owners."

"Many of my people suffered because of your actions."

"Many of my people died because of Saxon aggression." I leaned forward, "I was showing kindness when I did not slaughter your people. Aethelfrith would have done so."

"I am not Aethelfrith."

"That remains to be seen but you are a Saxon and therefore I distrust you."

Aella's hand went to his sword. "Touch that sword Aella of Dunelm and Saxon Slayer will claim another foolish Saxon leader." I stared at him so that he knew I was speaking the truth.

King Edwin held up his hands. "Keep your hands in plain sight old friend. We are talking. I need to persuade my people that you are no threat. Will you swear not to raid my lands again?"

Aella gave him a look of disgust which told me what he thought of the proposal. "When I became Warlord I swore an oath to protect Rheged. The land of Rheged reaches beyond the divide. I cannot swear an oath that I had no intention of keeping." I shrugged, "As far as I am concerned I will not rest until every Saxon is back across the waters. This is Rheged."

His warriors were becoming angry but the king was calm. "You know that I have the might of Mercia and East Anglia behind me. You and this handful of warriors would be destroyed if I brought the full force of my army to deal with you."

"And yet you have just brought three hundred warriors. Why is that? Do the rest fear us so much? But no matter how many warriors you bring we will fight you. You may be an honest Saxon, if so you will be the first, but you are still a Saxon and my sword is Saxon Slayer."

The silence was eloquent. I knew that the warriors with Edwin were itching to draw their weapons and fight but this young king kept both himself and his men in check.

"Very well. No one can say I did not give you a chance." He looked at me trying to read my thoughts. My face was like a stone. I kept it impassive and I had spoken the truth.

Aella gave me a venomous look as he turned his horse and rode back over the bridge. I knew that he would happily have fought me on the bridge if his king had supported him. They rode back across the bridge and I waited until they were back with their army before I led Myrddyn and Lann Aelle back to our lines.

I spoke to all of our men when I said, "Ready yourselves. They will attack."

Chapter 7

I looked at Daffydd. "I want their horses dead. Let us put this Saxon king on his backside."

He grinned. Horses were much bigger targets and we could hit them from further away. Normally we liked to protect horses and use them ourselves but it would give us the advantage to have the Saxon king and his chiefs walking rather than riding.

The king allowed his shield wall to precede him while he watched from the rear. I noticed that Aella had joined the shield wall and was leading it. Daffydd did not need my voice to tell him what to do. He and his men waited until the Saxons had crossed the bridge and were adjusting their lines to make the shields overlap once more. As they became disorganised my archers chose their targets well. A dozen men fell to the ground and I knew we had had hits on others. They kept loosing until the Saxons were all across the narrow bridge and had a solid shield wall once more. When the king and his horsemen came across the bridge a shower of arrows rained upon them. One of the chiefs saved King Edwin's life at the cost of his own as he held his shield over his leader's head; his own neck was pierced by a plunging arrow. The horses were all struck. Two of them threw their riders and galloped east. The others fell dead.

I heard Aella order the charge. Daffydd and his men continued to harass the Saxons as they lumbered up the slope. When they were just a hundred paces from us I ordered the retreat. The Saxons whooped their delight as the Warlord of Rheged fled before them.

"Warlord, why do we not charge them?"

"Because, Prince Cadwallon, we would lose men and we do not need to. They will follow us and we will keep stopping and whittling them down. By the time they reach the ford they will be angry and they will be tired. They will wish to end the battle quickly and they will do something reckless."

The Saxons seemed in no hurry to close with us as we headed west towards Hogan Lann and Pasgen with their equites. There were twenty or so bodies lying around the bridge and the crows were already feasting on the flesh of the horses. We retreated in good order. Aedh and his scouts kept between us and them.

"Aedh, send a rider to Hogan Lann and tell him where we are." Our plan was a simple one. We would make the Saxons think that we were fleeing into the safety of the new fort at Penrhyd and when they broke formation then the one hundred equites and squires would fall upon their flanks. The weight of horse and man would wash away the sea of Saxons. Perhaps we could end it all here on this one day.

When we were just a mile from the fort I halted the men and formed them into two lines. It was a flat piece of ground and the Saxons would be uphill from us. Once again, I was tempting them. If they advanced downhill there would be a tendency to run and they would be likely to break formation.

"Captain Tuanthal, draw javelins!" I wanted the Saxons to think that we would be charging.

They quickly formed their shield wall and advanced toward us.

"Charge!" The eighty riders rode towards the Saxons who prepared to receive the suicidal charge. At thirty paces the whole line wheeled to the left and each man threw his javelin and then retired. As I had expected we only caused a few casualties but the sight of the retreating horsemen made them increase their pace. Daffydd and his archers sat patiently on their horses. They would not be as accurate as if they were on foot but it would have to do.

The horsemen galloped beyond us to form a line a hundred paces further west and the archers loosed three flights before they too turned and ran. More warriors lay dead and wounded on the slope and the road. Still, they pursued us. As we headed west I saw the wooden walls rising above the ford. The trap was almost complete. The Saxon warband was angry and keen for revenge. Hogan Lann and Prince Pasgen would have an easy time when they attacked.

I could not see the equites but I knew where they were. They waited on the hillside above the small wood. Inside the fort were the forty local men who would defend its walls. Aedh and his men were already heading towards the wood to aid the equites as the archers trotted towards the gate. Aella and his men came purposefully on. The slope down to the ford helped them and they began to gain ground on us. They would be thinking that they could catch us before we reached the safety of the wooden walls of Penrhyd.

I turned to Lann Aelle, "Now, the buccina." As the Roman horn sounded, Tuanthal ordered his men to halt. They wheeled around and began to hurl their javelins at the Saxons. We were doing it in hope rather than expectation but we needed their attention on us so that our horsemen would have a better chance of catching them unawares.

Cadwallon asked, "Warlord, why does one half of the warband hold back."

I looked at where he was pointing and saw that he was right. Less than half of the Saxons had been committed and I could see King Edwin with the half who waited well above the ford. Then we heard the eerie wailing of Prince Pasgen's dragon standard. I saw the Saxons look fearfully to their right and then the wall of metal erupted from the woods. The long lances of Hogan Lann reached almost a horse's length before them and even Prince Pasgen's spears would be able to kill and keep the rider safe from the swords of the warband.

The Saxons turned to face this new foe. It was brave but futile. As the horses rode over the front ranks the rear ranks fled from the lances. These were seasoned warriors and they ran in better order than I had expected. This king had brought some of his best warriors. They ran to the protection of the warband above the river. Something was not right. I looked at the warband but I could not detect what it was. The equites wheeled to pursue them and wreak havoc on them. The two leaders dressed their ranks so that, as they climbed the slope, they would hit together.

"Captain Tuanthal, take your horsemen and support the equites." The horsemen eagerly joined the squires who were following up the heavier horsemen. When the warband broke they would be able to pursue them for longer.

Suddenly it all went wrong. The warband at the top of the hill now held long spears, longer than the lances of my son's men and they began spearing the horses. The armour they wore on their heads and chest gave them a little protection and I saw, to my horror, horses falling and their riders falling to the ground where axe men raced out to butcher them.

Before I could react Daffydd galloped out to see me. "Warlord! A despatch rider has come from Civitas Carvetiorum. There is a second warband and they are besieging the fortress!"

I had been duped. "Sound the recall!"

My men were well trained enough to obey signals, even if they disagreed with them. The last two to reach the fort were my son and Prince Pasgen. The prince was furious. "We had them beaten! Why did you recall us?"

Saxon Slaughter

"Firstly you were not winning. Look at your dead equites. And secondly, the Saxons are attacking your fort. You two take Tuanthal and Aedh. Ride west and destroy the warband. Leave the squires here with me."

Hogan Lann looked at the warband which was making its way towards the ford. "You do not have enough men."

"If you two destroy the other warband and raise the levy then we might still survive. It is our only hope."

He looked determined as he said, "We will return." He grasped Gawan's arm. "We will come back for you little brother."

"Inside the fort." The Saxons jeered the horsemen as they rode away and we slammed the gate shut. We were now trapped in our fort and we were outnumbered.

I raced to the gate tower. I saw that Daffydd had placed all his archers on the front wall and in the tower. The local men were guarding the other three walls. "Lann Aelle, spread the squires out between the archers and the other men. Einar, keep the two boys close to you."

Before he ran off Lann Aelle handed the Wolf Standard to Gawan who clutched it proudly. "Myrddyn, what can we do?"

Myrddyn glanced at the walls. The local men all had a weapon and half of them had a shield of some description but only a few had a helmet. "It will be up to the archers and the squires to hold on. We have no artillery here. They will soon close with the walls and hack their way in. Our only advantage is that this is green wood and may not burn very well. We will need to be clever" He looked at Gawan, "Gawan give that to Cadwallon and come with me." My son looked disappointed and ready to argue but Myrddyn smiled as he said, "Or should I take the prince to help me make magic?" Cadwallon had the banner thrust into his hands as Gawan hurried after Myrddyn.

I heard the arrows being released as Daffydd's archers tried to pick targets where their arrows could do the most good. The wedge which crossed the ford was filled with mailed men. Targets were hard to find.

I drew Saxon Slayer. If we held, it would be because we refused to give in and die. We were outnumbered and facing a seasoned warband. I needed to encourage my men and discourage the Saxons. "Behold the bane of the Saxons, Saxon Slayer. Today, my brothers, my blade will taste Saxon blood again and they will hurl themselves in vain at our wooden walls. Do not let them gain entry to the fort and we will prevail."

I then shouted in Saxon. "Today you die, Aella, and it will be at my hand!"

Lann Aelle had returned and asked me, "Why did you not say that King Edwin will die today? It would have disheartened his men."

In answer, I pointed to the knot of warriors behind the rest. King Edwin stood there under his banner. "He will not fight today. He is in no hurry. He knows he has a whole day to create a hole in our walls and then he and his oathsworn will flood through and take the glory. It will be Aella of Dunelm who will challenge me."

The wedge came closer. "Have the pila ready." We had a very small supply of Roman pila. We used them with our shield wall. The two halves of the spear were joined by a piece of weak metal. When it struck the metal broke and the spear dragged down shields and was unusable. We only had forty of them but the squires held them ready with a larger supply of javelins. They would have to aid the archers. The problem with the javelins was that the Saxons could throw them back at us!

"Throw the pila!"

The Saxons had not encountered these weapons before. They held their shields up to talk the blow and then found that it became heavier and dragged their arm down. Daffydd and his archers had been waiting for such an opportunity and they poured arrows into the gaps which suddenly appeared. Soon there was a pile of bodies over which the other Saxons had to climb.

Aella showed that he was a wily old fox. He had his men throw the bodies into the ditch which gave the attackers a wider front as they could step on their dead comrades. And now we had no more pila.

"Now use the rocks!" We had gathered a limited supply of rocks to hurl down but nowhere near enough. We had all assumed that the battle would be between our horsemen and their shield wall. I knelt down to pick up a rock which was as big as a man's head. I hurled it down and it struck a shield with a boar's head design on the front. I heard a scream. A crack appeared and I knew that I had broken his arm. Even if he still fought he would not last long. Others were more fortunate with their rocks and managed to smash Saxon skulls.

Even with all our efforts and the many dead Saxons before us, they made the gate and I heard them swinging their axes. Daffydd and his archers now had more of a target and he began to pick off the men with axes who hacked at the gate. We did not stop the work but we were able to slow it down.

Saxon Slaughter

"Daffydd, you take charge here." I turned to the prince and Einar, "Let us go down and make ready for when they break through."

Cadwallon and Einar followed me. The young prince still clutched the standard in his left hand and held his seax in his right. He looked nervous. I put my hand on his shoulder. "Do not worry Prince Cadwallon. You guard my back. Einar will watch over you."

He seemed reassured and I saw the smile on Einar's face. He was a warrior through and through. He believed, as I did, that he could defeat anyone who came through the gate. I saw Myrddyn and Gawan hurrying by with two pails filled with something. He laughed as we went by. "We have put the water onto boil but this will give them something to think about."

He and Gawan raced up the stairs and they poured the contents of the buckets down to the ground before the walls. I was surprised when I heard no screams but the axe blows on the door lessened. As he passed me I held out my hand and asked, "What was that magic?"

"Pig fat! It will make the entrance a little slippery. Oh, it will not stop them but it will buy enough time for us to get the boiling water. I have another surprise too. Come, apprentice, we still have much to do."

Gawan went off happily with the wizard. I turned to Lann Aelle. "Bring down ten warriors from the rear wall we will meet them with a wedge of our own." He hurried off and I took my helmet off. "Einar, you and the prince stand directly behind me. I want the banner to stand quite clearly above me. I must be the target for their attack. You stand on the right and Lann Aelle will take the left." I paused. "Have you stood in a shield wall before?"

He nodded, "Once or twice. I prefer to fight alone. The shield wall is not used as often by my people but I know what to do. I will protect your side."

The axe blows on the door increased which meant they had rid themselves of some of the pig fat. Myrddyn, Gawan and four of the women who had sheltered in the fort came by with steaming buckets of boiling water. This time, when they emptied the contents, there were screams of pain as the boiling water found its way through mail and armour.

Lann Aelle and my diminutive wedge appeared. We formed up and waited. I was pleased to see that he had ensured that his ten warriors all had spears as well as swords. It was not much but it would give us a slight advantage in the initial encounter. I hoped that their better warriors would be dead before they breached the gate. The discipline of my men would then carry the day.

Myrddyn's tricks worked but, inevitably, the cracks began to appear in the door. I shouted up to Daffydd. "How goes it?"

"They are paying a high price Warlord. The ditch is filled with their dead. We are using many arrows."

He did not say it but I knew that meant they were running out. Once the threat of arrows was gone then the Saxons would use all their warriors. I hoped that Myrddyn had something else planned. As the rents in the gate became larger I moved my men a little closer to the gate. "Keep your shields locked tight. I know that you horsemen do not usually fight this way but it will do no harm to try it just once eh?" Their laughter told me that they would do as I had asked.

I turned when I heard the commotion behind me. Myrddyn had brought out a long object. He stopped when he was next to me. "This is *wyrd*, Warlord. It seems the men of Penrhyd had killed a wolf last week and were preparing a surprise for you. I sewed the head onto a pig skin. It is filled with pig fat, seal oil and kindling. It will burn well." He tapped the side of his nose, "It also contains a quantity of Greek Fire. I always have enough ingredients for a small demonstration. If they try fire then they will get a shock."

I could see how that would work but I was not sure of the wolf's head. "And the head?"

"That was your son's idea. He will be a wizard warrior one day believe me. He said that if you stood there and said you would fly amongst the Saxons and slay them then it would frighten them. You could duck down and we could send the corpse to burn them. The survivors would report that you flew amongst them, killed them and then reappeared on the walls."

"And, of course, the legend of Myrddyn the wizard would be enhanced."

"Of course. We will stay on the walls and advise you. We have more water to boil and I will use that when I judge the moment to be right."

I knew that I could leave the walls in the hands of my wizard and my archer captain. When they broke through, and it would be soon, the warriors who would be waiting beyond the ditch would race forward. They would come as a rabble and my men would be able to kill more. When they crowded near the gate then the boiling water would be even more effective. Of course, all of that hinged on me and my thirteen men stopping their attack. The followers of the White Christ believed that the number thirteen was unlucky. I hoped it would be, for the Saxons.

The gate was now almost in pieces. I wondered at the cost the Saxons had paid. As I saw daylight through the gate I resolved to make a double gate and have a gatehouse. The Roman forts were able to attack the men trying to force a gate. We had not had enough time for that. We would have to make time.

"Brace yourselves. As soon as I give the command we march forwards and throw them back. Sword leg first!"

I had seen plenty of shield walls collapse when men marched with the wrong leg first. We were too few to be able to afford such disasters. Lann Aelle, Einar and I all held our swords above our shields. We would be stabbing the first Saxons through the gate.

Suddenly the gate gave way as an axe sliced through the bar holding it. I saw the Saxon who would die first. He had used the axe two handed and he stood triumphantly with the axe above his head screaming his war cry. He grinned as he saw my wolf banner and shield. Before he could move I shouted, "Forward!"

We were only four paces from the gate. We moved swiftly and Saxon Slayer went through his open mouth and out of the back of his head. I saw Einar do the same to the mailed warrior before him. He managed to stab through the mouthpiece of a face mask to kill his man. The press of men behind me and the dead before us allowed me to step forwards and bring Saxon Slayer down onto the helmet of the warrior trying to get close to me. They had no cohesion. They had been so concerned with smashing through the gate that Aella had not had a wedge ready to exploit their advantage.

We marched through them all the way to the ditch. They tried in vain to get to our flanks but the archers and equites kept them back. I watched as Aella tried to organise his men. He stood at the head of a newly formed wedge. They began to advance. We had achieved our objective. "Back. Keep it steady. Sword leg first. Cadwallon, keep that banner waving."

I wanted them to come on again as recklessly as the first time. We had severely reduced their numbers. If we could hold out for the night then we might have a chance when the equites returned. As we stepped through the gate I saw the squires ready with wood and the bodies of the dead Saxons. Even as we stepped back through they were filling the gate with a new, grisly and macabre barrier. Some of the bodies had fallen down the other side which would allow the Saxons to climb. I hoped that they would for we could deal with that.

"Lann Aelle, stay here with the spearmen. Keep them at bay. I will go to the walls and annoy them a little!"

"Yes, Warlord."

"Come Einar and Cadwallon." I glanced down and saw blood on the prince's short sword. "Your first kill. Well done."

"I am not sure he was dead, Warlord."

Einar laughed. "He was, my prince. You gutted him like a fish." Cadwallon swelled with pride at both the deed and the praise.

I stood on the ramparts. I could see Aella forming his men up into a shield wall. Beyond them, I saw King Edwin and his oathsworn on the hill, framed by the slowly setting sun. I took off my helmet and shouted in Saxon. "I had thought to fight warriors today and not women. I have two boys here who have not lived sixteen summers and yet the three of us could have dealt with the rabble you sent at us."

Lann Aelle laughed and Prince Cadwallon asked him what I had said. When Lann Aelle told him he took out his bloodied sword and shook it at the Saxons.

"Do you see? The boy is keen to get at you again. It is a pity that your king is not made of sterner stuff. He sits and watches while you and your women die. At least Aethelfrith fought us, warrior, to warrior."

Aella raised his sword. "We will soon get to you and I will split you from the nave to the chops."

"How about you and I settle this matter here and now? We will meet in the middle and save men's lives."

I thought for a moment that the old warrior would do as I asked but one of the men behind him spoke urgently to him. I could see that he did not like what he was being told but eventually he nodded. "No Warlord, my king forbids it. But fear not. I will fight you before the night is out."

I put my helmet back on. "It is a pity you have not got a better king. Perhaps when I have slain you I will slay him. Perhaps I could be King of the Saxons eh?"

Gawan asked me, as the Saxons prepared their assault, "Why did you insult him so much? You have always told me to treat your enemies with honour."

"It gave me no pleasure for I think Aella is a noble warrior but I needed to goad them and plant doubt about their king at the same time.

They will attack us tonight and, with Myrddyn's magic, we will defeat them without the need for Hogan Lann and Pasgen."

They began to advance. "Make sure you have some fire arrows ready." Daffydd nodded. I could see that they were determined this time. They sent their best warriors, all of them mailed. They did not use axes this time; they had swords and shields.

Myrddyn said, "Wait until they are all in the gateway and then we will begin our magic show!" I could see that he was enjoying this but Einar's face showed his lack of understanding. He would soon see the power of Myrddyn's magic.

Aella was attacking with about two hundred men. They funnelled in to the gate. The squires and my archers thinned them out a little but the main effect was to make them even tighter and without a gap between shields. It would make them hard to defeat in a conventional battle.

Myrddyn said, "Stand, Warlord." I did so. Myrddyn stood. Behind him, Cadwallon and Gawan held the wolf pig ready to throw. Myrddyn shouted, "I am Myrddyn the greatest wizard in the west and I transform Lord Lann, Warlord of Rheged into a dragon to destroy Rheged's enemies!"

I dropped down and the boys hurled the missile. Four of Daffydd's archers pierced it with flaming arrows and it suddenly erupted into flame. The oil and fat ignited and shot out covering the front fifty warriors and making them burn. The ones behind tried to douse the flames but it was in vain for the Greek Fire kept burning.

"Now Warlord!"

I descended the stairs and climbed out through the shattered gate. I stood on top of the bodies slain earlier and I roared, "The Warlord of Rheged strikes down all of his enemies thus!" I raised my sword and Daffydd's archers launched the last of the fire arrows at the fleeing Saxons. I turned and walked back into the fort to the cheers of my men.

"Begin rebuilding the gate. Collect the weapons from the dead."

Daffydd looked at me and asked, "What about the fire?"

"Feed it. It will prevent an attack and we can still collect the weapons. Have half the men sleep and then change over halfway through the night. If the smell of burning flesh hasn't put them off then feed the men too."

We had a half-finished hall and I led my five companions to rest there. "I will bring some food."

"Thank you, Einar."

He nodded seriously and then said, "I have learned much from watching you, Warlord. I had heard the stories of Myrddyn and thought that they were made up."

His comment took Myrddyn by surprise, "But you saw how it was done! You saw it was a trick."

"No, that was magic. You made it burn with many colours; you made it burn even when men tried to put it out. And the disguise; that was clever too. No, it was magic. When I have my own men to lead I will have my own wizard."

Gawan became animated, "I will be your wizard, Einar. Myrddyn has promised to teach me."

As Einar and Gawan went to get food I asked the wizard, "Have you?"

"He has ability Warlord. I think he could be both a warrior and a wizard. Think how powerful he would be."

I knew he was right but I still worried about my son. Magic and wizardry were the dark arts. How would it change my son? It might make him forget his responsibilities as a leader.

Myrddyn sensed my dilemma. "Remember who I talk to in the Otherworld."

"My mother."

"Would she allow your son to turn to evil? Her grandson?"

He was right. "I am sorry Myrddyn. Perhaps I am tired."

Cadwallon just watched us mesmerised. I think I was doing more for him as a leader than even his father would have expected. Lann Aelle helped me off with my mail. "What will they do next, Warlord?"

"If I was Edwin I would attack now while we are resting."

"But you think not."

"I think not. Aella was the fighting leader and his charred body lies before my walls. Myrddyn's magic has put doubts in his men's minds. It will be hard to motivate them again. Had Aella lived then they might have risked it. As it is I suspect they will be gone by morning."

Einar and Gawan appeared with the food. "Warlord, Daffydd has a gate in place and the weapons and arms are collected. The fire still burns."

"Thank you, Einar." We devoured the food and ignored the smell of human roast wafting over to us. I watched them all fall asleep and then I donned my wolf cloak and ascended the gate. "Daffydd, get some rest. I cannot sleep. I will watch for you."

"Thank you, Warlord."

As I watched, I reflected that I could see nothing beyond the fire. But at least we would see any attack. The sentries looked tired but they all peered into the darkness watching for the movements of a shadow.

I had wanted to know about this King Edwin and now I had learned what he was like. He was careful. He did not waste his warrior's lives but most importantly, he was clever. He was what the Greeks called a strategos. He planned and he plotted. I had almost underestimated him. Had we not built the fort at Penrhyd then we would have lost Rheged for a second time. I should not have gone home. I knew now that I had a job to do here. I might miss my family but an oath was more important than a family and I would keep my word.

The fire slowly died and then, behind me, I felt dawn's early light. It flickered over the dying fire and the bones of the dead and then it revealed an empty camp beyond. King Edwin had fled. He had returned to Dunelm to plot and plan once more.

Chapter 8

We had the unpleasant task of removing the burned bodies and making a pyre of the others. We were not doing so out of kindness; we did not want a plague of foxes and rats feasting on the bodies. I sent a patrol of ten squires to shadow the Saxons. I was not taking it for granted that they would just go home. There was an unpleasant thought lurking in the recesses of my mind that they might go to Wide Water to cause some mischief there. As much as I was desperate to learn what had transpired at Civitas Carvetiorum; I had to make sure that my new fort was stronger. I set the equites and the levy to work deepening the ditch and building a better gatehouse. The men who had fought in the battle were all rewarded with arms and armour from the dead Saxons. We found some better mail for Einar and the boys gained good Saxon swords.

It was Gawan who came up with the idea that we incorporated into every fort we had. "We could have a continuous ditch and a bridge which we lowered across the ditch to allow us into the fort. We would then have a double door. If we use the Warlord's idea of a room behind the gate and another gate, it would make the gatehouse the strongest place in the fort."

Myrddyn was impressed. I think Gawan expected derision or some flaw identified but it was a good idea.

"Perhaps I will have you for my wizard, my lord. Should I take the boys and cut some trees for the gate." Einar pointed to the ridge a few hundred paces away which had a fine stand of trees.

"Aye. Lann Aelle, take the Roman Horn and signal if you see aught."

By the time evening came, the fort had a better gate but still lacked our new gatehouse and a rider had returned from the east. The Saxons had retreated to the high ridge and had made a defensive camp. They had not gone home. I had done the right thing by working on the fort. I still wondered why Hogan Lann had not returned. This Edwin was a clever man.

"I think they are waiting for word from the west."

"So do I Myrddyn. Tomorrow I will take Lann Aelle and the boys and we will ride to the fortress."

Saxon Slaughter

In the event it proved unnecessary. Aedh, Tuanthal and his riders rode in early the next day. He looked admiringly at the blackened earth. "I see you survived. We thought that, perhaps, it had ended badly."

"As did we. I wondered why it took two days to return." I tried to keep the criticism out of my voice but I failed.

"I am sorry, Warlord. We found the warband. They had not breached the walls but they were prepared for us and had the long spears Edwin's men had had. They had built boats to cross the river and they fled north. By the time we had crossed, they were ravaging the countryside just north of the wall. They used the Roman wall as a defence against our horsemen. The prince and your son were frustrated that they could not use their heavy horses against the men on the rocks and on the wall. It was left to my men to winkle them out."

"Did you account for them all?"

He shook his head. "Most of them were killed but we had to sleep and some slipped away during the night. We returned directly here and your son is following. The prince is returning to his fort to repair the damage."

"I must ask you to choose your best men and go with Aedh. King Edwin is fleeing east. He is waiting for those you routed. Make them pay for every inch of land. Do not risk your men but make sudden attacks with javelins. I want them to remember the day they came to Rheged. I want them to count the miles home by the bleached bones of their dead. Take fifty of the squires with you. Their horses will be fresh."

"Aye my lord and I am sorry that we let you down."

"You did not. I was outwitted. It will not happen again."

My son and his equites arrived at noon. I could see the frustration on his face and in the way he rode. His shoulders sagged and he looked as though he had had the life sucked out of him. He did not take failure well. Even before we had time to speak Gawan had proudly told his elder brother of the new gatehouse. His enthusiasm was such that Hogan Lann brightened visibly. Eventually, Myrddyn had to order him back to work on the gatehouse just so that I could speak with Hogan.

I told him of the battle and Myrddyn's trick. He chuckled, "I can hear that tale being told and retold. How the Warlord was turned into a dragon and flew across the battlefield consuming all in his path."

"That was not how it happened."

"No, but it is how they will report it. I wish I had seen it."

"I hear that your attempts to bring the Saxons to fight were thwarted."

"Aye. I will make sure the men have their bows the next time we ride. And the horses tired. We had no squires and no remounts."

"If we had not had the squires then we would have lost." I had already reached my decision and now it was time to tell my son. "We will go on the defensive for the rest of the year. I want our defences building up and I want you and Prince Pasgen each to have an army of your own. You will need foot as well as archers and light horsemen. I intend to ride with Tuanthal and Aedh and act as an early warning for the Saxons. He will come again. He nearly succeeded this time and, but for a trick, he would have done."

"Does he know that it was a trick?"

"You spoke with him. He is a very clever man. He might not know how we did it but he will know."

"And how did the boys do?"

"Well. Prince Cadwallon killed his first warrior and your brother has a desire to be a wizard."

Hogan was taken aback. For him there had only ever been one course he wished to sail and that was the course of a warrior. "Really?"

"He has the aptitude. He will still continue to train as a warrior but we might have an assistant to Myrddyn and that is no bad thing is it?"

"No. Two Myrddyns, that would worry some of our enemies. It is good that my little brother chooses his own course."

"Come, my son, let us walk together. We need to talk."

We left the fort and headed along the Roman Road towards Castle Perilous. I had loved my first command. It was where Hogan had been born and his mother and sister had died. I had faced the Saxons here many times and it felt right to speak with my son there. I also wished to be away from prying ears. I needed his honest opinion.

"I said to you before that I wished you to form an army. That was presumptuous of me. You may well wish to take your men back to Mona. I would not blame you."

"But you will stay?"

"I gave my word."

"What do you expect of me, father?"

"Expect of you?" The question was so unexpected that I did not know what to say. I repeated the question to give me time to think.

"When you are in the Otherworld, what will I be?"

I felt better now that I understood the question. "Why, you will be Warlord of course."

"But I did not take the oath."

I was taken aback. Was my son about to desert me? I had given him the opportunity. "The Warlord is not just about an oath to the King of Rheged. I promised the Emperor I would be Dux Britannica."

"But I did not."

This was depressing me. "So what would you have for your future?"

"I would be Warlord but I would need others to know that I was chosen. I would want them to know that it was not an accident of birth. I would swear an oath."

I felt relieved and terrified at the same time. My son was willing to take on an awesome responsibility with little or no reward for himself. "You know that you would have to fight for another man's land. You would have to fight for Prince Pasgen."

"I know but I also know that I would be fighting for all the other people as you do. The Kays of this world and the Aedhs."

"You would have to put your family second." I looked at the ground. The grass suddenly seemed interesting. "As I had to."

"My son will realise, as I did, that you can still have the best father in the world even if he is not wiping your nose all the time. Lann Aelle had such a father and yet he chose you to follow. Does that not tell you something?"

I nodded. "Well, we will arrange the ceremony then."

"What ceremony?" We had reached the ruins of my castle. "I will swear now on Saxon Slayer, here where my mother is buried and so many others who fought for you. I need not an audience to witness my oath. This will be my oath and I am the one who will have to keep it."

He was right, of course, and we made our way to his mother's grave. I took out Saxon Slayer and gave it to him. "It is your oath and should be your words."

He nodded and took the sword. Kneeling, he bowed his head, "I swear to protect Rheged and Mona and to fight for those who cannot fight for themselves. I will not betray my word nor my friends, and I will give my life for those that I love."

He gave me the sword and rose to his feet. "You said nothing about Saxons."

"And that was deliberate. There may come a time when I will have to fight alongside the Saxons if it means protecting Rheged."

I saw then that this was *wyrd*. I was the past and Hogan Lann was the future. This was good. My mother's words were coming true.

I sheathed the sword and we headed back. I felt a relief as though a weight had been lifted from my shoulders. I was no longer Rheged's only hope. There would be a Warlord to follow me.

By the time Tuanthal and Aedh returned from their hunt the gatehouse was finished. I was proud of my son, Gawan, and his clever idea. It was simple and yet it would make every fort we had better protected. Myrddyn took some of the squires to improve every fort we had. Time was of the essence. Pasgen and Hogan Lann took to heart my comments about their own armies and went to building them up. Daffydd went back to training archers but I stayed with Lann Aelle at Penrhyd waiting for my captain of horse. I was anxious to discover what my foe had done. Einar took the boys hunting as often as he could. We both agreed that it would make them both better warriors, without Myrddyn. Gawan seemed a little lost.

Tuanthal had lost only three men which I viewed as a miracle. "We did as you asked, Warlord, and we killed as many of them as we could." He smiled grimly. "They could not leave the camp for a pee without expecting to be ambushed. Barely two hundred and fifty made it home. We halted a few miles from Dunelm."

"You have done well. Now you and Aedh will be based here. You need to keep patrols out watching for the Saxons. I do not think they will come soon but we must be vigilant. You can use those men who are rested to begin the patrols. And I want you two to stay here for at least two days. I cannot do my work without you two."

They both seemed touched, I do not know why but I valued both of them as much as my sons Hogan and Gawan.

Hogan Lann used Penrhyd as his base. He used the levy from the surrounding area for his warriors. They were hardy folk. They toiled in the harshest of lands and they survived. What they lacked were the skills in arms. Pol was, like Lann Aelle, a tough taskmaster and they soon showed rapid improvement. In any battle, they would not be the deciding factor but they would fix the enemy and allow Hogan Lann's horsemen to use their immense power and destroy them. The archers were more difficult. We had the bow and we had the arrows. In some cases, we had strong men but they did not have the skill which came from using a bow from an early age. We would have to wait four or five years until the young boys matured into young warriors.

In the long summer's evenings, we had taken to walking to the small hill which overlooked the ford. It was not high but it allowed us to watch the sunset over the land of the lakes stretching to the west of us. Those were pleasant times. The two boys would join us. It was Myrddyn, Lann Aelle, Pol and Hogan Lann who formed the nucleus of the group. Of course, Einar and the two boys would be there and, if they were not on patrol Aedh and Tuanthal would join us. It was good for my son and Prince Cadwallon to hear us debate our strategy and form our opinions. This was not the way of most leaders who made their own choices and their men followed. I always wanted my captains to feel part of the decision making.

We did not always talk of war and the Saxons. Sometimes the conversation came down to more mundane matters but the two boys were still learning. I say boys but the recent months had seen them sprout into young men. Hogan and Pol had had a particularly hard day and were full of aches and pains.

"Wizard, why cannot we have a bathhouse and a heated floor for this fort as Prince Pasgen has at Carvetiorum?"

"Alas, we know how they work but we have neither the skills nor the materials to build them. When we built the ones at home we had the parts from Byzantium. We can build a bathhouse but it would not be the same."

"Besides, my son, if we built one then it would mean the defences of the fort would not be improved." I pointed behind us to the silhouette of the fort. Already we had added two towers at the corner and a second gate at the rear. The deeper ditch at the rear would allow us to sortie and use our cavalry.

"I suppose you are right. Do you think we will ever have peace for a time to allow us to become more civilised?"

I laughed, "It was not long since you were moaning about the lack of action."

"You are right but I do miss the comforts of our fortress."

As we watched the sky turning redder in the west I wondered about the future. Hogan Lann had made it clear that he was willing to compromise with the Saxons. Was I wasting my time fighting them? Suddenly Myrddyn looked at me and I felt a shiver run down my spine. He was reading my thoughts once more. I went back to watching the reddening sky become blue, then purple and, finally black. We headed back across the ford.

"Warlord, a word if you please." I slowed down and walked with Myrddyn. "When your son is Warlord he will not do things the way that you do. No son follows his father exactly. Look at Ywain and Urien; Iago and Cadfan. Your lot in life is to be the sword which the Saxon fears. You, alone, have turned the tide of Saxon expansion and you have reclaimed Rheged. Your son will do things his way and that is as it should be. It may not be your way but it might be just as successful."

"Thank you old friend but I find it disconcerting the way that you can read my mind."

"I have told you before that I read your face and your body. And I know you as well as any man."

"Still, some of the ideas my son has are good ones. Perhaps I should talk to others."

We had just crossed the drawbridge. I still enjoyed the reassuring sound as it clanked shut. The lights from the torches showed me Myrddyn's face. He was smiling too. "King Urien was not averse to alliances. Remember the last one in the last golden age. We nearly defeated them then."

The picture of the treacherous Morcant Bulc came to my mind and spoiled my mood. "Aye and little good it did us then."

"It did not fail because of you, Warlord. You warned the king of Morcant Bulc. The idea was a good one but the king's judgement was not." He saw my face and held up his hand. "King Urien was a good king; he was not perfect. You are a good leader but neither are you perfect."

"Hubris?"

"Hubris. I think that you should make an alliance."

"But who with?" Elmet had gone. My brother Raibeart was married to the daughter of its last king. Bernicia and Deira were now Northumbria. "You are not suggesting the Irish? I would as soon get into bed with a bagful of snakes."

"No Warlord, but what of Alt Cult. When Mungo came south it was because the Saxons had conquered his land but they had conquered Rheged too and yet here we are."

That night as I lay, unable to sleep, I pondered my wizard's words. I knew that Riderch Hael had died. I knew that his sons had died but could there be another ruler to the north of us? If I could secure an alliance there then it meant we could focus all our efforts on the east. I would return to my wife one day and when I did then we could join with Cadfan and make inroads to the east there too. The lands to the south of the land of the lakes were fertile but hard to defend. We needed strong armies to the north and the south and then that devastated part of Rheged could be reclaimed. I found that I slept once I had made up my mind.

The next day I organised the ones I would take. I chose Aedh and his scouts as my escort. Tuanthal was disappointed. "My lord, no disrespect to Aedh and his scouts but you will be travelling in a land which might be hostile. You need my warriors."

"I agree father. It is dangerous." Hogan Lann had become very protective since I had been wounded.

"It will be more dangerous if I take away the fine warriors who can warn you of a Saxon attack. I am taking Aedh because he can warn us of danger and we will be a small enough party to hide. There will be Lann Aelle and Myrddyn with me and that is all."

Then it was the turn of Gawan and Cadwallon to complain. "We should come with you. We need to learn too."

I nodded sagely, "True and I think the learning should be with Einar. I will not be away long and when I return you will both be better swordsmen."

We left both well-armed and with spare horses. I knew that the old stronghold had been the fortress of Alt Cult. Sitting on a high plug of rock it was said to be impregnable. It lay four days or so to the north of us. I had no idea what lay between but, as it was summer, I made the assumption that the people who lived in the land would be too busy gathering the fruits of their labour to be suspicious of strangers. We rode the Roman Road. It was straight and it was fast. We made sure that we paid for everything we consumed. We were lucky in that Aedh was the most affable of men who had a smile which allayed any fears. He and his men wore no armour and, as they preceded us, we had little difficulty in traversing the country. When we stopped Myrddyn and I would ask about Saxons and about the king. They all remembered and revered Riderch Hael and many of the older ones had heard of the Warlord of Rheged. A few old soldiers asked to see the sword which had held such sway in times past. It was reassuring that there was no Saxon presence.

From this, we gathered that there was a king. His kingdom was called Alt Cult and based upon the fortress to which we were heading. It seems he was the result of a union between a Pictish king and one of Riderch Hael's daughters. His people seemed happy with him although his borders to the north caused him some problems.

As we approached the river which marked the end of our journey Myrddyn speculated about the king we would soon meet. "King Necthan

Nepos Uerb sounds like an opportunist. The Picts were always a little belligerent and unpredictable. If he has managed to unite those two kingdoms then he has done well."

"It seems the Saxons were only here briefly."

"Yes Warlord, but they did as they did in Rheged; they stripped what they needed and then left. When we were in Constantinopolis I read of an insect they have in Asia and Africa. It is called the locust and when it comes to a land it completely strips all that can be eaten and then leaves. That is the Saxon way."

"So long as this king is on our side then I am happy."

We saw the castle long before we saw the river. It stood on a high craggy rock. I have seen some impressive sights for castles but the only one which came close to this one was Din Guardi and even that was dwarfed by Alt Cut. If Riderch Hael had been content to sit within his walls he might not have been killed in battle by the Saxons. I smiled as I remembered that larger than life king. There was no way he would have sat and waited while an enemy devastated his land. The river was too wide to ford and there was no bridge. Our problem was solved when a raft pushed off from the opposite shore. It came to a stop some fifty paces from the shore. There was an old man on the oar and a younger man at the prow.

"What is your business, sirs? I see that you are armed."

"I am Lord Lann, Warlord of Rheged and I am here to speak with your king. We come in peace."

The older man came forward. "I remember you. I fought alongside you against the Saxons." He looked at the young man. "He is not a threat, Guipo. He fought alongside Riderch Hael."

The journey across the river was not comfortable. Mona was calm enough but some of the scouts needed all their skills to calm their mounts. We had no opportunity to talk with the boatmen. The people we had spoken to hitherto had only heard of this king. I was anxious to get a picture of him before I met him.

As we stepped ashore the old man tugged at my arm and said, quietly, "This new king is a good man but he is no Riderch Hael."

"Thank you for that information."

"You saved us more than once my lord. I often heard the old king speak highly of you." He chuckled, "We heard the old wizard Myrddyn had entranced you and imprisoned you beneath a mountain in Cymri."

I laughed, "Do not speak too loudly, for that is Myrddyn ahead."

His face went white. "Please Warlord, do not tell him of what I said. I would not like to be turned into a stone."

"Your words are safe with me." I caught up with the others. The legends about the wizard just grew and grew. I had no doubt that, long after I had died, men would still speak of Myrddyn the wizard.

We led our horses up the steep road to the castle. I was aware of being watched. I wondered if there was another entrance to the castle for this one was too steep for an invading army to use. There was a welcoming party at the gate and I was glad that I had led the horses. It would convince the king of our peaceful intentions.

"I am Menteith, the steward to the king. What is your business?" He studied me as he spoke and, before I could answer he smiled, "You are the Warlord of Rheged. I thought I recognised the cloak and banner." He frowned. "What brings you here?"

"I would speak with the king. We have returned to Rheged."

His face beamed, "Then that is cause enough to celebrate."

He led me through the gatehouse which bristled with guards. "Your men will find stables and the warrior hall yonder. If you and your adviser will come with me, I will take you to the king."

I hid a smile as Myrddyn glowered at the steward's back. We were led through many smaller buildings to a large hall. We stood outside its doors while the Steward said, "I will go and announce you."

"Adviser indeed!"

"I thought that had annoyed you. Take it as a compliment that you are able to hide in plain sight. Would you have everyone recognise you?"

He stood back and looked at me. "You are becoming far too clever Warlord. I doubt that you need me at all."

"And that is not true. I would have you watch the others when I speak with the king. I need to know how his closest advisers stand."

The door opened and we were led into a dimly lit hall with a fire roaring, despite the warm day, at the end of the room. Necthan was dressed quite plainly and seated on a raised chair. He stood and extended his hand to me. "I have long wished to meet with the famous Warlord of Rheged."

He had a firm hand and his eyes looked into mine. I liked a man who could face you without flinching. "And I am pleased that a king sits once more on Riderch Hael's throne."

He nodded and then looked at Myrddyn. The question was in his eyes. "This is my nephew, Lann Aelle, and this is Myrddyn the wizard. You may have heard of him."

There was an audible gasp from the others in the room and Menteith paled. The king smiled. "You are as famous but I am a little disappointed that you did not fly in through one of the towers."

Myrddyn laughed graciously. "Some of the stories of my exploits are a little exaggerated."

I saw then that the king was wise, "And yet they must have some basis in truth. The story of King Morcant Bulc's death can only be explained away by magic. But we can talk of such things as we eat. Would you like to wash before we eat?"

"That would be most welcome."

"And please, bring your famous sword to the meal. I have some questions to ask you about that blade."

I had brought clothes other than those needed for war and when we entered the hall for food I was pleased. They had all made an effort to impress us and there were many rich coloured garments adorning the men. There were no women present. I had heard that this was the practice. It would not have sat well with Myfanwy but different cultures had different ideas.

I was seated to the king's right hand, the place of honour. I deposited Saxon Slayer on the table and I watched as every man's eyes were drawn to its jewelled pommel and inscribed blade. Before the food was served the king stood and raised his chalice. "A toast to our allies, Rheged, and the famous Warlord, Lord Lann."

My work had already been done for me. I had come for an alliance and it was offered to me without condition. I drank the heady wine and then resolved to drink more slowly for the rest of the night. It would not do to get falling-down drunk.

"May I hold the sword?"

"Of course, your majesty."

He was a warrior; that much was clear when he balanced the sword in his hand. I could see the envy in his eyes.

"It is everything I have heard and more. You are a lucky man. May my warriors hold it? I know they have dreamed of this."

"Of course." I hesitated, "Just so long as it returns here."

Saxon Slaughter

They all laughed. As the food was served the king began to speak. "I said allies, for once we were. Does Rheged wish that alliance to continue?"

"We do, most heartily. We have driven the Saxons from Rheged and before we can think of attacking their lands to the east, I needed to be sure that my northern borders were safe." He gave me a quizzical look. "A few years ago Mungo and some of your lords took refuge with my people. We thought until I arrived here, that the Saxons still ruled."

He seemed satisfied. "No Warlord, they stole many slaves and they killed many men but they did not settle, I promise you that your northern borders will be safe and my men will do all that they can to help drive the Saxons from our land."

"Then I am relieved."

"There is something you could do for me in return."

I had wondered what he wanted to cement the alliance. Perhaps every man wanted something for himself.

"You know that Riderch Hael had a sword called Dyrrnwyn?"

"Yes. I saw it when he used it on the battlefield. It was supposed to flame although I never saw that."

"You are right. That sword disappeared after the battle in which the king died. It just vanished from the face of the earth."

"Most likely one of the victors took it."

"I agree that is more than likely but as they were Saxons it is hard to know for certain. The new owner may not know of its power and its name."

"How would I know it? It is many years since I saw it although I remember a green jewel in the pommel."

"Yes and the blade is inscribed, 'Flame of the dragon' in our language. If a Saxon took it he would not know what the words meant."

"I have not come across the blade yet but we will now seek it out. When I find it I will return it to you."

"You seem confident that you will be able to do this. What gives you this confidence?"

"The warrior who took this blade must be a good warrior to have beaten your king. He was old but he was a fierce fighter. I intend to defeat the Saxons. I will come across this warrior sometime and I will defeat him."

"Again you are confident; why?"

"Myrddyn has not dreamed of my death."

The king looked at Myrddyn. "You can predict when a man will die?"

"No, but my path and that of the Warlord are intertwined. I will dream when he will die and when I will die. I have already dreamed of my own death."

I had not heard of this. The whole table became silent. The king asked, in a hushed voice, "And what will your death be?"

He finished chewing a piece of meat and said, quite calmly, "I will fall, I will be stabbed and I will drown."

"Then will you not avoid being in places where you can fall?"

"If it is meant to be it will happen no matter what I do. I have not yet dreamed when I will die, only the manner of my death."

The king shook his head. "I am mightily glad that you two came to my court. I have learned much and I now have hope for the future."

Chapter 9

We stayed longer than I had wished for the king was keen to show me his kingdom. Eventually, we begged our leave and left. The journey back was much more relaxed. The king sent ten of his men as guards. We had told him that we had been treated well by his people but he was worried about the Irish pirates. It seemed they still bothered him too.

The passage to Carvetiorum was a pleasant one and when we saw the improvements made by Prince Pasgen I was delighted. He too was pleased to see me. "Tuanthal has seen no Saxons and I have deemed it safe enough for my wife. She is coming with Daffydd."

I hoped he had judged the time right but I smiled anyway. "Excellent, and we will try to make her both safe and welcome when she is here."

He was also delighted about the alliance. "My army is building well but we will not be ready for an attack until next year."

I knew what he meant. There was a balance between an efficient army and a full larder. We would all eat well this winter and it was up to my men to keep the food and the people well protected. Of course, the presence of Prince Pasgen's family brought even more problems. He would always have one eye on them. Hogan Lann would have much more responsibility upon his shoulders. Perhaps this was *wyrd*; perhaps this was a good thing which would make him a better leader.

Although we had been away less than a month autumn was already on the horizon. We could see the summer crops being harvested. I was pleased that the rains had held off as well as the Saxons. I was pleased I was not a farmer. It was bad enough fighting Saxons without fighting nature too. The two towers at the fort of Penrhyd were finished. We had stayed overnight at Prince Pasgen's and so we arrived just after noon. The fort seemed almost deserted. There were just six of the levy there and Daffydd busily training archers. Lann Aelle and Aedh took the horses and I went to speak with my captain of archers.

"Any problems?"

"Not with the Saxons but Einar has had his hands full with the two boys. It seems they were desperate to go hunting rather than working and he finally relented. They will be happier when they return this evening."

I laughed at the image of Einar being pestered by the two youths. "The training of the archers is going better. Some of the young boys, especially the ones who live in the hills, have a real eye for archery. We will have half a dozen that will be able to give the Saxons something to think about."

I was pleased. Our archers were a major advantage we held over the Saxons. The more we had the more secure we became.

When Einar returned from his hunting trip he brought disturbing news. "My lord I found the tracks of men. Saxons. Their footprints were in the woods and on the muddy paths."

That was potentially worrying. The last thing we needed was a band of Saxons who had survived the battle raiding my land. "Where were they?"

He pointed to the west. "They were in the woods some five miles away. Where the small stream comes from the hills."

I knew the spot. I now became even more worried. The Saxons who had fled Prince Pasgen had gone north and I knew that King Edwin had gone east. Who were these Saxons?

"Thank you, Einar. Aedh, mount your men. We go hunting Saxons." Although the days were getting shorter the place we would search was close.

Aedh was a good tracker and he found Einar and the boys' tracks easily. He too found the Saxon tracks. "They came from the south, Warlord." I could hear the concern in his voice. He pointed to the east. "They headed east."

We followed the tracks until it became dark. "We will return here in the morning and follow them to their destination. I do not like unknown warriors wandering freely in Rheged."

We discussed it as we ate our evening meal. "I can see why they were heading east; they would be trying to join up with the others but where did they come from?"

Hogan Lann was right. The land to the south had no Saxons. We had travelled through that land. We kept no watch on the trails and roads which traversed that part of Rheged for it was the safest part of the kingdom.

"Tomorrow take some of the squires and travel as far as the sea. Look for signs along the way. We will see where they have come from."

It was not to be as easy as that. The autumn rains began that night. It was as though the gods had been saving all their water and decided to drop it upon us. It felt as though we were swimming in Wide Water. There was little point in searching as we could not even see beyond the end of our horse's heads. It rained for two days and when we emerged from our fort it was to wade through a muddy morass which sucked your feet into the ground.

"You had better take your men and search as far as the sea but I fear we will see no tracks now. I will take Myrddyn and go with Tuanthal. We will ride and search to the east. They will have suffered in the rain as much as we have. Perhaps they will have reached Edwin's lands by now. Lann Aelle, go with Aedh and his scouts. These Saxons may have come from the battle at the wall."

"What of the boys?"

"Einar can work on their sword skills." I saw the disappointment on the faces of my son and the prince but they had learned to obey my commands.

We spent a fruitless day riding along a sodden, soaking land. The crops which had not been gathered in, and there were mercifully few of them, had been ruined. We saw many farmers repairing the storm damage. None had seen any sign of Saxons. That was a relief; I would not have wanted the farmers and their families to suffer. However it was also a worry, for where had the Saxons gone? I still worried about the purpose of this mysterious band.

As we rode disconsolately back to Penrhyd, Myrddyn tried to deduce what their purpose was. "How many men did Aedh think there were?"

"He thought that there were at least fifteen."

"And they were armoured too?"

"Some were. We had seen where their prints had sunk deeper into the soft earth suggesting that they had mail on them. They had no horses."

Myrddyn shrugged, "The Saxons rarely do. This has me perplexed. There are too many together to be survivors from the battle and their route does not fit a pattern. If they were raiders they would have raided the villages along the way."

Penrhyd loomed up ahead. "Perhaps they had raided to the south and were heading home. Hogan Lann may have information which will shed light on this."

"He may but you would have seen evidence of that. There would have been pack animals or captives' footprints. Still, we will have a clearer picture when we speak with your son."

Lann Aelle and Aedh were waiting for us. "We saw nothing. We spoke with the farmers along the wall and they said they had seen Saxons but it was only one or two and they were heading east. None had been seen in the days before the rain."

That left just Hogan Lann. He had had the longest journey and it was almost dark before the sentries saw him. As I peered south I suddenly realised that I had not seen Einar or the boys. "Have you seen my son?"

The sentry grinned, "Not since this morning Warlord. I saw them heading yonder." He pointed to the west. "They were dragging your Dane with them. I think they were eager for a lesson."

I laughed, that was typical of my son and the prince, and then the thought struck me that they should have returned. I would have to speak with Einar. He knew better than to keep the boys out too long. I knew that he was inordinately fond of the boys but he had to be in charge of them. I descended the stairs to greet Hogan Lann.

His worried face showed me that he had news and it was not good. "When we reached the coast we found Daffydd and our ships. It seems they came upon a Saxon ship on the night of the storm and they attacked her. There was one survivor who told our men that he had come from Man."

"Where is he?"

"He died of his wounds."

Myrddyn nodded sagely, "It explains the raiders but what were they doing so far from their ship? And why did they not do anything? We have found their tracks and yet they seemed to do nothing. This has posed more questions than it has answered."

I felt a chill run down my spine; the boys were in danger. I knew it. I had done Einar a disservice. He would have returned before now. Something had prevented him from doing so. "I want every man not on guard duty ready to search with a lighted torch. Einar and the boys have not yet returned from their training. We will search the woods to the west. It is where they went hunting. I fear they may have run into this band of Saxons."

As the others ran off Myrddyn said, "Or that may have been the purpose of the raid?"

That thought was unpalatable but suddenly made sense. It would have been typical of King Edwin and his cunning plans and yet the fact that the ship had landed in the west did not make sense. Something was not right.

I grabbed a torch and joined the men who ran from the fort. Einar and the boys had gone on foot. They could not be far away. I kept thinking of reasons why they would be late and therefore safe. The thought which dwarfed all of the others was that Myrddyn was right and this Saxon incursion had a purpose.

We heard a shout within moments of entering the wood. I ran to the sound and found a sight which filled me with both horror and fear at the same time. We found the bodies of two Saxons. They had been killed by sword strokes.

"Spread out and go carefully. Look under every bush. My son and Einar are somewhere close by. These dead Saxons are not the only ones. We seek a war band."

I scoured the ground before me. I could see churned up tracks and broken branches. Someone had moved at speed through the undergrowth and they had not worried about secrecy. This was the sign of a flight and a fight. I saw blood spatters on the leaves and branches. Prints in the soft ground seemed to radiate in every direction.

One of my men up ahead gave a cry. "Warlord!"

I ran through the woods in the direction of the voice. Einar hung, barely alive; he had been nailed to the tree like the White Christ. The wounds on his body showed that he had fought his attackers bravely. There were many cuts and injuries. Myrddyn was at his side in an instant and he ordered the men to support his body while he removed the nails. My faithful Dane opened his eyes and murmured, "I am sorry my lord. I have failed you."

"No, you have not." I was about to ask him where my son was when Myrddyn removed one of the nails and Einar passed out. It was a mercy as we were able to take him down quickly. We laid him on the ground and Myrddyn began to patch him up.

"The rest of you search the woods and find the boys."

Aedh said, "Watch for tracks and be careful."

I nodded my thanks. Aedh was right and I should have thought of that but I was angry. Anger always clouded your judgement. I was angry at what they had done to Einar; I was in no doubt that this was the work of Saxons and I was angry that I had not watched my son and the Prince of Gwynedd more carefully.

Myrddyn shook his head and said quietly, "He is beyond saving, Warlord. I do not know how he has lasted this long. Most of these wounds would have killed a normal man before now."

Einar opened his eyes. They were filled with pain. He began to speak and we had to lean close to him to hear. "They gave me a message. They said you can have your son and the prince back when they get Caestre. If you follow then they will disfigure the boys. You have until the Yule." He winced in pain, "Warlord, a sword!"

He knew he was dying. I handed him Saxon Slayer. He smiled as his hand gripped the hilt. "I will wait for you in the Otherworld, Warlord." When his fingers released my blade we knew that he was dead.

"Carry this brave warrior back to the fort. We will bury him with honour."

Myrddyn looked at me. "This then is Aethelfrith and not Edwin."

"I know." Edwin had no interest in that fortress on the Dee but Aethelfrith knew its importance. If he could regain that then he could carve out his own kingdom and regain Northumbria that way. I was not bothered about Saxon politics. I wanted my son and Cadwallon back. This also explained why they had come on a ship from the west. He had moved from Hibernia to Man.

The others returned. Hogan looked angry too. "The three of them put up a good fight. We found seven more dead Saxons in the woods. They took my little brother south."

"I know. Einar died but he told me that it was Saxons who took them and they will be heading south. They will go to the coast for their ship and then they will head for the Dee. They are holding the boys as hostages in return for Bor's castle at Caestre."

"We will hunt him down and kill him."

I shook my head. "No, my son, I will hunt him down. You will be needed here. This may be a ruse to lure us away. It may not be just Aethelfrith but a complicated plan devised by the wily Edwin. It would be foolish to risk all that we have regained just to chase a will o' the wisp over Rheged. I will go with some chosen men. This does not need an army and one of us must stay here to safeguard Rheged. I gave my word to King Cadfan that I would care for his son as though he was mine. Besides I am the one who must avenge my oathsworn, Einar."

They all tried to dissuade me as we headed back to Penrhyd but I had made up my mind. I knew Aethelfrith and I knew his mind. It would have to be me who followed him.

"Myrddyn, I need you to stay here and advise my son. He will need your help."

Alone out of all of my men Myrddyn neither begged to accompany me nor to dissuade me. He knew my mind better and he understood my reasons. "Be careful, Warlord. This Aethelfrith has gambled once and lost to King Edwin. He will not care if he hurts Gawan and Prince Cadwallon."

"I know. Aethelfrith may not even be with them. He may have sent some men to do his bidding."

"I am thinking it will be either him or his sons. He had already lost much face. He could not ask others to risk the Warlord's wrath. Who will you take? "

"Lann Aelle, Aedh and ten of Tuanthal's warriors. We need to move swiftly. I do not need equites; they would only slow me down. I will take the ten best that Tuanthal has. We will need to ride hard. They have a head start on us."

"You will leave tonight?"

"Aye. We may be able to overtake them. They will go to the coast first. When they do not find their boat then they will head south and we may well be able to ambush them by heading due south."

"You risk losing them."

"I know where they will be heading but we can move northwards anyway. There are only a couple of passes south that they can use."

"Warlord, take my advice. Follow their trail. Your son is clever and he knows you will follow. He will leave signs if he can, for you to follow."

I was now on the horns of a dilemma. My heart told me to get ahead of them but my mind trusted Myrddyn and his wisdom.

"If you follow them you will still have opportunities to get ahead of them but you need to find their whereabouts."

"Very well." Later on, I thanked all the gods that I had heeded the wizard's advice. Had I not done so then my son would have been lost to me forever.

It took some time to gather the men and the spare horses. When we did leave it was almost moonrise. Aedh was confident that we would be able to pick up their trail. "The rains have left the ground muddy. This will be the only large body which has travelled south since the rains. When we come to the mountains it will be more difficult but by then it will be daylight."

And so I set off with twelve warriors to rescue my son and the Prince of Gwynedd. We were not the largest force I had ever led, but we were the most determined.

Chapter 10

The men we chose were all good warriors who had fought the Saxons many times. I could rely on them not to panic, even when faced with overwhelming numbers. The enemy numbers were still uncertain. We took bows as well as javelins; it was one of our major advantages over the Saxons. I needed to be able to fight the Saxons wherever I found them. The spare horses enabled me to take my mail shirt. Although we had only seen the tracks of fifteen men it did not mean that Aethelfrith did not have more warriors waiting for him. The numbers did not worry me. My only worry was that something would happen to my son and Cadwallon before I reached them. The taking of a hostage did not necessarily mean that they would be returned unharmed.

We reached the site of the ambush and we followed the trail which was as clear, in the moonlight, as though it was day. The mud had been churned up by many feet. I let Aedh do his job and we rode in single file behind my hawk-eyed scout.

As dawn broke we found ourselves in the craggy land to the north of the two lakes. The Saxons were leading us through the highest peaks of this land towards the coast and we would not be able to use the advantage of our horses. I smiled grimly to myself; Myrddyn had been right. In many ways, the route the Saxons had chosen made it easier for us to follow. There were few places where they could deviate from their path. I now had a good idea where they were headed. The coast south of Alavna was sparsely populated and the Saxon ships could land unseen.

We were approaching the peaks known as the Roman soldiers when Aedh held up his hand. "Warlord, look!"

We saw a line of stones made into the shape of an arrow. They pointed towards the old Roman Fort in this steep pass. We had been going in that direction but it was good to know that either Gawan or Cadwallon had their wits about them. It confirmed that we were headed in the right direction.

"I hope they are careful, Warlord. If the Saxons know what they are doing it could cost them dear."

Lann Aelle was right and it spurred us on. We passed the fort and I wondered why we had not thought to fortify it ourselves. Then, as I looked around, I answered my own question. It was a bleak outpost. Its only purpose was to stop an invasion from the west and to guard the pass. I was really thinking about what I could have done to protect my son and the answer was that there are some things beyond our power. It did set me thinking. The Romans had known how to protect what belonged to them. It was when this fort had been abandoned, over two hundred years ago, that the problems had begun. When time permitted I would sit with Myrddyn and Brother Oswald to examine all the places the Romans had built their forts.

My reverie was interrupted by Aedh. "I think we should rest, Warlord."

My captain of scouts was right. We had to conserve our horses but I was loath to let the lead become too great. I nodded. "But just a short break. They will not halt."

"They will, uncle, as soon as they get to the coast they will have to stop and await their ship."

We fed and watered the horses and chewed on dried meat. I tasted nothing. My mouth moved and swallowed but it was an unconscious act. I was picturing the warriors who were heading west. I was seeing them prod and poke their captives with their weapons and I could imagine the terror the two boys were experiencing. I just wanted to leap on Mona and gallop to the coast. I would slay them all. Then I stopped my speculation. They would kill the boys as I watched. I knew that as surely as I knew that the sun rose in the east and set in the west. We not only had to catch them we had to do so without their knowledge. Aedh was right to counsel caution. I had brought the right men with me. Hogan Lann would have fed my fears and we would have galloped in recklessly.

We had not ridden more than half a mile when we saw the sea. There was a small settlement of fishermen who lived by the shore and I wondered if they might have seen the Saxons. We proceeded cautiously towards their cluster of huts and left the road. There were woods and copses which we used for cover. Aedh took us towards the village. It was north of the route the Saxons were taking but we had horses and we could use the sands to get ahead of them.

The smell of putrefying flesh assaulted us. This time it was not the flesh of Saxons which had burned but the villagers. The men lay where they had fallen but the women and children of the village had taken shelter in their huts and they had been fired. Their burned bodies turned the stomachs of even the hardest warriors. Some of the women had not had an easy death and we saw their bodies showing what they had suffered before they had died. My men were grim-faced as we searched for survivors. They were used to seeing men slaughtered but not women and children. It hardened their hearts even more against the Saxon kidnappers.

We found no survivors. "Looking at the bodies Warlord, they did this when they first landed. They are beginning to decay already."

I nodded. Aedh was correct. "Take the bodies to the beach and we will bury these fisher folk close to the sea." It was not just a romantic gesture. We would be able to bury them quicker.

We left the desolate and devastated village and headed south. Soon we found evidence that the eight men we pursued had been joined by others they had left at the beach. "It looks like there are now eighteen of them." Aedh pointed to the slightly smaller footprints. "See, this is Gawan and this is Cadwallon. They have different footwear to the Saxons."

We were all relieved that they were still alive. We pushed on harder now. The rest at the fort and the burial had increased the Saxons' lead and we hurried south along the coast. It was easier going but it would be just as easy for the Saxons. They would be making good time too.

We had travelled less than five miles when the trail turned inland to cut the corner of the estuary. This was our chance to gain the initiative and lay an ambush. "Aedh, take two men and keep after them. We will get ahead of them, on the other side of the estuary."

Aedh knew me well enough to know I would be able to communicate with the three of them. The rest of us rode hard along the coast. It was a longer route than the ones the Saxons would take but our horses could maintain a faster pace. I was pleased, yet again, that I had chosen Mona as my mount. She just kept going and was the most comfortable of my three horses to ride.

I knew where the Saxons were heading. The coast began to turn south about sixteen miles from where we were. We were heading east and they were travelling towards the south-east. They would have to camp before they got there. I could probably predict their campsite. The forests came close to the shore and there was a stream. It was not far from the small village of Cark. I hoped they would leave those people alone. Once they camped then we might have a chance to rescue the hostages. That was now my priority. All the work I had done to secure King Cadfan his kingdom would mean nothing if I lost his son and heir. The Saxons I could kill any time but first I had to have my son and my ward safely in my hands again. I pictured the estuary and began to plan how I would trap them. They would camp close to the forest and the stream. We would be able to see them from our vantage point on the other bank. I had Aedh who would stop their retreat. Soon I would have my son and the prince back.

I pushed my men and my horses hard. I had more on my mind than the condition of horses. My son's life was at stake. I was relieved when we reached the small wood overlooking the estuary. The Saxons would have to pass close to the wood in order to carry on their journey south. We could see no sign of them which allowed us time to set up an effective ambush.

We secreted the horses towards the rear of the woods and then began to construct a natural barrier made from hazel branches and blackberry vines. It would enable us to use our bows and prevent the mailed Saxons from closing with us. We were outnumbered and we would need to whittle their numbers down.

As the afternoon settled towards evening one of the warriors watched from the top of a tree. Suddenly he whistled and pointed to the west. They were coming. "Ready your bows."

I hoped that they would camp and allow us to recapture the boys that way but if they pushed on then we were ready. I shinnied up a tree to get a better view of them. Aethelfrith was there, I recognised his helmet and his shield. The two boys were in the middle of the war band and each was led by a warrior. The boys both had a tether around their necks. There were nineteen Saxons in all. I wondered where the extra warrior had come from. A small outcrop of rock hid them from our sight for a short way. We waited for them to emerge. It soon became obvious that they had stopped. Aethelfrith had not chosen the campsite I had expected him to.

I was about to order my men to follow me to their new camp when I heard a whistle from above. The sentry pointed out to sea, to the south. A Saxon ship was edging into the estuary. They were not camping; they were going to sail away.

"Get your bows and horses."

I had anticipated too much and my son would pay the price for my arrogance. I shook my head; there was no point in feeling sorry for myself. I had to deal with this new situation. Time was of the essence. We were a mile away and the ship was arriving rapidly on the rising tide. By the time we reached the beach, the first of the warriors were already wading out to the ship. As we galloped up the rest turned to face us. I heard Aethelfrith ordering the warriors to hurry.

"Use your bows and stop them!"

Lann Aelle had the best horse and he hurled himself to the sand before the rest of us were close. He loosed an arrow and the warrior holding Gawan fell to his death in the foaming waters. Gawan did not flee but tried to help Cadwallon. It was his undoing and Aethelfrith grabbed his tether and tugged him from his feet. He was dragged unceremoniously towards the waiting ship.

I reached my nephew and I drew my bow. My arrow thudded into the back of Aethelfrith's shield making him stagger but he kept going. One of the warriors on the ship ordered those in the sea to attack us. There were twelve of them who obeyed and they turned to advance towards us. We had no choice but to loose our arrows at them. Aethelfrith was sacrificing his oathsworn. Three fell to a foamy death but the other nine charged us through the surf. I drew Saxon Slayer and threw my bow to the ground. I ran at them and I used my sword two handed. I swung the blade in an arc. The first warrior was struggling to gain secure footing in the treacherous sand and my sword sliced through his throat.

A second warrior tried to gut me with his sword but I twisted Saxon Slayer in the air and parried his blow. I put my shoulder into his shield and pushed hard. He too struggled to find purchase in the sand and I brought Saxon Slayer down. It smashed his sword in two. I hacked at him as I passed and felt the blade bite into flesh making the darkening sea redder. I had to get to my son.

Aedh and his two warriors had ridden along the surf and they crashed into the last of the Saxons. I turned to the ship and saw, to my horror, that Aethelfrith had the two boys on board already. He stood at the stern-looking triumphant. The Saxon took out a knife and grabbed my son's left hand. "I told you what would happen if you followed me!" He raised his hand slowly and then brought it down. His knife sliced across Gawan's hand and chopped off his third and fourth fingers. They dropped into the sea and I saw blood spurting. His scream was masked by the sound of the surf. Aethelfrith pointed at me, "I will come to Caestre at the winter solstice. The fort will be empty or these two will die!"

"Aethelfrith, you cowardly dog! Come and fight me like a man!"

As the ship edged back towards the sea I heard him laugh. "And why should I do that? I have your son and the young prince. Your days are

Saxon Slaughter

ending, Warlord; let us hope that you are wise and save your son or he will be waiting for you in the Otherworld."

My shoulders sagged. I was defeated. I would have to do as he said. I could not risk the life of Cadwallon and I would not risk my son. I watched as a torch was applied to my son's wounded and scarred hand and I heard his screams across the water. It felt like a knife cutting into me. My son had paid for my arrogance. By the time I had turned to wade back to shore Lann Aelle and Aedh had the two survivors. Both were wounded.

My men had dragged them clear of the surf. Lann Aelle held his dagger to the throat of one of them. My nephew could speak Saxon as well as any man and he chose his words carefully. "I will ask you a question. If you answer me honestly then I will put a sword in your hand and give you a warrior's death. Do you understand?" The man nodded. "Where will Aethelfrith take the boys?"

Without hesitation, the warrior said, "Hibernia."

Lann Aelle nodded and slit the man's throat. He went to the other warrior. "He lied and he has paid the price. I will ask you the same question." I saw the terror in the man's eyes as he watched his comrade's blood drip down the edge of the blade to make dark blobs on the sand. "Where will Aethelfrith take the boys?"

"I cannot betray my lord."

In answer, Lann Aelle pricked his throat with the dagger. He broke the skin. "It is your choice. Tell me the truth and you will get a warrior's death." He leaned in and spoke as a friend, "Besides would not Aethelfrith like to get his hands on the Wolf Warrior? If you tell us then the Wolf Warrior will go to Aethelfrith's home. Your king can kill him."

I could see the torment in the Saxon's eyes. It sounded plausible and he knew that he would die anyway. Aedh held out the warrior's sword for him and he smiled sympathetically. I think it was Aedh's face which convinced him. He closed his eyes and said, "The island of Man. He has a camp there."

Lann Aelle nodded to Aedh who handed him his sword. The warrior smiled his thanks as my nephew ended his life.

Aedh said, "How did you know the first one lied?"

"He answered too quickly and there was no truth in his eyes."

"Get their weapons. We head north. Hopefully, we will find a ship to take us to this island."

My men never questioned my orders. There might only be a handful of us but they would follow me anywhere. Loyalty was something created over many years. Our horses were tired and it was depressing to travel back along the same road but there was no other way. I had to get to Alavna and hope that Daffydd would call soon.

It was deep into the night when we reached the port the Romans called Alavna. The sound of our horses brought the headman and his men, armed, to the gate. I was recognised immediately and welcomed into the stockade.

"Have any of my ships been here in the past week?"

"Aye, Warlord. Two of them put in five days since and when they saw a Saxon ship they left."

I worked out that they must have been patrolling to see if they could find the Saxons. It was just bad luck that they had missed the second ship but a hope rose within me that they might be fortunate and come upon them now. We were all so tired that we collapsed in the headman's hut and slept like babies.

I had bad dreams. I kept seeing Aethelfrith cutting pieces from Gawan's body and I could do nothing about it. It was as though I was sinking in the estuary sands and watching my son dying piece by piece. I awoke sweating and breathing heavily: it was still dark. I rose quietly, without disturbing my warriors and went to watch the sun rise. I was still peering out to sea when Aedh and Lann Aelle joined me.

"What I cannot understand, Warlord, is why Aethelfrith is doing this. It does not get him his kingdom back and it risks your enmity."

"He has that anyway and it makes sense for him to capture Caestre. He was the one who conquered Man. It makes sense that the people there would support him rather than Edwin but if he is to challenge Edwin he needs a base and Caestre is perfect. He knows how strong it is and I would guess that he has scouted it and seen that Bors has made it strong again. We have done the work for him. Do you think that we could retake it if we gave it back to him?"

Aedh shook his head, "The Saxons could never take it. Bors would be too strong for them."

"And what of the hostages? Will he return my cousin and the prince as he has promised?"

"He said it in front of his oathsworn but he does not have to return them whole. We have pursued them; he told us the consequences and that will give him licence to mutilate them as he chooses. It is why we must get to the island as quickly as we can. Aedh, send a rider to Penrhyd. He can tell Myrddyn and my son what we are about." Aedh nodded and left. We would be one warrior short but it could not be helped. I had to let the others know where we were going.

I know that it was impulsive but waiting has never been something I have been good at. I like to be active and I paced up and down the beach. My eyes scanned the horizon until they became sore from the salt and the wind. Aedh and Lann Aelle tried to keep my mind on other things but it was difficult. They talked of anything save the Saxons and my son. It did no good. I was my own biggest critic. Hogan Lann had been a cause for worry when I had had to leave him at home but he had been safe within the walls of my fort and behind the shields of my men. I had tempted fate by bringing Gawan so close to the battlefield and into the stronghold of the Saxon.

Eventually, the two of them decided to distract me by asking about my plans for our assault on Man. "Do we know what the island is like?"

"No. I would imagine that Daffydd would have an idea." The memory of the attack by the Saxons when I had last sailed south suddenly surfaced. Why had ignored that attack? I could have done something about it. This made me even angrier with myself. I knew that the Saxons were there, less than half a day from Mona and I had left them undisturbed. I was paying the price for that omission.

"We will be going into the lair of our foe. Every man will be a potential enemy." Aedh was a scout and we were now making him a warrior who would have to fight warriors in the shield wall.

Lann Aelle shook his head. "Not necessarily. The Saxons have only been there for a few years. The people who lived on the island before the time of the Romans will be there. They may have no love for the invader."

Aedh was right. I knew the island was small but we would have to find where they kept the boys quickly. We would need all the help we could get. Another day passed and there was still no ship. When we saw Hogan Lann and the column of horsemen approaching I knew that my message had got through.

My son dismounted and embraced me. "Your message made Myrddyn angry. He is fond of Gawan. He would have come with us but I told him we needed speed." Myrddyn had never been a good rider; he could stay in the saddle and that was about the extent of his skill. "We have brought another ten men for you to take with you."

"This is a task for a small group of men and not an army."

"I would be happier if they were aboard the ship. The last time you sailed you were undermanned. We are using the squires to patrol with the other horsemen. It is good we have not compromised our strength."

I felt happier knowing that I was leaving a safe Rheged. Perhaps the good feelings we had felt had transmitted themselves to the gods, for a sail filled the horizon. It was Daffydd. We had all our weapons ready. We would board as soon as he reached us. We would leave the horses. It would have been too difficult to board the ship with them anyway, especially if we had to leave Man in a hurry. That was a likely end to this madcap adventure. I did not think that the Saxons would just allow us to go in, rescue the hostages and leave easily. We would have to fight our way out.

The reception party he viewed made Daffydd leap ashore before the boat was even tied up. I told him what had happened and asked, "Did you see the Saxon ship?"

His face fell. "I saw one yesterday but it was on the horizon and close to Man. Had I known...?"

"Had you known, you could have done nothing. This will need warriors and not sailors. Do you know where Aethelfrith will go on the island?"

"Not for certain but there are four settlements on the coast. Two are so small that Aethelfrith would not use them. The other two have jetties for boats. One is on the southern coast and the other faces east. That is the one I believe he will use."

"Can you drop us close enough for us to walk there?"

"The island is so small that you can walk its length in a day and its width in half a day. I could sail along the coast and see if the ship is there."

I shook my head. "No, I do not want him alerted. I believe he would kill them if he knew that we were on the island. We will need to be in and out so quickly that he will not have time to react. We will need you to be on hand so that we can escape."

"If I drop you at night I could sail into the harbour and pick you up from there."

"Good. I will leave you half of my men to boost your crew." I looked at the sky. "And we have wasted enough time. Get the men on board. Hogan Lann, you are in command until I return."

His voice was husky as he said, "Make sure that you do return."

Saxon Slaughter

The men I chose to take on the island with me were all the most skilled at both hiding and killing silently. Apart from Lann Aelle and Aedh, I took Tadgh who, small and lithe could move as silently as a fox. There was Drugh who had been with us since he had been a despatch rider. He was skilled in all types of weapons but he was as good with a bow as any man. The brothers, Garth and Wem made up the seven. The two brothers were as strong as bulls and yet they could hide almost in plain sight. All of us had the ability to both adapt and change to unforeseen circumstances. We all took out shields, swords as well as bows and daggers. Aedh and Drugh even took the slingshots they had used when they had been despatch riders. The rest of our force we would leave on the ship.

I asked the captain what he knew of Man. "My father told me that there were people like us on the island but the Saxons came there when they could not capture Mona. I do not know what happened to the people."

"Tell me more about this island of Manau?"

"It is a compact rock not far from our land. There is one larger hill in the middle of the island." He smiled, "If it were ours I know that you would have placed a watchtower there for I have been told that from its peak you can see the whole island."

Once again I had not defended some of the people of Rheged and, as on the mainland, they had paid the price.

"We will find where the hostages are held and we will wait until they are all asleep. If we can take out the guards, when it is quiet then we can recapture the boys. Garth and Wem, your task will be to guard the boys and get them to the ship." I looked earnestly at both of them. "We will buy you time to get to the ship. I trust you both and I know that you will not let me down."

"We will get them to safety, Warlord. We so swear."

That left four of us to be a shield wall while the wily Aedh watched for anyone coming from the side. We would be a small group but we had all fought together before. We trusted each other and in the heat of the battle that was often worth more than mere numbers. It was important that every warrior knew his job well before he was called upon to carry it out.

The coast loomed up as the sun set on the western side of the island. We could see an occasional flicker from the northern settlement. Our captain told us that this was just two or three huts but we did not wish to risk being seen. We sailed along the coast as though we were just another trader. The fact that we had a sail and no oars helped. We passed a small stream which gave us a backup point for our rescue should the settlement prove too difficult.

"If I have to sail from the harbour without you I will come here. " Our captain pointed to the small hill. I will drop you on the other side of this hill." He ordered the sail lowered and we drifted, with the tide, toward the beach. His men dropped a small skiff into the water. "I will return at dawn."

Aedh, Drugh and Tadgh were rowed ashore to scout out the land. "If you are not in the harbour and I need you I will loose a fire arrow into the sky. I am leaving you with enough men to secure the landing."

"I will destroy any Saxon ships I see. It will distract them from your quest." He clasped my arm. "I pray that you are successful."

"I will either be successful or I will be dead. I do not leave this island, without my son."

The skiff returned and we descended. It was now so dark that I could not see the shore. As the sailors rowed I looked back and saw that the ship itself was barely visible. That meant that our arrival might escape notice. The water was icy as I stepped ashore. I swung my shield around and looked for Aedh. A figure slid down the rocky slope ahead of us. It was my captain of scouts. "There is a path leading to the town. Tadgh and Drugh are both guarding the top."

Lann Aelle placed himself at the rear and we followed Aedh as he climbed the slope. Drugh waved his arm and we flattened ourselves against the hillside. I took off my helmet to enable me to see the town more clearly. Below me, I saw the pinpricks of light from the roundhouses. Aethelfrith was so confident about his island that there was no wooden wall around the twenty or so huts and buildings. It was a sizeable settlement. We could see little else and we would have to descend to get a closer look.

The hillside was covered with gorse bushes and rocks. We used both for cover as we slid silently down the slope. When we reached a point a half a mile or so from the first hut, we halted, to get our bearings, and to get a better idea of the layout of the village. I could see that they had a warrior hall. It was in the middle of the huts. Its size clearly marked it out. That would be where Aethelfrith and his oathsworn were. There were two guards outside the front entrance which made me think that the hostages would be inside. There were also four men guarding the Saxon ship which was tied up to the jetty.

I signalled for Aedh and the two brothers to move around to the other side of the village. I needed to know if there was any danger from that quarter.

They had not been gone long when two warriors walked from the warrior hall and seemed to be making directly for us. I slid my dagger out. If they came too close we would have to silence them. None of us moved. So long as we were just shadows we would be safe. They were within ten paces of us when they stopped. They began to urinate and I wondered why they had come so far from the huts to perform this common act. Normally they would have just stepped beyond the last hut and then they talked.

"We left some good men behind today, Rolf."

"I know but we had to have the hostages. King Edwin has too much power for us to defeat him in the east. Our lord is right; we need to build up those who follow us and use our strength in the west. King Cadfan and his men have made Mercia weak. It is like a chicken ready to be plucked."

"I had fought with those warriors who died the other day in the shield wall. We could have turned and defeated them. There were but a handful and only two had mail."

"Aye, but one was the Wolf Warrior himself and the other was his standard-bearer. I would not like to go against either of them; at least not in shifting sands and on their land."

"You may be right but will this Warlord hand over the fort for the boy? I would not. A man can easily father another brat but he cannot retake a fort as easily."

"No, but this Lord Lann believes in family. Had his wife still been on the island we would have taken her when we sought a hostage. Have faith, the gods favoured us and allowed us to take the richest prize we could and we have the prince too. We can use him to get what we want from his father."

"The gods weren't with us when that Dane laid about him with his sword. There were six good warriors who fell to his blade."

"*Wyrd*, Raed, *wyrd*. Now come let us go back. We have the guard duty soon and I would like to have a little more ale beneath my belt by then."

The two men turned and returned to the huts. I watched them carefully and saw that they entered the warrior hall. Were they the guards for the hall or for the hostages? We would know when we saw the changing of the guards for I had marked them both. I also felt a shiver down my spine; they had been to Caer Gybi and looked for my family. I would need to be ever more vigilant from now on.

It became quieter and there was less movement. Suddenly Aedh and the brothers appeared behind us. "There are no guards on the other side but the hut behind the warrior hall has two guards there."

I pointed to the warrior hall. "When they change those guards we will head to the hut you have discovered. That may well be where they hold them."

The noises from the hall slowly subsided. When the two guards were changed and it was not Raed and Rolf who relieved them then I knew where the boys were. They would not guard an empty hut. We stood without any commands being given and we slowly and silently slipped around the outside of the village. Aedh led the way. I saw that the two guards were Rolf and Raed. I also knew that they had been drinking. I predicted that they would need to relieve themselves sooner rather than later. This time they would not go far but just slip around the side of the hut and that was where we would wait for them. I signalled for Lann Aelle, Tadgh and Drugh to move to one side of the hut. I took Aedh and the two brothers to the other side. Then we waited. I kept my sword in its scabbard for I would need a knife.

I could hear the two guards talking although they never mentioned what they were guarding. They spoke of their dead comrades and then their hopes for a future raiding the lands of the King of Gwynedd. I hoped it would be the hostages who were within the hut but it could be anything. Doubts began to assail my mind. Where would they have put the hostages? I did not think that they would have the hostages in the warrior hall. Aethelfrith would not want to risk a drunken warrior hurting them prematurely. Perhaps this was Aethelfrith's hut. If that was the case then the gods were definitely smiling upon me. I could rescue my son and kill Aethelfrith.

I suddenly heard one of the guards, I think it was Raed, say, "I need a leak."

Our daggers were already out and we waited to see if he came around our side of the hut. He did not. When we heard the soft sigh, such as someone makes in their sleep, we slipped around the front. Raed would be in the Otherworld already. Rolf was already peering around the far side to see what the noise was. Aedh was on him in a flash and his throat was slit before he could utter a sound. The two brothers caught the warrior and his weapons before he crashed to the ground. In the quiet hours, such a sudden sound would have alerted the other guards at the warrior hall and on the jetty. I stood where he had been. Lann Aelle joined me and we stood there while the bodies were removed.

Tadgh and Drugh picked up the dead Saxon's weapons and stood at the entrance to the hut. I couldn't hear any sounds from inside but that meant nothing. I nodded to Aedh who pulled the door open and I burst in. There was a dying fire in the middle of the hut. Before me, I saw a sleeping Saxon warrior. He must have felt the draught from the door for his eyes widened as he awoke. I fell on him and stabbed him in the throat. He too died silently. I looked up, anxiously, and there, on the far side of the fire were the two boys tied back to back. Prince Cadwallon's eyes were wide with terror. I took off my helmet and his face broke into a smile. I held my finger to my lips.

I cut their bonds. Lann Aelle helped Cadwallon to his feet and I turned Gawan over. His hand was covered in a dirty bloody bandage. His eyes filled with tears when he saw me. I clutched him to my chest and held him tightly. I whispered in his ear, "I am here to take you home."

He whispered back. "We knew you would come."

Lann Aelle gave the two boys the daggers from the dead men; we were few enough as it was and we needed all the weapons we could muster. "What now, Warlord?"

It was a vexed question. I had not expected it to be as easy as it had been but what were we to do now? If we left we risked the guards being missed. "How long until dawn?"

"It is not yet the false dawn. I would guess a couple of hours."

Men tended to get up in the early hours of the morning to relieve themselves. We had to stay for at least another hour and we risked discovery with each passing moment.

"Aedh get the fire arrow ready. If we are discovered then give the signal immediately." I turned to the boys. "We have a ship coming into the harbour at dawn. We will have to go past the warrior hall and that cannot be helped. We will need a great deal of fortune and silence to do so undetected. You will go with Wem and Garth and you will do all that they say. Is that clear?"

They both nodded relief and terror showing in equal measure on their faces. I smiled. Looking down I saw a jug of ale. I poured a beaker and swallowed it down then handed it to Lann Aelle. He passed it to the others. It tasted rough but at that moment my throat was so dry I would have drunk horse's piss.

Wem's voice suddenly came from the outside. "Two men just staggered out of the hall."

"Better get ready. If they get too close then we make a break for the harbour." I unsheathed Saxon Slayer and Aedh prepared his arrows.

Lann Aelle put his arm around Gawan's shoulder. "Do not worry, cousin. We will soon be back at home and you will be safe. Just follow the brothers and leave these Saxons to us."

It made me smile that just a few short years ago Lann Aelle had been the same age as my son and yet now he was so confident and assured. I glanced at the disfigured bandaged hand and knew that it was unlikely that Gawan would achieve the same level of skill as his cousin. Aethelfrith would pay.

Tadgh peered out of the door. "They are coming over."

"Lann Aelle, you speak Saxon, pretend you are the warrior we killed in the hall, take off your helmet and go outside. They will speak and neither Wem nor Garth can speak Saxon." My plan was beginning to unravel. "Aedh, ready the arrows."

I heard one of the Saxons shout, "Hey Ida, you haven't been touching the little boys, have you? "

They were both drunk. Lann Aelle played the part well. He spat and said, "Come a little closer, and I will show you a real warrior and not a blowhard."

I heard his voice and it was suspicious, "You're not Ida."

That was as far as he got. I leapt out of the door in time to see the two brothers spearing one while Lann Aelle was wiping the blood from his blade. We stood in the silence. To us, it had sounded loud but it must have been quiet enough not to wake anyone. "Now Aedh. Wem and Garth, take the boys. The rest of you, shields."

As the arrow soared into the night sky we hurried through the village. I kept glancing at the warrior hall but there was no movement. We had had a stroke of luck. The two guards from the hall had been the ones who decided to come and tease the dead Ida. We had a little more time than I had hoped. We had to buy as much distance between us and the warrior hall as we could. Daffydd and the ship could be anywhere. The wind and the tide were not under our control.

"Warlord, there are four guards at the jetty. They are sitting by the fire."

Saxon Slaughter

The four guards had not seen us but it was merely a matter of time before they did so. I said quietly, "We will need to kill them quickly and quietly. Aedh, can you see the ship?"

My scout had the best eyes but he said, "Not yet my lord. I know he will come."

The first job we had was to kill the guards as efficiently as possible. "Aedh, use your sling. The rest of you, get out your bows."

We stopped and took out our weapons. The guards had neither seen nor heard us. They were all staring at the fire and that spoiled your night vision; experienced sentries sat their watches with their backs to the fire. These men were lazy and it would cost them their lives. The light from the fire also illuminated them and made them better targets. Aedh's sling was accurate and one guard fell a moment before four arrows plunged into the others. They had been less than fifty paces away and we did not miss at that range. There was a groan from one as he died but I was sure that no one would have heard it. We raced to the wooden jetty and stared out to sea. The black sky and the sea merged into one save for a thin line of the whitening sky to the east. I knew we had to be patient. They would have been sailing along the coast but the wind was a fickle and precocious thing. We would have to wait. We stood so that the fire of the guards protected one flank and the sea on the other. When they came they would have no chance to outflank us. We would only have five men to face them but it would have to be enough. Two of us wore mail and that would give us the edge.

Prince Cadwallon asked as we waited, "What became of Einar? We saw what they did to him."

"He lived long enough to give us the message and he died with a sword in his hand."

"I am pleased. I will honour his memory for the rest of my life." The prince was as good as his word and the brave Dane was never far from the prince's thoughts when he went to war.

Suddenly there was a shout from the far side of the village. Our escape had been discovered. "You boys, stand behind us."

"I can use a bow, Warlord." I think the prince did not relish the thought of incarceration a second time.

"Here Prince Cadwallon, take mine. Gawan, watch for the ship."

He turned and ran. Was he afraid? "Gawan, where are you going?"

"I can help. Trust me." He ran to the Saxon ship at the end of the jetty and disappeared on board.

"Lock your shields and pray that Daffydd comes soon or this will just be a tale told around campfires about the Warlord and his heroes who died fighting a war band." Every time I fought the Saxons I believed that I would win but I knew that one day I would lose and this could be that day.

The Saxons were forming up. I could see that they had hurriedly donned helmets and held shields and swords but they had not had time to put on mail. That was not a quick process. I estimated that there were about thirty of them. Aethelfrith led them as they came resolutely towards us. He had managed to put on mail. I suppose they thought that they had us. The lightening sky behind us showed how few we were and the cunning king was not about to rush into a sudden attack. They outnumbered us and we would die. He could afford to be patient.

I smelled smoke and turned my head. Gawan was scrambling back from the Saxon ship. He grinned, "I might only have one hand but I can light a fire." There were flames licking around the base of the mast.

"Well done. Prince, Wem, cut the ship free. Perhaps they will try to save their last ship."

It was a thin thread that had been thrown to us but we would grasp it. If it distracted the approaching Saxons then we might have a chance. The line of shields was just a hundred paces away. Aethelfrith lowered his shield a little so that he could taunt me. "So you came yourself. That is good. I will kill you and then the fort will easily fall, for without you Rheged is nothing. You should have stayed away and saved your life."

I decided to keep him talking. Any delay aided us. "I came to punish you, Aethelfrith, for hurting my son and killing a brave warrior. I have come to show all Saxons that my retribution is swift and deadly. You should have stayed on this island. It would have been a kingdom big enough for someone as small as you. When I have rescued my son I will return and we will burn your hovels to the ground; as we have burned your ship."

Perhaps he had concentrated so hard on me that he had not noticed his burning ship. I saw a flash of anger in his eyes and he shouted, "Aethelread, secure the ship."

Ten men detached themselves from the shield wall. We loosed arrows at them to slow them down and two fell to the missiles. There were fewer men now to face us but still, they came and still they outnumbered us.

Saxon Slaughter

"The ship!" Gawan's voice told me all that I needed to know. Daffydd was approaching. I did not know how far away he was but there were reinforcements on that boat and we now had a chance.

Without turning and without shouting I said, "Wem, Garth, get them on board as soon as the ship touches the jetty."

The sight of my ship heading in was too much for the Saxons and the shield wall raced at us. I noticed that Aethelfrith hung back and was not in the first rank. The coward was allowing his men to be killed by me so that he could fight a weakened and, possibly, wounded warrior.

We held our swords above our shields. A blade in your face has a way of making a man more cautious. All of us, except for Tadgh were big men and were taller than most Saxons. It was a slight advantage. The other four were to my left and right and I was slightly ahead. We were the tiniest wedge it was possible to use. The Saxons would come for me. Each one would dream of the glory of killing the Wolf Warrior and owning the mystical sword, Saxon Slayer.

The Saxons tried to run at us for the last few paces. It was a cardinal error. They had not locked shields and two of them stumbled at our feet. Tadgh and Drugh despatched them with ease. The warrior facing me made the mistake of flicking his eyes to the side to see what had happened to his fallen comrades and Saxon Slayer slid into his forehead. He slumped dead before I had withdrawn my sword. Lann Aelle stabbed forwards too and then slashed sideways with his blade. The Saxons had pressed too many men forwards and they were so tightly packed that they could not use their weapons properly. Their weight, however, was pushing us inexorably back towards the water. If we fell into the sea then we would all die. We would either be drowned or dragged from the water to be executed. Neither was an attractive prospect.

Suddenly two things happened at once, Cadwallon began to use his bow from behind us and Gawan hurled burning brands from the fire into the air towards the back of the press of warriors. When they fell amongst the Saxons they made them recoil. The pressure decreased slightly, giving us a little breathing space and I yelled, "Push forwards!"

It was a well-practised move and we punched with our shields as we slashed with our swords. We were all able to do it in time. The effect was dramatic. Four warriors fell immediately and others slipped to the ground. I heard Aethelfrith giving his orders. I looked beyond the press of warriors and saw a depressing sight. His oathsworn had donned armour and there were eight of them coming towards us. The odds were now in their favour. These would lock shields and they would know how to fight. The odds swung dramatically in their favour. Only Lann Aelle and I had mail and Tuanthal's men and Aedh would not last long against such experienced warriors.

Aethelfrith ordered the warriors who had been pushed back to withdraw. Three were too slow and they fell to our blades. The oathsworn formed up with locked shields. Aethelfrith positioned himself behind the lead warrior and they began to march forwards. This was not an ill-disciplined charge, this was a measured approach. Gawan's torches had run out and would not harm the mailed men. Cadwallon's arrows now struck shields. We had had a small breathing space and we tightened our grip on our shields. It would soon be a fight to the death as the five of us fought the nine mailed men who were advancing toward us.

The warrior at the head of the small wedge had an open helmet and a long scar running down his cheek. It gave him a strange grin. His sword was held before him and he looked as though he knew what he was doing.

I wanted them to do something stupid and I taunted them. "Still hiding behind your men I see, Aethelfrith."

"They all want to kill you. I am a generous leader." Aethelfrith did not rise to the bait. He knew they would win. It was inevitable.

"When I have slain enough of them then you and I will try our blades." It was all bravado, of course. These were seasoned warriors. The warrior bands on their swords were testament to that. The leading warrior suddenly swung his sword overhand. As I put my shield up to take the blow Aethelfrith tried to stab me with his sword from behind. Lann Aelle knocked the edge down but the blade scored my leg where there was no mail. It did not hurt much but it made me angry. Lann Aelle then had to defend himself from the warrior to Aethelfrith's left who assaulted him. I would be fighting two men, so be it.

As the sword from the scarred man crashed into my shield I allowed myself to sink slightly and the move caught the warrior unawares He tried to stop himself from falling forwards and he opened his shield, it was only a marginal gap but it was enough. I stabbed Saxon Slayer forwards. I felt it strike the mail links. They were not as strong as they should have been and I pushed harder. I saw the exultation turn to fear on his face as the blade sliced through the mail as though it was not there. The tip entered his flesh and I pushed harder. He grimaced in pain and I twisted and turned the sword. When I saw the tendril of blood dripping from his mouth I withdrew it just in time to fend off another blow from Aethelfrith.

Things were not going our way. Tadgh lay dead on the ground and I could see that Drugh was wounded. Suddenly, with no warning, there was a whoosh from behind me and a bolt speared the two men on the end of the Saxon line just as they were about to finish off Drugh. It was my ship. Lann Aelle took advantage and killed his man.

"Wem, look after Drugh." I could see that Aethelfrith was now worried. A second bolt flew through the air and took out six of the warriors who were waiting behind the mailed warriors to join Aethelfrith's oathsworn. They fled back towards the huts. I had no idea how far away the ship was and I could not risk looking for it. The numbers were now slightly in our favour although we still only had two mailed warriors to fight Aethelfrith and his remaining oathsworn.

The other bodyguards realised that the bolt thrower could not be used if they closed with us and they did so. I had just blocked a blow from Aethelfrith when Garth went down clutching his side. Before the warrior could help his king, Cadwallon's bow appeared over my shoulder and he loosed an arrow from a sword's length. It entered the warrior's eye and erupted out of the back of his helmet spraying the bodies behind with blood and brain. It bought us more breathing space. There was just Aethelfrith and two of his men left. We were evenly matched in terms of numbers.

I noticed, for the first time that Aethelfrith's sword was Dyrrnwyn. "I see you have a stolen sword, Saxon. How appropriate that you use another man's weapon and use it without any honour."

If I was trying to irritate him it was working. He roared at me, "And it will end your life too!" He swung it overhand and I had to hold my shield up to take the blow.

Dyrrnwyn was a good blade and it bit deeply into my shield. My shield was well made and had both leather and metal to protect it. I swung my sword sideways with the full weight of my body behind it and I felt his shield shiver. His was not as good.

"Father, the ship is here."

"Get them aboard and I will finish Aethelfrith."

"You are confident. Let us see if Dyrrnwyn can defeat Saxon Slayer."

My men leapt from the ship to protect the boys and to allow them to collect the wounded. Lann Aelle and Aedh still guarded my right as they finished off the last of Aethelfrith's guards.

I knew that his shield would not last but I could also see more men coming from the village. We had to leave and leave soon. I swung at his head and he raised his shield. This time a lump of his shield shattered. Fear was in his eyes. Lann Aelle shouted, "Hurry Warlord, there are more warriors coming from the village and beyond!"

Aethelfrith's next blow was aimed at my head but I punched it away with my shield and smashed down with Saxon Slayer. It sliced off another piece of the shield and slid down the mail shirt to rip open his knee. I could see the white bone of his shattered kneecap erupt through the bloodied flesh as he fell screaming and bleeding to the ground.

"Lann Aelle. Pick up his sword!" I raised Saxon Slayer but before I could despatch the injured king, four men raced forwards to drag him to safety and my men dragged me back.

"I will return, Aethelfrith, and you will pay for the pain you have caused my son. This I swear."

As arrows thudded into my shield, Lann Aelle and Aedh led me over the side of the ship to safety. I was the last one to leave the island and I watched as the Saxons tried to protect Aethelfrith from the arrows of my warriors. The bolt throwers continued to hurtle towards the Saxons who had to pull further away from the jetty. As we edged away I noticed that the Saxon ship had settled deep into the water her hull ruined. They would need to build another one before they could raid my land again but by then we would be prepared. I also had the satisfaction of knowing that Aethelfrith would be crippled for life. I had repaid the mutilation of my son.

Saxon Slaughter

Chapter 11

"I am sorry we took so long, Warlord. The wind died on us."

I looked at the two dead warriors who lay on the deck. It was possible they might have lived had Daffydd arrived earlier but I doubted it. "It was meant to be and they both died warrior's deaths."

I saw that Gawan was shaking. I think it was the shock of it all. He would have steeled himself, while a prisoner, to be brave, but now he was free and his body took over. I was about to go to him when I saw Lann Aelle slip his arm around his shoulder and begin to talk with him quietly. Lann Aelle and I had almost suffered the same fate some years earlier. He would understand better than most. I could leave my son in his cousin's arms. We would honour the dead later but for now, I had decisions to make.

As the ship heeled around and headed away from the island Daffydd asked, "Where to, Warlord?"

"I think we had better get these two home where they will be safe."

Prince Cadwallon stood defiantly looking at me. "Have I done something to offend you, Warlord?"

"No, Prince Cadwallon. Why do you ask?"

"If you take me home now then it will be in disgrace. I will have failed you."

"You have failed no one but you nearly died."

"And next time something like this happens then I will be stronger." His face hardened. "Einar must not die in vain. I will work harder now to be the warrior he dreamed I would be. No more wasting time hunting. I was a boy then. Now I am a man and I will work to be the best warrior in your army."

I saw the nods of approval from the rest of my men. Those were the kind of sentiments of which they approved. "But what of Gawan? He needs healing."

Gawan stood and placed himself next to Prince Cadwallon. "And the best healer in the whole land is Myrddyn. Take me back to him." He held up his bandaged, mangled hand. "I can never be the warrior I hoped I would be but I can still be a healer like Myrddyn and I can still learn his magic." He pointed to Prince Cadwallon, "The prince is right. We were not committed enough before and it took the death of Einar to focus us. I swear we will not argue with you in future and we will work to be the best that we can be."

I looked at Aedh and Lann Aelle, their faces told me what to do. I closed my eyes. What would Myfanwy and King Cadfan say if any other hurt came to them? That decided me; I would have to ensure that nothing happened to them. "Set a course to Alavna then, captain."

As we headed north the two boys told us the full tale of what had happened. It soon became obvious that the Saxons had been stalking the fort looking for just such a target. They told us that the Saxons were waiting at the place Einar used for sword work. I worried about their knowledge. Someone had to have told them of the two boys. Was there a traitor amongst my men or a Saxon spy? Those questions would need to be answered when we returned. They both told me how bravely Einar had fought. We teased out of them how they too had fought as hard as they could but they had been overwhelmed.

Both boys had lost their mail and their swords. When we reached Penrhyd that would be the first order of the day. They needed better weapons too. When we reached Wyddfa we would have the new sword for Gawan that had been made for him by Hywel. The most important decision I made was that Cadwallon would not leave my side and Myrddyn would watch over Gawan. That way I would ensure that they were both well protected.

I remembered the sword of Rhydderch Hael I had recaptured. It was a prize as important as my son. I took it from the deck where Lann Aelle had laid it. It was magnificent and almost as good as my own. Its strength lay, however, in what it would do for our people. We would now have a secure alliance once the sword was returned to our near neighbours. It would also be a boost for our people. They would know that the Saxons were no longer invincible. The tide was turning against the Saxons. It was not rising, now they were ebbing. They were no longer having their own way. It had cost my son his fingers and three brave men their lives but we were winning.

I spent the rest of the voyage writing two letters: one was to King Cadfan and one to Myfanwy. I dared not let them discover the events for themselves. I told them all that had occurred and I explained why the two boys were still with me. I hoped they would understand. As I stood on the jetty at Alavna I said to Daffydd, "Deliver this personally, my friend. I know that my wife will have questions. Answer them honestly." I smiled, "It will be an ordeal worse than sailing into a Saxon firestorm but you are married and you know these things."

"I will, Warlord, and, for what it is worth, I believe you have made the right decision. If I stopped sailing every time a bad storm took some of my men then I would have given up the sea many years ago. It is these challenges and how we meet them that mark us as men. You, my lord, are a man."

The horses were well-rested and we made good time as we rode east. My men made sure that the two boys were surrounded by iron and men for the whole journey. We called in at Wide Water because I needed to speak with Kay.

He had heard of the attack and was concerned. It showed that he was both loyal and compassionate. I needed those qualities for the task I was to give him.

"I will be speaking with all my leaders of a hundred but you are a seasoned warrior and you can put these plans into action sooner, rather than later." I pointed to the west. "You will need to have your despatch riders become scouts who can ride this land and let you know of anything which appears out of the ordinary. We may have Saxon spies amongst us. I suspect they were watching us before Aethelfrith arrived. We need vigilance. This is a task for the rest of your life. I am giving you command of all the land as far as the sea to the west; to the two lakes to the north and to long water to the east."

"And the south?"

"For the moment Wide Water is our southern boundary. I have thoughts on the land to the south but they are not clear yet." I smiled, "I need the wizard's mind."

"I will do all that you ask. If it were not for you, I would be dead and my people still suffering. What we hold we keep."

I felt better knowing that Kay would guard this southern gateway to Rheged. I had not spoken of it to him but I had decided to make the south more secure, myself. If we left the eastern boundary as it was then King Edwin could be kept at bay. The land to the south was fertile farmland but lacked defences. I would work my way south building forts and settlements as I went. What I now needed was people. I was sure there were many who had fled the Saxons in Rheged and settled in the south. I just had to find them. It would not be a rapid settlement but it would make Rheged much safer than it had been.

Myrddyn's face showed the strain he had been under while we had been away. Hogan Lann also looked older. Their faces were wracked with anger and shock when they saw what Aethelfrith had done. We all knew that we could suffer wounds in war but to suffer such wanton mutilation was beyond the pale. I was still angry that I had not finished him off but I had maimed him too. He would never walk properly again. His days of fighting were gone.

I showed the sword of Dyrrnwyn to Hogan Lann. "I want you to take this and return it to King Necthan at Alt Cult."

"Why me? You are the one he should reward for you recovered it."

"I have plans to make here with Myrddyn; plans which will make Rheged much safer. Besides the king is of your age and you will be Warlord when I am gone. The bond should be between you two." He nodded. He could see the reasoning. "And if you take your knights it will show him another way to fight the enemy."

"Will he fight the Saxons then?"

"Aye but he is assailed from the north by the Picts and from the east by the Hibernians. He needs all the help he can get."

"And Prince Pasgen?"

"I will need to speak with him. He must now assume control of this land. King Edwin has retreated. The prince must keep him on the defensive."

I told him of my plans to give warriors like Kay control over large parts of Rheged. "It sounds a good idea but it may be dangerous. You are giving power to men who may decide to try to get more."

"True but if that happens, it is because I will have made an error of judgement. So far there is Kay who will be my lieutenant around Wide Water. Do you think he is a wise choice?"

"Of course."

"Good, and if I say that I am considering Pol as my second choice what would you say?"

He looked disappointed, "I think he would be perfect but he is my right hand."

"I know. That is why he is such a good choice and my third would be Lann Aelle who, as you know, is my right hand. We all must make sacrifices. The future of Rheged is not about our happiness; it is about the safety and security of this land. I beg you not to say a word. I will need to speak with Prince Pasgen."

"Of course." He gave me a curious look. "When did you think of this?"

"When I stood on the jetty at Alavna waiting for Daffydd and I wished to put all thoughts of your brother's pain from my mind I began to work out how we might have made the land so secure that this could have been prevented."

"Even your new plan would not prevent a small war band from causing trouble."

"But it would. When we pursued Aethelfrith I was thinking then that the land of Rheged has natural narrow points that men have to pass through. The Roman fort close to the coast is one such place. Somewhere along the long lake just south of us is another. We have done this at Wide Water and, so far, our enemies have avoided it."

"Where would Pol and Lann Aelle rule?"

"One would rule here at Penrhyd and the West Moors Land; the other the land to the south of Wide Water. It is harder to control and it needs someone who understands horsemen such as yours. I want Rheged to reach all the way to Mona. We will be an island against the Saxons. And now I must go to Myrddyn. He is looking at your brother's hand. I am anxious to hear his opinion."

Myrddyn was in his quarters. The room blazed with light and Gawan's bandages had been removed. The wound made me gasp. I had seen worse wounds but this was my child. It was red and angry. The two fingers had been taken off below the knuckle. The Saxons had used a torch to cauterise it but I wondered if that would be enough to save the hand.

Gawan saw the pain on my face. "It does not hurt father."

Myrddyn glanced up at me. "I can save the hand but he will have a weaker left hand." His eyes bored into mine. "He will never stand in a shield wall."

"I can hold a shield." Gawan was desperate to hold onto the dream of being a warrior.

"Myrddyn is right. You will find it hard to use a bow too. How would you ride and use a weapon? You could not. We will continue to train you with a sword but it may be that you do as you wished to do before this horror; you may become a wizard."

"I would rather have had a choice."

Myrddyn just said, "It is *wyrd* boy. Do not fight it. You accept what you are given and you make the best of it. He dabbed the wound with an ointment he held. "It has served both me and your father well enough. There have been times when it was not the blade which saved us but my mind and yours is as sharp as any."

I stepped back as Myrddyn continued to work on the hand. I knew that Myrddyn would also heal my son's mind. It amazed me that Gawan did not seem at all put out by what Myrddyn was doing. He was asking him questions and even aiding him. They seemed so close that I almost felt a little jealous. This would be good for them both and I had to accept that my younger son might follow someone who was not his father. My own words came back to haunt me. We often had to give up things we loved for a greater cause.

I left Gawan with Myrddyn when I rode to visit Prince Pasgen. Lann Aelle and Prince Cadwallon accompanied me. The prince never stopped asking me questions as we rode. Lann Aelle tried to shut him up at one point. "He needs to learn, my nephew. He is to be king and he will have to lead an army against the Saxons. He must understand not only how to fight but how to use his best weapons."

"Best weapons?"

"Aye, his warriors and his leaders. If you know your men then you can win. Look at King Edwin. He knew Aella would fight as hard as any man to get to me and that allowed him to watch from afar. Aethelfrith had to come himself because he did not trust his men."

Cadwallon nodded. "And you sent your son to see King Necthan because you trust him."

"Exactly."

As we rode the twenty odd miles north I noticed that the weather was changing. It would soon be autumn again. The year seemed to fly by. My daughter would be a grown woman before I returned home and my son would not even know his young children. At least I would be able to move further south and closer to my family once I had spoken with Prince Pasgen. I also needed to send for a monk. I had written to Brother Oswald asking him to journey north to serve the prince but he had begged to stay where he was. He was getting old and he did not like change. I understood that. He had promised me that he would find someone who could do the job that he did. We needed someone who understood writing, map-making and how to organise armies. Prince Pasgen could lead but he could not plan. Myrddyn could plan but he would be with me. I needed someone in whom Prince Pasgen and my son could confide and who was completely trustworthy. The monks of the White Christ were such men.

Prince Pasgen was also concerned about Aethelfrith and his attack. "What can we do to stop that happening again, Warlord?"

We were in his great hall and Prince Cadwallon and Lann Aelle were both there. This would be a lesson for both of them. I watched Prince Pasgen carefully as I explained my ideas. He had, in the past, shown a reluctance to delegate but his face appeared at ease with my suggestion. "This way, my prince, you can worry about the whole kingdom but you will have warriors who will watch the smaller parts."

"And have you any leaders in mind?

"Kay is an obvious one. He already controls the vital artery to the south."

The prince frowned slightly. He had wanted him punished for desertion not so long ago. How would he take this promotion? I would not allow him to dissuade me from my decision but I needed him to approve it. The frown changed to a smile and he looked at Prince Cadwallon, "The Warlord is right and it is good to know that some bad decisions can be changed. I think that Lord Kay will be a perfect choice. And the others?"

"I have a couple of warriors in mind but I would prefer to speak with them first. The responsibility is a great one."

"It is." He hesitated and chewed his lip. This was always a sure sign that he was worried about something. "Will you be wintering here?"

"No, I will depart when the leaves begin to fall. I will wait until then in case Edwin tries something."

"And you will return home?"

"No, Prince Pasgen. We need to make sure Rheged is secure. I will take a small army south to build forts and reclaim that part of Rheged. I hope that, by spring, your land will reach the Dee."

He looked surprised. "That would be a larger Rheged than my father ruled."

"True. Are you up to the challenge?"

He seemed to sit taller, "I am, Warlord."

We dined together that night. I was not certain when I would be able to visit with him again and I needed him to be confident to act without me looking over his shoulder.

"I will leave my son at Penrhyd for a while. The return of the sword to Necthan should ensure a secure northern border. What are your plans?"

"I think I will advance along the wall and establish a fort there. We have the advantage that many of the Roman forts still stand. With Penrhyd in the south and one at the wall it would enable me to control the two major routes into our land."

I liked that plan. The roads south of the wall were in good condition and the Saxons appeared to have left that part of the land untouched. It was, however, sparsely populated. He would have few men to defend the fort.

"When will you begin?"

"When your son returns would be a good time. We will still have time before winter to make a start."

"My son should be back within a few days. I will return to Penrhyd for him and Myrddyn. I will join you and begin my journey south from there."

As I headed back to Penrhyd with Lann Aelle and Prince Cadwallon I began to rehearse the words in my mind. I needed to ask Lann Aelle to leave all that he loved and be a warrior lord controlling a new land. In the end, he made it easy for me by bringing it up.

"Warlord, who do you have in mind for these new commanders? Will you promote warriors such as Kay?"

"As I said before, I need to speak with them first but you were one such."

He seemed genuinely surprised. "Me?"

"When we travel south I was going to make you commander of the land between the lakes and the Dee. It would be Lann's land. How would you feel about that?" He hesitated. "You can refuse. I know that you wished to rule at Wide Water. I can understand that. I would ask no man to do this if he was unhappy about it."

"No, Warlord. I am honoured that you should entrust this to me. I can see that the land south of Wide Water will need someone who is a strong leader. I am honoured that you think of me." He paused. "What about your son?"

"Hogan Lann will be needed to replace me. I am getting old."

They both laughed. "No Warlord, I have seen no sign of that and I have fought beside you for many years."

The truth was that I was feeling the recent combats more than I had. I could not have fought much longer when I had defeated Aethelfrith. Had Daffydd been late then I would have weakened and might have lost. My days of fighting were ending and I would be a strategos. My son had seen that and perhaps that was a good thing. That was a sign. "Well, I notice my weaknesses. But back to your new role. Does it not daunt you?"

"When you first mentioned it then yes but I remembered that you had done something similar at Castle Perilous." I smiled at the memory of those early days with a handful of men. "I would just ask that I could have some of my comrades to aid me."

"Of course. You will need captains. You will need to ask for volunteers; equites and archers as well as warriors."

"You have given me much to think on."

Prince Cadwallon had listened with keen interest. "How have you made such warriors who are loyal and whom you can give such power to? I know that Lann Aelle and Prince Pasgen will never betray you. How did you know this?"

"Your father, when he was ejected by your grandfather, took Dai with him. That was his start. All the other warriors were chosen to lead his men because they fought alongside your father and Dai. When you begin to fight then you will do the same. You see a man's heart when you stand beside him and protect him as he protects you."

The prince was learning and I was doing what I had promised his father. I was making him into a king.

Gawan was much improved and pleased that we would be moving on. I spoke with the commander of the fort, Ralph. "I will be appointing a commander for these West Moors. You will know him but I leave you in charge until he arrives. You will have much to do when he begins his role. You will have all the land to the high peaks to control. Train your men well."

Just as we were about to leave I saw two friars trudging along the road from Alavna. They had two ponies laden with goods. We halted at the gate.

"I am Brother Gryffydd."

"And I am Brother Stephen. We have been sent by Bishop Daffydd as your new scribes. We have just come from Alavna."

"This is a most beautiful land."

They both had the same thin face of Brother Oswald and the same beatific smile.

"We also have a letter from your wife, Lord Lann." He handed over the sealed parchment. Was there just a hint of criticism in his tone? Myfanwy would have spoken to him when she gave him the letter. I expected the letter to be critical and I tucked it away to read later. I would delay reading it; if at all.

"You have both come at a most propitious time for we are heading for Civitas Carvetiorum."

They positively bobbed with pleasure. "We have been told so much by Brother Oswald about it that we cannot wait to see our new home."

I rode next to them. They were a connection with my home and I asked them about the state of affairs there. It all seemed to be peaceful. King Cadfan kept encroaching on the Mercians and increasing his land and Bors had had to repel one or two minor assaults. It seemed I was not needed there.

"You know, I take it, from Brother Oswald, that we want none of our warriors converting to this White Christ. I cannot have warriors turning the other cheek and worrying about killing."

Brother Stephen grinned broadly. "We held a conclave at the monastery and Brother Oswald attended. He explained your position and we discussed it at length. When we read the Holy Scriptures we could find no reason why warriors should not kill other warriors. There were many occasions when this occurred in the past. The consensus was that Christians could kill other warriors but should abstain from killing those who were not warriors."

"Does that satisfy the Warlord?"

"It interests me Brother Gryffydd but I will discuss it with Myrddyn before I allow it."

Their faces darkened. "We have heard that he is a wizard and communicates with dead spirits."

"He is a wizard and I too have spoken with the dead." I smiled as they both clasped the crosses they wore about their necks as though the devil himself was present. "You know your duties?"

"We are to help Prince Pasgen and Lord Hogan Lann to administer this land and ensure it has a solid foundation."

"Good. That means organising what they trade and keeping track of it."

"Brother Oswald also asked us to keep his maps up to date."

"Yes, you will be using the same cell as Brother Osric who began the maps long before I was born."

Brother Stephen's voice showed his awe. "We have heard of this man. Some say he should be as St. Asaph and be canonised." I gave him a puzzled look. "Made a saint."

I laughed, "I do not think that Brother Osric would have worried about that."

"You knew him, Warlord?"

"Aye, it was he who taught me to read and sharpened my mind for me. You have a large pair of sandals to fill." I was not sure that they understood my image. "You realise that you will be here for the rest of your lives?"

"Yes, and we are honoured to serve. We will be the only outpost of Christianity north of the Dee."

"Not true. I believe that there are monks at King Nechthan's court but that is many leagues from here. You are surrounded by a sea of pagans."

Strangely that seemed to please them. They were a peculiar pair but I liked them and my experience of such men was a good one.

"There is your new home." I pointed to the towers of Carvetiorum.

"It is even bigger than Deva."

"It is a fine palace but it will need work. The heating system needs repairs. I hope that Brother Oswald told you how it works."

They both looked doubtful. "He told us but we thought it would be working and we would have time to discover its workings."

"I am afraid that here you are on the edge of the world and time is a luxury."

As we entered the gate I pointed to the left. "That will be your office. If you take your ponies over there with your equipment I will get someone to show you around."

I had not spoken with Myrddyn and the others on the way across. The four of them were busy behind me discussing how the Land of the West Moors would be run and speculating who would be given charge of it. Myrddyn, of course, knew but the mental exercise was good for the three young men.

I made sure that Mona was looked after and then went for the monks. They were delighted to have their own space and I had to tell them to follow me or else they would have happily stayed there all afternoon. Hogan Lann and Pol were with Prince Pasgen. Here they had no table which allowed you all to see the other's faces but they had a long oblong one which would do. I bade them all sit. The two monks were a little uncertain at first. Hogan Lann laughed, "You will have to get used to this, brothers. Here you will need to work with Prince Pasgen on a daily basis. You will be as close to him as his family."

Brother Stephen stood excitedly, "That reminds me. Prince Pasgen, your family will be coming before Yule. They had decided they miss you too much."

We all laughed and the monk sat, blushing. "Well Prince Pasgen, it is even more important that we make your land secure." I stood and nodded to Myrddyn who unrolled a map. The two monks almost drooled when they saw the detail. "As you know I have decided, with Prince Pasgen's permission to create lords who will control the lands around this fortress. Each lord will answer only to the Prince and to me." I smiled, "If you remember, King Urien had such a system. If you are going to steal an idea make sure it is from the best." Prince Pasgen nodded his thanks.

"Lord Kay will command the land of the lakes to the coast. Lord Lann Aelle will command the land we have not conquered yet; the land between the land of the lakes and the Dee. I call it Lann's Land." They all smiled at my self-indulgence. Hogan Lann patted his cousin on the back. It was well done. "The land around Penrhyd I give to Pol as lord of the West Moors Land."

Pol looked surprised. I had wanted to speak with him first but time was of the essence. He looked at Hogan Lann who nodded and then rose. "Warlord, I am honoured. Do you think I can do what you ask?"

"If I thought otherwise I would not have asked you." I looked him in the eyes. "Do you accept?"

"Aye my lord."

I was aware that they were looking at Tuanthal, Daffydd ap Miach and Hogan Lann who appeared to have been overlooked. Hogan Lann will remain here until the borders are secure and then he will return to our home in the south. Captain Tuanthal will be with me and Lann Aelle. I have great need of both my archers and my horsemen."

They all began talking at once. Myrddyn coughed and tapped the map. "You will see that we have marked in red the key forts. Here in the northern half, they are already built and just require maintenance. When Prince Pasgen has rebuilt one on the wall then we will be secure. Lann Aelle will have to build them in the south."

"Prince Pasgen and Hogan Lann; Pol and Lann Aelle will be asking for volunteers from your equites to serve with them. Daffydd you will need to leave ten archers to allow them to build up their strength. The squires will have to be used to replace the equites. We need an elite force of horsemen and archers for every time you fight the Saxon you will be outnumbered. It is in our strength of arms that our power lies and not our numbers.

Chapter 12

Pol, his five equites and five archers returned south to Penrhyd. It was a sad parting. Pol had fought at either my side or my son's since he was a boy. He had travelled to the Emperor's court with my son and now he would be alone; he would have to make the decisions now. I had confidence in him but I knew how hard it would be. He would have Kay and Pasgen as near neighbours but he would be on the front line in the war against the Saxons.

Prince Pasgen had taken fifteen of the squires who remained and given them the task of defending the new fort. It left Pasgen and Hogan Lann with just twenty-five squires. They would all become equites sooner than they had expected. Aedh and his scouts found the fort we were seeking. The Romans had called it Cauldron Pool or Chesters and it was exposed. It was the furthest east of any of our forts. It lay just on the other side of the great divide but it was a well-placed fort. A river surrounded it and high ground lay behind it. Any enemy would have to spend time destroying it before advancing west.

As we rode east Myrddyn pointed to the turrets on the wall the Romans called Hadrian's. "Do you see how they all have a clear line of sight to each other? If you get the local people to watch them we could send a signal from our new fort to Civitas in less than an hour. You would have to impress upon them the need to keep dry wood to hand."

I was aware of how parlous the position of this small garrison would be. There were ten volunteers from Tuanthal's men. These were warriors who had lived close to the wall before and wished to begin families. For the rest of the garrison, the commander, Bedwyr, would have to find men willing to serve for whatever booty he could loot from the Saxons. It would not be an easy task.

"Warlord, we have found the fort and it is unoccupied."

We set up camp around the crumbling ruins of this once great fort. We had fought close to here when I was younger and I remembered that this was where Lann Aelle's father, my brother Aelle, had lost his arm. I had slain King Aella just on the other side of the bridge. The bridge still stood but it was weak. While the camp was being built we descended to the bridge to inspect it.

Bedwyr nodded as he saw how poorly maintained it was. "We would have to rebuild this."

"Why?" The rest looked at Myrddyn but I continued to peer east. He would have a good reason for his question and he would explain it. I was trying to decide what to do next.

"We need the bridge to cross the river."

In answer, Myrddyn said, "Gawan, ride your horse to the other side and then come back."

The wooden structure shook but showed no signs of breaking. "You and your men cross as Gawan did one at a time. What do you think would happen if a large number tried to cross at once?"

"It would collapse."

"And therein lies your best defence against the Saxons. If they try to cross it will collapse and many will fall into the river and die. They could repair the bridge but by then Prince Pasgen could be here. Leave the bridge as it is. Come we will look at the rest of this building and I will advise you."

They all left with Myrddyn, save Hogan Lann who came next to me. "What is on your mind, father?"

"I am remembering crossing this country to kill Morcant Bulc. It is no further to the sea than crossing Mona. If we can hold this place then we could drive a wedge into the Saxon defences and hold the land from coast to coast as we once did." I smiled at my son, "This will be in your lifetime and not mine. My last task will be to join Rheged to the Dee."

He laughed but I could see the worry in his eyes, "You are not old and you will outlive us all."

"Of the warriors I grew up with how many are left?"

"Prince Pasgen."

"He was Gawan's age when I held Castle Perilous. There are just your uncles and they were both younger than me. I have already outlived them all as well as all of my friends and foes. Edwin was not even dreamed of when I killed Aella here."

I watched as my son took it all in. I was not being morbid. I hoped I would fight for many more years. Myrddyn had not dreamed of my death and he would give me ample warning but I was not immortal and I wanted my son to make plans for life without me. He looked at me with new eyes. I was still the same father I had always been but I had grown wiser. The young Wolf Warrior who thought he could save Rheged alone had now grown into the pragmatic Warlord who knew that change which came slowly brought lasting change.

We stayed just seven days and in that time we seemed to work miracles. Myrddyn and Gawan appeared more capable when working together. They saw each other's ideas and adapted them. I had no doubt that this fort could be held by the small number of men of Bedwyr's command. Hogan Lann and Prince Pasgen remained after we had left to try to increase the number of local men who could fight. The prince was also keen to rebuild some of the towers. It was just fifty miles between Pol's fort and this one. Reinforcements could reach it in a day. Of my leaders, I was only taking Daffydd and Tuanthal back to Mona. When we left Lann Aelle he would be on his own.

I walked Mona to the bridge. Hogan Lann asked, "Where are you going?"

"I am going south and I do not want this bridge to break yet."

He pointed to the west. "You could go that way."

I nodded, "True but I want to go this way. I have a yearning to see Stanwyck again and the Roman Road which goes south passes through it."

"But there are Saxons!"

I laughed and pointed at my men. "And I have these warriors. Do you think I fear a foe that fights on foot? I know the land and I would see how much the Saxons have taken." I turned and walked across the bridge. As Gawan had discovered it was a disconcerting experience but that was all. When we were all gathered on the far side I waved. "I will send a despatch rider north when we reach our destination."

"Look after yourself Warlord; we cannot do without you yet."

"I will still be here and I promise you that I will watch out for your brother and the prince in the land of the Saxons. They will not come to harm."

This was not mere bravado. The route I would take would be quicker than travelling west and then south. I also wished to see the Roman fort where I had first discovered weapons. In my mind, I saw that as one of our forts but I knew that would be a fort too far.

The road was unerringly straight. The two boys had never travelled on such a straight road. "Did the Romans have engineers as road builders?"

"No, Prince Cadwallon. They used their soldiers. Every Roman soldier knew how to build a road and they built well. This one is over five hundred years old."

"They must have been mighty builders. Could we ever build roads like this?"

"If we had peace for a time then it would be possible."

Myrddyn rode next to me. He pointed east. "You do know that Dunelm is less than thirty miles in that direction?"

"It is my son who is your student, not me; do not teach me how to suck eggs. I know perfectly well where it is. I need to know how vigilant this King Edwin is. Has he built defences close to the road? Does he patrol the road? We are horsemen and can outrun anything." I waved an irritated hand down the road. "Aedh will spot anything which is ahead of us. Let us enjoy this journey."

"You are definitely becoming more bad-tempered, the older you get."

"Perhaps I am aware of the passage of time and how little time I have left to achieve what I want to."

We rode in silence and I enjoyed looking at the land. There were farms and small hamlets along the road. Aedh, and the men with him, investigated each one and discovered that many of them were the people of Rheged. There were also Saxon communities but none had defences up. Their king held his army at his main forts. There were no Saxons defending this part of Northumbria. I had gathered some valuable information already.

We reached the old Roman Fort of Morbium on the Dunum by dark and we camped there. "Tomorrow Gawan and Lann Aelle, you will see where your grandfather and grandmother were murdered. Those who did it paid with their lives but it did not bring them back to us."

That evening I showed them the fort where I had dug up the caligae, the nails and the swords.

"Why did you take the nails? They could not have seemed important."

I shrugged, I had asked myself that question many times over the years. "Perhaps I thought that if someone had buried them then they must be important. They turned out to be for we used them to make better shot for our slings. I think I was meant to find them and they saved the lives of your uncles and me."

When we saw Stanwyck the ancient ditches and ramps impressed all three. I had seen it recently but I was not sure that I would ever see it again. It was strange because it felt smaller than the last time I had visited. I sent Aedh to scout out the small road which headed over the moors towards the south-west. He came hurrying back within an hour.

"They have built a fort on top of the high cliff overlooking the river. It will make passing it without being seen difficult."

Myrddyn said, "We can go south. There is another road close to the Nidd." He looked at me with a strange look on his face. It was the look he normally had when he read my mind. "This is *wyrd*, Warlord."

"Why?"

"I had hoped to visit a cave where a witch was said to have lived but could think of no reason to deviate from our path. It seems we were meant to go that way."

While Gawan was excited Cadwallon was worried. "A witch? Living in a cave? We should avoid it."

"Just because it is unknown does not make it dangerous Prince Cadwallon. Watch and see what we can learn."

It took us most of the day to reach the river. We travelled over low hills and shallow valleys. We saw no Saxons. We did not even see any signs of them. It still looked like Elmet when we had ridden in this land. The houses looked the same and the people, before they fled in fear, also looked the same. We could see the cave high on the southern bank. There was a small settlement there nestling at the foot of the cliffs on the northern shore. The villagers hid in fear. I took off my helmet and dismounted.

"I am Lord Lann, Warlord of Rheged. You have no need to fear me. I swear by my sword, Saxon Slayer that we will not harm you."

The men were the first to appear and they bowed. The women and children hid in fear behind them. I looked over my shoulder and saw why. My men were all armed and had their weapons at the ready.

"Sheathe your weapons and dismount. You are frightening them. Who is the leader?"

The headman came over and began to speak. He spoke our language. "I am Geraint. What can we do for you, Warlord?"

"I would know of the cave and ask you if the Saxons visit here?"

"The Saxons come for tribute twice a year but they fear the cave and its power. They do not take everything and they do not stay long."

"Rheged is returning. Soon the Saxons will be like the tide and they will begin to ebb." I could see Myrddyn bursting with questions, "This is Myrddyn the wizard. He has some questions for you."

"The cave up yonder. Does a witch live there still?"

He shook his head. "No longer. Legend has it she lived there before the Romans arrived and she came from a holy island far to the west across the darkening sea. Some say that they have seen her flying through the sky at night. But none can visit the cave for there is an aura of death about the place. We live here because the Saxons fear it and we are better off than most of the other people of the valley."

I looked at Myrddyn and saw his surprised expression, "*Wyrd*. That is Mona. One of my following lived here in times past."

"What happened to her?"

"It depends which legend you believe. Some say she murdered a Roman soldier and was crucified. Others say that when the Romans came for her she changed into a bird and flew back to her island home."

"What is the cave like inside?"

The man shook his head and looked fearful. "No man ever goes inside. It is said that you turn to stone if you stay too long in the cave. No one has ever visited it in my lifetime."

Myrddyn suddenly looked like a child again. "Well, tonight we shall sleep there."

There was a collective gasp from both the villagers and my men. I smiled. I knew my wizard. We had nothing to fear from a night in a cave. I clasped the headman's hand. "Thank you old one. We will leave you now and cross the river."

We camped on the opposite bank. I left Tuanthal, Daffydd and Aedh to set up the camp; they looked grateful that I had not asked them to come with us. I went with the others up to the cave. Lann Aelle had little fear for he had spent a night in the cave at Wyddfa and Gawan was excited but Prince Cadwallon looked terrified.

"Do I have to go in with you?"

"No, of course not; it is your own choice. There is no shame in not facing an unknown danger. Of course, if you do come in and survive then there is nothing on this earth that will be able to frighten you."

Gawan nudged him, "Let us do this. It will be safe and think of the stories we shall tell." He pointed to the horsemen below us, most of whom were staring up at us. "They will be impressed by this as much as killing a man in combat."

I think it was the last argument which persuaded him. He knew that my men were all true warriors and he yearned for their respect. "I will do it."

Myrddyn stepped into the cave. He had to bend a little beneath the overhanging roof. We could hear the steady drip of water as we entered. The light from our torches lit up the cave throwing strange and sinister shadows. The cave was filled with peculiar misshapen rocks and they were all around the glistening pool as though they had been placed there. We could see no sign of human habitation. Once we were all in with our lighted torches the cave looked white.

Suddenly Cadwallon gasped and pointed at a rock. "It is a woman! It's the witch!"

He tried to flee but Gawan prevented him. "Then she is stone."

I saw what he meant. There was a rock which looked like an old woman bent over. The rock was round in places but the similarity was uncanny.

"The prince is right, Warlord, it does look remarkably like a woman." We all went closer to examine the rock. It was wet and slimy to the touch. Prince Cadwallon would not touch it but I did. I touched the other rocks and they had the same slimy feel.

Myrddyn walked around it and examined it from every angle. He looked up at the ceiling. Then he caught a drop of water which fell and tasted it. He nodded and smiled. "Gawan, go and ask Aedh for his small war axe if you please."

My son raced from the cave. I sensed that the Prince of Gwynedd considered following him. "What are you up to, you cunning old goat?"

"I think I know what this is and if so then we might well find some treasure here." He went around all the other rocks which were sitting around the pool. None was as big as the one which looked like a woman.

Gawan raced in, his eyes aglow with excitement. "They all wanted to know what we had found."

Myrddyn's hawk-like eyes fixed on him, "But you did not tell them."

"Of course not."

Myrddyn turned to Prince Cadwallon and wagged a warning digit at him. "We keep this a secret from the others and preserve the magic." The prince was so frightened that he just nodded.

I was fascinated. I knew the wizard well but I had no idea what he was up to. He turned the axe so that the blade was facing away from the rock and then he brought the head down onto the slimy, dripping stone. To my amazement it shattered, revealing a crumbling skeleton beneath. Prince Cadwallon was dumbstruck and even Gawan was bereft of speech.

"How did the woman get inside the rock? Was it magic?"

Myrddyn pointed to the ceiling. "She died. She died a long time ago and the water dripped onto her head. It deposited something which became rock again. This may well be the witch they spoke of."

"Should we go lest her spirit harms us?"

Myrddyn smiled at Cadwallon and then closed his eyes. After a moment or two, he said, "Her spirit is not here but she is in torment." He frowned, "She is on Mona."

That surprised even me. How did he know that? He would tell us more in the fullness of time. I then saw what he meant about the other objects. "So all of these rocks contain objects which have turned to stone?"

"Yes. Of course, those made of living things will have rotted away but other objects should still be here. Shall we look?"

I suspected that he was as excited as my son whose face was as bright as a summer's morning. "Yes, Myrddyn."

"Remember, Prince Cadwallon. Not a word of this to any others." The prince nodded and Myrddyn tapped one of the taller rocks. The rock crumbled as though waiting to reveal what it hid. A rusty Roman Spatha stood there embedded in the ground. When Gawan tried to pull it from the rock the rusty tip broke. He looked disappointed. Myrddyn shook his head. "The sword can be mended and it must have been here for a purpose. Look at the writing on the blade. We will keep whatever we find here, safe."

I knew that a sword drawn from stone had to be magical in some way and there was a story here. The next four objects all turned out to be bones. Myrddyn examined one closely and said, "I think that these must have been cats or another small animal. This witch had real power if she was able to make the cats all stay here even when the others had died." He stood and stroked his beard. "When we were in the library at Constantinopolis I read of the Egyptians who revered cats. They believed they aided the passage to the Otherworld. She may have been trying to ensure her own safe passage. Fascinating."

The next four rocks all revealed treasures of different types. There was a pile of jet that the ancients had placed great value on and there were three piles of Roman coins. Some were copper, some silver and there were some large gold coins. Myrddyn slipped them into his leather pouch. "More for me to examine."

Some of the smaller piles had nothing but dust beneath but there was one which had not completely rotted away and was a piece of calfskin with writing upon it. We could read nothing and I saw the disappointment on Myrddyn's face.

The wizard stood and went to the walls of the cave. They too were shiny with the watery deposits. He held the torch as close as he could get to the wall and then said, "Gawan, the axe."

When Gawan had handed him the axe he swung it at the wall. To the horror of Prince Cadwallon, a skull fell from the wall, shattering on the floor and we could see the rest of the skeleton. Myrddyn repeated this action a number of times and we found eight bodies. He stopped and shook his head. "This was not a woman to be crossed. She put her enemies here and turned them into stone." He shivered. "Let us leave this place now."

I pointed to the bones we had uncovered. "What about those?"

"The cave will turn them into stone." Myrddyn waved an airy hand around the cave. "These followers of the White Christ would not understand that here it is Nature which has the power. This is a special place. We were meant to come here."

When we emerged and entered the camp the warriors just watched in silence. Tuanthal approached, nervously and asked, "Are you hurt?"

Gawan laughed, "We are unharmed. It is a cave filled with..." he glanced at Myrddyn, "rocks and a pool. There is nothing living within it."

We put our treasures in the saddlebags on the spare horse. Myrddyn wanted to examine them but back in the safety of his room I somehow felt better too. We had been meant to find the precious stones, coins and sword. I did not know why but my life had changed when I had found Saxon Slayer. Perhaps the Roman Spatha would have the same effect.

We headed southwest. We were travelling in an unknown country. Even when we had visited Elmet before we had not crossed this part of the country. Unusually, this Roman Road had more twists and turns than they normally did. The moors had many valleys and they were steep and, in many cases, dangerous. The road had crumbled over the years and parts had fallen into the torrential river below. It was not an easy day but, by late afternoon we had left the wild passage of the moors and descended into a green and verdant land filled with woods and gentler streams.

Myrddyn smiled as he said, "The Saxons can have that land. This is Rheged." He had been making notes as we went and he showed me a rough map he had compiled. "I think that the coast lies less than fifty miles from here."

I looked at him sceptically, "And how do you know that wizard?"

He laughed and pointed, "If you look to the west you can see where the land ends and that sparkle in the distance must be the sea."

I grunted, "I suppose you are right. Aedh, send two of your scouts north-west, two more to the west and two to the south-west. I want to know what we are likely to find in the next forty miles." I looked at Myrddyn, "We will see if the wizard is correct."

The first scouts returned the next day. "Warlord, we rode west and there is a river which reaches the sea some forty miles from here. We crossed the river when we headed north. It is not far from Wide Water."

The next two scouts confirmed their findings. We had reached the land we sought. That night we summoned the four scouts and Myrddyn tried to make a map of the land. When we had questioned them about what they had seen we realised that there were no Saxons to the north of us. All of the farms and villages they had passed through had been our people. This was Rheged still. The hills gradually stopped and became a huge fertile plain where there were many farms.

Myrddyn fixed Lann Aelle with his sharp eyes, "My lord of Lann's Land, where would you build your fort?"

Lann Aelle knew the wizard well enough not to be intimidated by his hawk-like stare. In my mind, I had already pictured the fort. I knew where we should build one. My nephew looked at the rough map in Myrddyn's hand.

"We need to have one close to the river which runs west to stop invasions from the south. If my memory is as good as yours then I believe there was a Roman fort close to the river." He turned and pointed to the north. "Just a few miles north of here."

One of the scouts forgot himself and shouted excitedly, "Yes my lord, it is quite close."

Aedh's irritated look made the man subside. Myrddyn smiled and clapped my nephew on the back. "Well done Lann Aelle. I can see that those years as Lord Lann's squire stood you in good stead."

I looked at the sun which was dipping in the west. "Scout, do we have time to reach the fort before nightfall?"

The chastised scout was eager to please. "Yes, Warlord."

We headed north. The visit to the cave appeared to have brought us good fortune. This was going far better than I had dreamed possible when we had set out from Penrhyd. The fort was in an even worse condition than I remembered it but at least it still stood as did the bridge. We crossed the bridge, which was firmer than the last one we had used, and found the fort. Lann Aelle looked at his new home somewhat nervously.

"Remember nephew, that you do not have to start anew. The Roman legionaries did the hard work four hundred years ago. We just have to repair what time and the land have tried to reclaim."

Myrddyn pointed to the river where stones had fallen in. "There are materials to hand."

Gawan suddenly grinned, "And cousin, this is the best site we have seen so far."

"Why is that cousin?"

Gawan pointed to the river. "Our ships can sail here and bring other materials from Wyddfa."

I was pleased with Gawan. He was using his mind. "Indeed Lann Aelle, that means that we can use the Roman cement. This will be a formidable fort."

Myrddyn pointed to a small ruin close to the river, "And unless I am mistaken, that is a Roman Bath. Who knows, you may have a fort to rival Carvetiorum?"

Later that same day, while the warriors all toiled to repair some of the walls, the last of our scouts rode in. "There are no Saxons to the south. We almost reached the Maeresea and we saw none."

The other scout pointed south, "There are many farms and the people there are our people. They speak our language." He nodded eagerly. "This is a good and fertile land. The people are pleased that the lords of Rheged have returned."

With a low wall completed around the damaged sections, we slept easier. While we ate a frugal meal using the last of our rations we held a meeting. "Send two of your men to Wide Water to bring some food for us. Two more should go to Brother Oswald. We need Daffydd to sail here with some building materials and arrows. You may need to defend this land over the winter."

"But the scouts have reported no Saxons."

"Aethelfrith is not far away and we have not yet scotched that snake. Vigilance, Lann Aelle." I looked at the map Myrddyn had. There were many gaps and blanks. A red line marked the Roman Road and a couple of red dots the villages we knew of but that was all. "Tomorrow I would go and see what lies close to here. I will take Tuanthal, Aedh, Lann Aelle and Prince Cadwallon. We will just need Aedh's scouts. The rest can work under Gawan and Myrddyn. We can make the ditch a ditch once more and not a repository for rubbish. Perhaps my wizard and his apprentice can make this fort the strongest in Rheged."

Gawan's face showed that he was up for the challenge.

We donned armour when we rode. I was still smarting over the ambush which had cost Einar his life. The ten warriors we took were all heavily armed. Their role would be as escorts.

We headed southwest, towards the coast. It was the least explored of all the land. We rode steadily, passing small farms and houses which were dotted about the land. The people hid when we rode by and I could not blame them. By noon we had travelled twenty miles or so and were ready for a break. In the near distance, we saw the smoke rising from a small village. It lay on a low ridge. This was a large village. They had no stockade but they had a small river for water and the land overflowed with crops. I was a warrior but I could see the value of such land.

As with every village the people hid. I took off my helmet and dismounted. "I am Lord Lann, Warlord of Rheged."

As soon as I spoke the people came out. An old headman, older even than me, came towards us. "Welcome, my lord, I am Osgar the headman of this village. We do not have much but would you break some bread with us. My wife has just made a batch."

The rules of hospitality were quite clear; I had to take some or risk offending him. I nodded to Tuanthal; he would take care of the men and ensure that we were safe.

"This is my nephew and the lord of this land, Lann Aelle." Lann Aelle nodded at him and the man narrowed his eyes. "This is Prince Cadwallon of Gwynedd." The title impressed both him and his wife and they bowed as they led us into their hut. This was not a roundhouse but a long, oblong building. There was a fire but it was at one end and I noticed that there was an oven above it.

There were four rustic chairs made of larch. I wondered if they would take my weight; I was wearing armour. Hospitality dictated that I should sit. Osgar's wife brought us a wooden platter with bread and homemade butter. Osgar gestured with his hand for us to eat. The bread was still warm and although the flour was coarsely milled it was delicious and reminded me how long it was since we had eaten.

Osgar said, "Lord Lann you said earlier, lord of this land. I did not know that there was such a lord."

I was about to speak when Lann Aelle did it for me. "You are right headman. There was no lord but Prince Pasgen has returned to rule

Rheged and we have defeated the Saxons in a battle far to the north. The Warlord defeated the Saxons at the old Roman fort at Deva and we now have men there. So I have been asked to guard this land."

It was a well-delivered speech and Osgar was impressed. "I hope you were not offended by my question. It is just that I remember when you left the last time Lord Lann. I was tempted to follow you to Mona but I stayed with my brothers. The Saxons killed them and for the next few years, we had to pay tribute. Then we had a few years of peace, save for the Irish who raided us. Two years ago the raids and the tribute began again."

Those events tied in with when we had been successful and defeated the Saxons. "We are back now and Lord Lann Aelle will be building a fort to the north of you. But tell me, why have you no stockade?"

He shook his head ruefully. "We had one but the Saxons took it as a sign of defiance and punished us. They destroyed each one we built. We cannot fight them."

Lann Aelle's face became angry. "That stops now!" I think he took Osgar aback. The headman had been deceived by my nephew's youth. He did not know his inner strength as I did. "We will bring you weapons and teach your young men how to fight. How many men are there in this village?"

"Fighting men?"

I laughed, "You mean there are men who would not defend their homes because they were either too young or too old? My brothers and I fought the Saxons when we were children. All of your men can fight. It is how we stopped the Saxons. There is no difference between a farmer and a warrior."

"I am sorry my lord. It is just that when you have never won it becomes harder to fight and easier to lie down or bow your back."

"And that is my fault for I deserted you but I am back now. How many men?"

Thirty. Five are like me old, fifteen are boys or young men and the rest can fight."

I stood, "Come Osgar. Let us speak with your men."

We left the hut and I saw that a crowd had gathered around Tuanthal and his warriors. The boys and the young men were looking at their weapons and their horses and I could see the admiration on their faces. Aedh was not there and I knew that he would be scouting.

"I am the warlord of Rheged and I am here to ask the men of this town to help us to defend this land against the Saxons and the Irish."

Most of them looked happy about that but one surly looking man spat and said, "Fight? With what? We don't have fancy helmets and iron shirts like you do."

His tone was insolent and I was tempted to smash him into silence with the back of my hand but I needed their compliance and I did not know how many of the others would side with him.

I pointed to the scouts. "These men do not have armour and all of these began fighting when they were," I looked around and saw a boy no more than seven years old, I drew him to my side, "the same age as this boy." I pointed at one, Miach, "How did you fight Miach when you were a boy?"

Miach stared at the insolent man. I knew he too wanted to hit him. "I used a sling and rode a pony carrying messages. When I became older I learned to use a bow and became a scout. It is easier to fight than to let a Saxon walk all over you."

I pointed at Prince Cadwallon. "This youth has fought and killed Saxons. If you wish it then it can be done. We will provide you with weapons and we will bring men to show you how to use your weapons."

The insolent man was still not convinced although the other men all looked eager. "And where will you be? Miles away in safety I expect."

Lann Aelle began to move forward, his hand on his sword. "Yes I will but you will have Lord Lann Aelle here and his fort is but two hours ride away to the north."

"He is but a boy!"

Miach had had enough and he leapt towards the surly faced man and picked him up with one hand. The man was not small and I could see that he was shocked. "I have had enough of your insolence. You are not fit to kiss the ground these two lords walk upon. One more word from you and the Saxons will not need to kill you for I will."

"Put him down Miach. The man obviously does not understand that he has a chance to make his village and his family safe."

The man spat on the ground and shouted, "This is not my village and I will not stay here to be insulted by bandits." He stormed off.

Miach said, "I am sorry my lord. I should not have lost my temper."

Before I could say anything Osgar said, "He only arrived seven days ago. He was hungry and we fed him."

I did not like that. I gestured Miach over. "Follow him but do not let him see you. I mistrust him. And, Miach, you did not do wrong. My men must speak for themselves. It is our way."

He smiled, "I will find out where he goes."

I turned back to the rest of them. "Will you fight?"

They all cheered and the insolent man, who was at the end of the village, turned to see what the noise was. I nodded to Lann Aelle. He clasped Osgar's hand. "Would you command the men of this village for me?"

"I would be proud to."

Chapter 13

We spent the next few hours giving basic instructions to the men of the village. We found that all the boys had slingshots and many of the men had bows. I would soon bring them swords and show them how to make shields. This was a good start.

Tuanthal drew me to one side. "We could begin to make a stockade. It would give them something to do and I noticed that they have already begun to cut their hedges and trees. Instead of making a fire with them, they could make a wall."

Lann Aelle agreed and we told Osgar of our plan. It soon transpired that their idea of a stockade was just a fence around the outside. It was no wonder it had been destroyed so easily. We showed them how to dig a ditch and use the earth to make a mound. With the larger branches placed equally on the top and the thinner ones between they soon had a defensible village.

"I do not wish to anger you, Warlord, but this will not stop them."

"No, because it is unfinished. We can do this in an afternoon but it will take many days to cut bigger trees and put them on the inside of this wall. By Yule, you will have a sound fort and you can defend yourselves. Nature has given you this ridge and this water."

Just then Aedh rode in. "Warlord, there are Hibernians. I found a village to the south of here. It has been destroyed sometime in the last seven days. The men were killed and the women and children taken as slaves; at least I assume they were. I found only dead men. Their trail led to the sea."

Osgar was appalled. "They were good people!" he looked around in panic. "What can we do? We will be next."

It was too far to the fort to be able to take the whole village and if we were caught on the road then we would all die. "Aedh, send a rider to the fort and ask for twenty men. We will hold them here until they arrive."

The scout selected looked at me, "But Warlord we will not be able to get back before morning at the earliest."

"I know. We will be here." As he rode off I said, "Get the horses under cover. Osgar, get your men here and we will organise them."

The headman hurried off, pleased to be able to do something to help prevent this catastrophe.

"Will they come today, uncle?"

"I do not know. If they took their captives back to their ship then they would have then been searching for another village. I hope not. If our men can reach us by tomorrow then we can find them and stop their raid."

There was the sound of a horse and we all drew weapons. It was Miach. He threw himself from his horse. "That man I followed, we should have killed him. He is a spy. He went to a Hibernian war band just three miles away. He is one of them. They are heading here."

I turned to Osgar. "Get the women and children to collect stones for the slingers. Make sure we have food and water to hand." I saw the worried look on his face. "Do not worry. If wyrd brought us here in time to face these slavers then we were not meant to die. At least not all of us!"

When he had gone I said, "Miach, how many?"

"At least fifty and perhaps seventy. I saw them moving and it is just a guess. I am sorry."

"Do not be sorry. You may have saved these people and this village." My men did not need to be told what to do. Aedh took four men and went to the west wall. Tuanthal took the other four and went to the east. There was no gate but there was an entranceway. "You two will be with me. Prince Cadwallon, stand behind me to the right. Lann Aelle, you will stand to the left. Osgar, spread your men out between mine and support us."

I heard an, "Aye my lord," but I did not turn.

I strung my bow. "The spy will have told them our numbers and who we are. They will rush here because they will hope we have gone and the village will be an easy target." I looked at the sun. "We have plenty of time left for killing. Use your bows and take them out before they reach the ditch. Tuanthal's men are brave but they have little armour and are not used to this type of fighting."

As they strung their bows I made sure that my shield would slip around quickly and I slid the dagger I had sheathed on the shield in and out of its scabbard. It was a secret weapon which had stood me in good stead before now.

Aedh shouted. "They are here!"

The war band jogged up behind their leader. They were typically Hibernians. Only the leader had a mail shirt and it was only a short one. Most were bare-chested, showing their tattoos and scars. I was glad that I saw no bows. Most of them had a helmet and all had either a sword or a spear. They outnumbered us by at least fifteen men and in terms of armed men they outnumbered us three to one.

I notched an arrow. They were a big target. In my prime, I could have loosed an arrow more than four hundred paces but these days I was not too sure. I waited until they were three hundred paces from us and loosed one arrow and then two more in quick succession. My men all did the same. Over thirty arrows sped through the air. Some men were hit by more than one arrow but we still felled a number and they raised their shields. The next shower did less damage but they were moving slower now and they were not as confident as they had been.

It was now time for accuracy. We only had twenty arrows each. I saw the villagers loosing their arrows and the boys slinging stones but they were an uncoordinated force. They did make the Hibernians form a shield wall which was a good thing but they caused few casualties. They had to move more slowly. They took weapons and shields from the dead so that the forty-five who advanced on us were all armed with a weapon a shield and a helmet.

The three of us were exposed and suddenly Prince Cadwallon yelled, "Slingers!"

I pulled my shield up just in time and felt the stone crack off the metal boss. I was wearing my helmet but the blow would have stunned me and disheartened my men. "Thank you, squire. You are doing well."

He looked nervous as he asked, "What if they rush us?"

"They will rush us and soon. When they do drop your bow and lock your shield behind mine. You have mail and a good shield while they have no mail and piss poor shields. Your sword can break them. They will try to push us back. Show them you are stronger."

"Yes, Warlord."

"And now let us tell them who we are eh nephew?"

He grinned, "Yes Uncle."

"I am Lord Lann Warlord of Rheged. Leave now and you may live. I have killed almost as many Irish as Saxons. Fear me for I am merciless." I pointed Saxon Slayer at them and they halted. I had destroyed a whole village after they had raided my home. Every warrior had been slaughtered and it had kept us safe for many years. I hoped they would be intimidated.

The leader stepped forwards, "I am Brian son of Felan and I am not afraid of you. You killed my father but now you are alone and without your knights. I will kill you and eat your heart."

Tuanthal's arrow thudded into his shield and made him step back. I heard Tuanthal's voice. "Fourteen warriors are more than enough to deal with a rabble like you."

That enraged them and they hurled themselves at the three of us. I knew that Brian had not planned that for they came at us piecemeal. A bare-chested, red-headed warrior with a crude tattoo on his chest roared at me and thrust his sword at me. I deflected the sword with my shield and swung Saxon Slayer to decapitate him. The blood-covered those following and the head bounced in front of those on the side. Because they had attacked us in the opening of the stockade they were funnelled into a small area and Aedh and Tuanthal were able to attack their flanks. The slingshots from the village boys also did more damage as they rained down on those at the rear.

Lann Aelle was dealing easily with the Hibernians. He was experienced and knew the weak spots of an enemy but the prince was under pressure from the men to his left. He was holding them but he was not killing them. In battle, you needed to kill more of the enemy. I half turned, Lann Aelle could cope with the men he fought, and I swung Saxon Slayer sideways at the warrior fighting Prince Cadwallon. It bit into his neck and carried on. The man fighting me tried to take advantage and he lifted his sword to strike, as he thought, when I was unprepared. I punched my shield boss into his face and his nose erupted in a gory mess of blood, bone and gristle. As he slid to the ground I stabbed him with Saxon Slayer and stepped forwards.

Prince Cadwallon took heart from the death of his enemy and he took a blow on his shield and then stabbed underneath. The Hibernian looked in surprise as his guts began to spill onto the floor. I looked and saw that we had reached the gate. "Halt."

We now filled the space where the gate would be and Tuanthal and Aedh began to whittle down their numbers. Brian, son of Felan, suddenly shouted and the warriors fled back beyond arrow range. I looked and saw that the sun had almost set. They would wait for the night.

I lifted my helmet and felt the rush of cool air. "Lann Aelle, get some of our men and collect the weapons of the dead, give them to the men of the village." As he did as I bade I turned to the young prince, "You did well, Prince Cadwallon. I hope that you never have to face as many foes again without help."

He took off his helmet. "

"Warlord, you saved me. I was lost and then you took off that man's head."

I shook my head, "It is all down to experience. Look for the enemy's weakness. These had no armour. Any blow to the neck or body would be fatal. Use your weapons. Our shields are stronger. Hit with them. Never pull back on a stroke. You always follow through. That way it has more chance of being a killing stroke. You have a fine sword which can go through metal. The enemy had weak ones which did not even dent your shield."

He turned his shield over to examine it. There was barely a mark on the leather cover.

"They were not trying to destroy your shield they were trying to kill you and you are armoured. A good sword would pierce it but these," I picked up a sword and bent it, "are worse than useless. The ones who wield them can get lucky and stab you or cut you but have faith and you will prevail."

I turned and looked around, the wounded were being tended to but we needed to prepare for the next assault. "Aedh, Tuanthal, Osgar here."

The three men ran over. Osgar looked a little wild-eyed but he gripped the sword he held firmly. "We have done well. Have we lost any men?"

Tuanthal shook his head, "They did not get close enough. We have some wounded men but nothing serious."

"Good. Lann Aelle is distributing the weapons from the dead Hibernians. They are poor but the shields will afford the village men some protection. They will not try a frontal assault again. They will sneak over the stockade. We knew it would not hold them. Osgar I want one of your men allocated to one of mine. We will get no sleep tonight but at least with two men together we have a better chance of spotting them when they do come." Lann Aelle had returned. "Lann Aelle, you stay with the prince."

"And what of you, Warlord, who will watch with you?"

"I will be alone tonight. I intend to patrol the perimeter." Before they could argue with me I went on, "Osgar, tell your people that tonight they must be totally silent. One sound could alert the enemy. I want them to wonder where we are and if we sleep. We light no fires and we listen for danger."

My men nodded. Osgar looked at them and then he smiled and he too nodded. "One night without sleep is a small price to pay. Thank you, Warlord, for stopping this day. If not for that chance visit we would be dead and our families would be slaves."

"Thank me when my men arrive in the morning eh?"

There was a flurry of noise as the instructions were given and then pairs of men and boys were placed around the flimsy wall. I had left the dead Hibernians where they had fallen. They were an obstacle but the superstitious warriors might not wish to pass the dead. As I walked around I smiled at the villagers looking at their newly acquired weapons. I had told the prince that they were poor quality and they were but they were better than nothing. I nodded to each pair as I passed and I patted the villagers on the back as I gave a reassuring smile. We did not have much chance but the confidence might make the difference. I was trying to calculate how many men Brian son of Felan had left to him. There could still be forty warriors if Miach's original count had been correct. This time we would not be able to use arrows. It would be close in work which would suit the Hibernians.

When I had completed a circuit I sat close to the gap in the stockade. There was an old tree stump they used to chop wood upon and it made a good seat. I put Saxon Slayer into the ground so that I could grab it quickly. My shield was over my back and I held my dagger in my left hand. The dagger was a Roman pugeo and I had had it since I had first discovered the horde of Roman weapons. I remembered when it had been my proudest possession and yet I could not remember the last time I had used it. The discovery of the Roman Spatha had brought it to mind. I wondered what was so special about that sword. Myrddyn and I had not had a chance to examine it. Apart from the broken tip, it had looked to be in perfect condition. Once again I was tied to the past. Rome and the Warlord were never far apart. When would I be able to sit and reflect on my life?

My reverie was broken by the slightest of noises. It came from beyond the stockade. I did not stand but I reached out to grab my sword. I could see nothing but I knew there was someone out there in the dark. I kept looking at one shadow in the dark and then it moved. It was a man. Once I had identified the man I saw others close by. I dared not stand and I waited as they crept forward. I had not put on my helmet for I needed my ears as much as my eyes. I hoped that my white face would not give me away and I took satisfaction in the knowledge that I could not see their faces. That meant that it was unlikely that they could see mine. Suddenly one of them tripped over a body and I took the opportunity to stand. My movement appeared to have gone unnoticed. Their shapes were a little clearer now but it was still hard to estimate distances.

Closer they came and I was able to count them. There were six killers. I heard a cry to my right and a sudden clash of metal on metal. There was no longer any need for silence. I stepped forwards and slashed in a wide arc before me. The blade bit into flesh and a warrior screamed. I jabbed forwards with my pugeo and felt it grind into a face. I quickly stepped back and the blade which would have taken my head cut the air instead. As I moved back they advanced and I saw them a little more clearly. They had shields and swords. All around me, I could hear the sounds of battle and men dying but I had my own little war with four men; each one eager to take my life.

I felt my foot touch the stump on which I had sat and I stood on it; the tree had been a big one. I now had the advantage of height. They lurched forwards to get at me and I swung Saxon Slayer using all of my force. The edge dug into the neck of the warrior on the left of the four men. Two of them tried to slice off my legs with their swords. I jumped in the air and, as I came down brought the sword onto the helmet of one of the men. My weight, the fall and the heavy blade sliced his head and helmet in two. When I landed I took the offensive. I leapt at the two men with my pugeo held before me. As I hit the ground the wind was knocked from me and I found that I could not move the dagger. It had impaled a warrior to the ground. I stood and, as the last man tried to rise, I stabbed him in the heart.

I sheathed my dagger and pulled my shield around. Pausing only to don my helmet I moved towards the gap in the fence. The ones I had slain had obviously been sent to secure the entrance whilst others had climbed the flimsy stockade. I moved out of the enclosure and along the ditch. There were men hacking at the walls while others jabbed at the defenders with spears. They did not see me coming. I brought Saxon Slayer down on one man laying open the side of his head and his arm. I punched away a second man who had turned to face me and I stabbed him as he lay prostrate.

I heard a shout behind me, "Wolf Warriors!" I did not turn for I knew that it was Lann Aelle and the prince. As the Hibernians turned to rush me they were faced by three warriors, all in mail. I felt a sword strike my shield while another slid along the mail of my byrnie. The two warriors died at the hands of my nephew and the prince. The others fled.

I turned to my saviours. "Thank you both."

Lann Aelle laughed, "You did not need our help. We just wanted to fight alongside you."

"How goes it inside?"

"There are many dead but these were the last."

"Good, get their weapons and join me inside."

By the time I returned to the village the first hint of dawn was lightening the east. I went to the bodies of those who I had fought at the gap. The surly faced warrior lay there. He was the one whose face I had split. He now had a strange grin which made him look happier than when he had been alive.

As I walked through the village I saw dead bodies, both villagers and Hibernians. Osgar's people had fought well. I also saw three of Tuanthal's men lying dead. They would be hard to replace. Aedh and Tuanthal were relieved to see me.

Tuanthal shook his head, "I did not like that my lord. You had no idea where the enemy was. Each shadow could have been a friend or a foe."

"I know but that gave us the advantage. Collect their weapons and put the bodies on the other side of the ditch." Leaving my men to do their work I sought out Osgar. I hoped the old headman had survived. Lann Aelle would need such brave leaders.

I found him being tended to by his wife and his daughter. His head had been laid open by a blade. He grinned, "We showed them, Warlord. They will learn to leave my village alone next time."

"Hopefully there will be no next time." I put my hand on his arm, "You will have lost people."

"I know but that is the price we have to pay and now that we have a lord we can learn to be warriors as well as farmers."

There was a clattering of hooves as my horsemen rode in. I turned and saw that they were led by Myrddyn and Gawan. The two of them leapt from their horses. Myrddyn nodded at me but Gawan looked concerned. The light was filling the village and the blood-stained ground and bodies told a grim story.

"Are you hurt, father?"

"No Gawan. This is the blood of others. There will be those who need healers. See to them." I looked up at the leader of my horsemen. "Bal, I will get my horse and we will run these Hibernians down."

"Aye my lord."

We had left our horses saddled in case we needed to leave in a hurry. I mounted Mona and rejoined my men. Lann Aelle was speaking with Myrddyn. "Lann Aelle, take charge until I return. I will make sure these pirates rob no one else."

Tuanthal threw me his spear as I passed him. "You will need this, my lord."

It was now light enough to see a mile or more and we rode south-east. Aedh had spotted their camp in that direction and I guessed that would be where their boat would be moored. We followed their trail by their dead and their dying. We despatched the wounded as we went. Inevitably that slowed down our pursuit but I could not let any warrior suffer a lingering death. These men had struggled as far as they could. Their bones would remain and rot in Rheged.

By the time we reached the sea, it was daylight and we saw their ship as we emerged through the pine forest into the dunes. I urged the men to try to catch them. I thought it might be too late but I had to try. There were ten warriors wading out to her and another six still on the beach. We rode hard at them. The sand slowed us almost as much as it slowed the fleeing warriors. I saw Bal lean forward to spear one man while a second of my men took the head from another. As we struck the water one of the fleeing men fell and Mona's hoof cracked open his head. The last two warriors were hauled on board. Those of my warriors who had bows launched arrows at the ship. A cry told us that one had struck its mark but the ship slowly turned and we hit no more.

As it headed west I saw a wounded Brian shake his one good arm at me in anger. His words were lost in the wind but I knew that he was cursing me. I had been cursed before and still, I lived. We returned to the village laden down with weapons. Many were only good enough to be melted down but they were better than nothing.

Osgar already had his men mending the stockade. They all cheered when I rode in. Tuanthal gave me a questioning look. "They are fled but it will take him some time to gather a war band big enough to trouble us again. By then Lann Aelle should have enough warriors to stop him."

The villagers had lost ten men. Sadly they were mainly the old men. Osgar was philosophical about that, "They have given their lives so that their sons and daughters might live. And they died as warriors. It is not a sad event." He pointed to the weapons his men now carried, "We will now be able to defend ourselves."

Lann Aelle clapped him on his back, "This is the first of my defenders. Osgar has told me where the other villages are. I will now take Aedh and Tuanthal's men and complete my inspection."

I was pleased. My nephew was ready for his new role. He had not asked my permission. He had made his own decision. "And I will take the prince with me. He and Gawan have learned much but let us not tempt *wyrd*."

I rode back to the Roman fort with my four companions and the scouts who had fought in the village. They had earned a rest. I was not worried about an ambush and I was keen to see what progress had been made. I was anxious to return home. If Aedh's scout had not had any problems then Daffydd should be at the fort within a short space of time. I would travel back by sea.

Chapter 14

Gawan was impressed by Prince Cadwallon's deeds. Lann Aelle had told them of his bravery when fighting fierce, although badly armed warriors. Myrddyn told me of the fort and the land. "The fort will be finished by Yule but it is defensible already. This is fine farmland, Warlord. With the protection of warriors, it will encourage people to settle here."

Tuanthal asked, "Are there enough people from Rheged?"

Prince Cadwallon had been listening and he said, "Many of my father's people try to eke out a living perched on steep valley sides. There will be some who wish for an easier life if they are offered protection."

"There is your answer, Tuanthal. It is not just Rheged folk who will come. It is the free peoples of this island; the ones who are neither Saxon nor Hibernian."

Myrddyn offered a word of caution. He gestured to the hills to the east. "At the moment our Saxon foes are well beyond those hills and we have bloodied their noses. If we are to keep them on the defensive then we need to keep their attention in the north. Your son and Prince Pasgen will need to go on the offensive in the spring. If not then Lann Aelle will be surrounded by a sea of Saxons."

He was right. We had travelled the most difficult route from east to west but there were other, easier routes I knew. We had made a good start but that was all that it was a start.

As we headed back Miach asked, "My lord, can I ask a boon?"

"Of course Miach. Your tongue and your mind saved that village."

"Osric and Ludd had served with me since we were boys. We grew up in the same village." He paused and looked skyward. "They were amongst the warriors killed last night."

Then I remembered that we had lost warriors and I berated myself for not asking their names. There would have been a time when I would have known them all.

"You wish to leave my service?"

"No, no Warlord. I am your oathsworn until death. Captain Tuanthal will be taking the warriors off to war in other parts of the land. I would like to serve here. I would like to stay close to where the spirits of my brothers in arms wait. And I would not be able to do my job for I would always be looking for them. Let me serve Lord Lann Aelle here. I swear I would be a good servant."

"I will grant your boon and I am sure that my nephew will use a warrior such as you wisely."

He nodded his thanks and rode to the rear with a huge grin on his face.

The local villagers soon heard of our presence and we had a trickle of visitors. Although Lann Aelle was away he had reliable deputies from amongst the equites. Some of them, like Mawn, were much older than my nephew and had served Hogan Lann for many years. I also used Miach for I saw in him wisdom which was sometimes absent from other warriors. I made a point of speaking to them all. Some of them were at the fort to see what we could give them. Despite the supplies from Wide Water we still did not have enough for our own men and we had to send out hunters each day. Myrddyn had made sure that the granaries were rebuilt and we would have to buy some grain and fill them.

Six days after our return Daffydd brought two of our ships up the river. He was a fine seaman and he brought them as close as he could get to the fort. In the end, we only had to carry the supplies for half a mile and the men did not mind. We also had a surprise, for my wife and daughter were both on board.

Daffydd's face told me of the argument he had had with my forceful wife. She took one look at my face and said, "Do not blame the captain. It has been such a long time since I have seen you and I wished to see my son." She glared at me. "The one with the maimed hand, remember?"

"When the supplies are unloaded I will turn the ships around, Warlord."

I smiled at him; we would talk later. "Thank you Daffydd. You have done well." I paused, "Did you see any Hibernian ships on your voyage?"

"No, my lord, why?"

"A ship raided the land to the south of here. We will have much work to do later."

I led my wife and daughter to the fort. Myfanwy's face fell when she saw the conditions in which we were living but brightened when Gawan looked up from his work."

"Come here bairn; let's see what they have done to you." She gasped when she saw his hand. "If I get my hands on the Aethelfrith it is more than two fingers he will lose." One or two of my men smirked but were silenced by a glare. She looked at me."Well, when are you coming home?"

"We will leave as soon as Lann Aelle returns from his patrol. It will only be a couple of days."

"Well don't expect us to sleep in that ruin."Nanna was just as precocious as ever.

"Daughter I did not ask you to come here but you can sleep on the boat if you wish."

"That is as bad as here."

I spread my hands in exasperation. "Sleep where you will. We leave when I say!"

I saw the twinkle of a smile on my wife's face and knew that I had done the right thing. Nanna still thought that she could wind me around her little finger. I was too tired and too irritated for that. I had had enough of the spoiled child.

Prince Cadwallon came to her rescue. "I am sure that Gawan and I can make something which is comfortable for you, my lady."

She changed in an instant and became coy with fluttering eyelashes. I thanked all the gods that I had been too busy with war when their age to worry about such things.

Myrddyn, of course, had already made four rooms in the old Praetorium warm and watertight. The rough furniture which Daffydd had brought saw service that night for my family. The warriors all made a fuss of Nanna. She was the only girl they had seen for months and she revelled in the attention. It made both her and her mother easier to handle and the next days were easier than I could have dreamed.

Lann Aelle returned in an excited frame of mind. He had travelled as far as the Maeresea and then inland as far as the old Roman fort of Mamucium.

"There are many villages and all are keen to be warrior farmers. We distributed some of the weapons we took from the Hibernians. I am hopeful we can withstand an assault."

Myrddyn was interested in the Roman fort. "Is it worth investing Mamucium?"

"No, I think that Caedwalestate would be better. It is closer to Caestre."

I remembered the town from our journey south. Many of the villagers at that time had fled south with us.

I pointed to the west. "There is a small stockaded village called Prestune. It is just a few miles downriver. The headman there is keen to be part of your army. I think you have all in place now to rule as we hoped."

He suddenly looked nervous and I put my arm around his shoulder and led him away from the others. "You can do this nephew. You have some good men here who will serve you well. The villagers like Osgar will support you and are worth fighting for." I pointed at a group of men busy building the gate. "There is Miach he is leaving his troop to serve here with you. He volunteered for that service despite the fact that he has ridden with Aedh and Tuanthal since they were children. That is the measure of the confidence the men have in you."

He looked surprised, "Miach? He is a fine warrior."

"If you take some advice from your uncle I would make him your garrison commander. You need someone here who can be relied upon. Your equites will be happier in the saddle with you." I shrugged, "But it is your decision to make, not mine."

He laughed, "And I am not so foolish as to spurn such good advice. I think he will make a perfect garrison commander."

We left the next day and sailed down the river to the sea. I had achieved more than I had dreamed possible in a short space of time. "Captain, take us along the coast of Man. I would see what Aethelfrith is up to."

Myfanwy was both worried and intrigued in equal measure as we saw the island of Man to the southwest of us. I went over and put my arm around her. "We will not be going close but I must know if he has ships. If he does then we are in danger."

She nodded. "I know but it angers me to be so close to the man who hurt our son so."

"He is young and he is resilient. He will bounce back from this. Look, he and Cadwallon are laughing and joking." The two youths were, indeed, at the prow of the ship with Nanna and you would not have thought that they had experienced such horror and so recently.

I was able to concentrate on the island more than on my first visit. It was daylight and I would not be risking lives in midnight battles. I could see how small the first village we passed was. There were barely a handful of huts. The sheep dotted on the valley sides told me what they did for a living. Higher up the hills were forests and woods. There would be hunting there. I smiled to myself. I was evaluating the land as a home for my people and I had not even driven the Saxons from it.

The burnt-out carcass of the Saxon ship still sat forlornly in the shallow water where she had sunk. Gawan glanced at me and nodded. He remembered, as I did, the fierce fight. The memory of how close we had all come to death would be fresh.

Myrddyn joined me. "I see they have not acquired another ship as yet." I shook my head. I was busily trying to see Aethelfrith's warriors. There were only a few and when they saw the ship they hid. The bolt throwers had had a profound effect on them. "I am surprised that they did not put a wall around it. You might have had more difficulty had they done so."

"It is either laziness or overconfidence. The captain tells me that the settlement which faces Hibernia has a wall. Perhaps that was the only place they felt threatened."

Myfanwy snorted, "Well, husband, they have learned the error of their ways."

Laughing I said to Daffydd, "Take us home, captain. We have seen enough."

After our journeys through Rheged the monastery, and then my castle looked like formidable structures. I felt reassured by the mountain rising protectively behind it. Then I realised that apart from my archer captain, Daffydd and Tuanthal, I had none of my captains within fifty leagues of me. There were warriors who commanded but I did not know them as well as those who had gone before. Mungo and Garth were both dead and Bors was young. I would have to get to know my warriors again. I still had much to do before I could hand over power to my son. I had not talked of this to Myrddyn and Myfanwy but I had wanted to be close to Wyddfa and my mother's spirit before I did so. It would be a momentous decision when I finally made it.

I felt relief when I entered the gates of my home. Here I was secure. More importantly, my family were safe. Myfanwy smiled, almost for the first time since this whole saga had started. It was not just the safe return and the fact that Gawan was home again; Nanna was less argumentative. The attention of all the young men had flattered her. I hoped that the worst was past.

I stabled Mona and told the stable master to give her as much attention as he could. She deserved it. I then wandered my walls talking to the sentries and getting to know my garrison again. I had been away for almost two years and I needed to become a warlord again. I ended up at Brother Oswald's office. He looked frail now but his eyes were as sharp as ever.

"Did the two brothers I sent prove to be satisfactory?"

"They did, Oswald, and I think that they were a good choice." I pointed to his lists. "How is our trade?"

He frowned slightly, "It would have been better had they had more opportunities to sail to Byzantium rather than attacking Saxons but we are in profit. Our stocks of metals and arms are high."

"How stand the granaries?"

"They are full." He knew me well. "Why do you ask?"

"We need to send some wagons with grain to Lann Aelle. Arrange it, please. Captain Tuanthal can escort them."

"It will take a few days to organise the wagons."

"The captain will need that time to choose his riders." I felt sorry for Tuanthal. His best riders were now either dead or in the service of Lann Aelle and the other northern captains. We had to hope that the ones who had remained behind had not lost their sharpness.

"And how does King Cadfan fare?"

"He is doing well and his borders appear secure."

"These questions are all leading somewhere, Warlord. What do you really wish to know?"

"You have managed without me for almost two years. Could you manage for longer?"

"Hmn, " He put his fingers together, almost as though he was praying. "I am no longer a young man my lord. I now feel much as Brother Osric did towards the end of his life. I can continue to manage affairs but I will need an assistant."

I felt relieved. I had hoped the suggestion would come from him. I did not want to offend him by telling him that he was too old. "If you could arrange for one. I am not planning on leaving for some time but we are all getting old and we need to plan for the future."

"Hogan Lann, of course, will take over as Warlord."

"You are becoming like Myrddyn. You can read my mind."

"That is a terrifying thought that I should be turning into a pagan."

"I doubt that, old friend."

That evening as we sat around the table Myrddyn brought up the problem of Prince Cadwallon. "I know that you were asked to be the prince's mentor but I think we should visit with his father and ensure that he is still happy about that situation."

I noticed that the three young people all looked unhappy at the prospect. I fixed Prince Cadwallon with my eyes. "And what are your thoughts?"

"I agree it would be rude not to visit my father and I would like to see both my parents but I have not yet learned all that I can from you." He looked at Gawan for help; my son shrugged his shoulders helplessly. He could think of no arguments to help his friend. "I know that we have suffered while learning but I need to know how to create and run an army. My father's army is a fine one but it does not compare with yours. I would have my army as powerful as that of Rheged."

"Well in that case we will visit your father and then spend the winter learning all that there is to know about being a strategos."

Gawan looked relieved as did Nanna. Myfanwy had a strange look about her as did Myrddyn. I was obviously missing something but I could not see what it was.

Daffydd and Tuanthal were set the task of selecting warriors to form their new companies. "We need forty archers and a hundred horsemen."

Both captains looked unhappy at the number. "Archers take time to be created, my lord."

"You are right. Tomorrow we will visit my brothers and see if they have any."

Daffydd brightened visibly. Both of my brothers had many archers and slingers. Tuanthal, however, was not going to be able to get horsemen there. "Our problem, Warlord, is that this land does not breed natural horsemen. Our best ones were the ones who came from Rheged when we moved south." He sounded bitter.

I put my hand on his arm. "I know how you feel Tuanthal. I did not give away your men recklessly. Lann Aelle and my son will need those men to control the vast distances in the north. Start with the scouts. They are horsemen and you can give them the skills of fighting warriors."

He looked happier at that. "Thank you, Warlord. I know you are right. It just goes hard to see the men you have trained using their skills for another captain."

He was right and I could do nothing about it. I was the Warlord of Rheged with huge responsibilities. I had to think of the kingdom but I felt for my men.

Saxon Slaughter

I left Gawan with Myrddyn and took only Prince Cadwallon with me and Daffydd. The island of Mona was as safe as any place in the land and I feared no ambush. We did not even ride in armour. Aelle was now a greybeard and his hair had almost gone. My little brother had aged. He had grown more portly too. That was to be expected. He was not a warrior and he did not live an active life. His face showed the joy in my presence.

While Daffydd and Prince Cadwallon went with Aelle's captain to select warriors. I told my brother all that had happened. He had heard of Aethelfrith's despicable act and it sickened him as much as it had us. "I do not like the thought of spies in our land. I will set my shipwrights to build another ship. The trade will come in handy and I would like to keep an eye on Man."

"You are wise, Aelle. Your son now rules a huge part of Rheged. It is the country south of Wide Water."

His face showed his pride in his son. "I am pleased. You have done well, my son and trained him to be a great warrior. I thank you. And how is Wide Water these days?"

"We have rebuilt it and Kay, one of Prince Pasgen's equites commands there. It is safer now that your son protects the south. We have also reinvested the fort where you lost your arm."

"That seems a lifetime ago."

"We were different then. We had few responsibilities."

"Aye, think of all the dead comrades we have buried."

"I would rather think of the people we have saved."

"You are right and we will hold onto this land. Neither the Saxons nor the Hibernians shall have it."

My brother Raibeart was just as welcoming and we rode back with the forty archers. Daffydd was as happy as I had seen him in a long time. He confided to me that they were as well trained as his own men. He had little work he needed to do with them. "I just need to train them to ride and then we can be a force to reckon with."

Tuanthal had managed to gather twenty trained horsemen and, with a dozen scouts and Daffydd's archers, we headed for Wrecsam and the court of King Cadfan. As we approached his town I could see that he had improved it in the years since we had captured it from the Saxons. The ditches were deep and the gatehouses were both strong. I saw the pride on Prince Cadwallon's face as he saw the changes wrought by his father in his absence. The prince had grown too. He was almost a man now and he carried himself with the easy confidence borne of a warrior who has fought for his life and lived to tell the tale. I was just grateful that there were no scars on his face to upset the queen.

We had with us Myrddyn, Gawan, my wife and Nanna. I wanted all of my family as close to me as I could. When I thought I had lost Gawan it had made my family even more precious to me. King Cadfan, too, had filled out. He was no longer the boy I had taken under my wing. He was a king who had increased his kingdom at the expense of the Saxons of Mercia. I was looking forward to seeing him again.

We were greeted like royalty and shown more respect than a mere warrior could expect. The king was grateful for all that we had done. The women left us to sit in the Great Hall and tell each other our information.

He was intrigued by Aethelfrith's raid. "I have heard that his sons, Oswiu and Oswald are still in Hibernia trying to carve out a kingdom there."

"I would have expected them to be with their father on Man?"

Myrddyn shook his head. "Aethelfrith is too cunning for that. He spreads his eggs about. He would regain Bernicia. He cannot do that with the men that you saw on Man. He needs a bigger army than that. He is up to something."

"And you, King Cadfan, how goes the campaign against the Mercians."

"We did have great success; especially when Edwin went to war with you but I think that the alliance of Mercia and Northumbria is at an end. He is now building up his forces against us."

King Cearl had been an ally of King Cadfan's father but he had turned against him. He was as cunning as Aethelfrith and I did not like this news. The buffer against Saxons from the east was Gwynedd. We could not afford for it to fall. I had committed too many men to the north to be able to withstand an attack. Myrddyn saw my concerned expression and he gave the slightest of shakes with his head. I knew that look. He would speak with me in private.

The politics finished with we drank wine and the king asked about the capture of our sons and their escape. "I would not have wished that on either of our sons but I am pleased with the outcome." He held his chalice to Cadwallon, "I salute you, my son, you have become a powerful warrior which was my hope when you left us."

The prince inclined his head. I heard the unspoken question. "I believe your father is asking if you are ready to return to help him to rule the kingdom."

When the king nodded the prince looked at the table as though he was trying to read an invisible message. "I still feel that I have much to learn from the Warlord. Grant me the winter to finish my education and I will return in the spring."

"Very well. I do not blame you for your decision. I still remember, fondly my times with the Warlord and his wizard."

Prince Cadwallon took a deep breath and launched into a speech he had obviously rehearsed. "It is not just that father," he looked at me. "Warlord, I would like to marry Nanna."

I think that I was the most surprised at that. The thought had never crossed my mind but I could see that Gawan was in on the secret and, of course, Myrddyn had divined the answer himself. My silence must have made them think that I disapproved.

"I will make a good husband, Warlord."

I shook myself. I was giving the wrong impression. "No, I do not doubt that but I am trying to take it all in. How does my daughter feel about this?" I looked at King Cadfan, "She can be a little moody."

"She approves of it."

"Then we just have to convince my wife."

Myrddyn laughed, "Warlord she is more than happy about this, believe me."

Gawan nodded, "You mean I am the last to know?"

Prince Cadwallon said, "You have had much on your mind, Warlord."

The arrangements were made for a Yule wedding. It would appeal to the Christians and Pagans alike. The ceremony would be held at my castle for all of the families wished Wyddfa to bless the union.

Chapter 15

There were fewer guests at the wedding than we might have hoped but Lann Aelle, Prince Pasgen and my son could not leave their lands in the middle of winter. Our watchword was still vigilance. But the ceremony went well and they both seemed enamoured of each other. I know that my wife hoped for more grandchildren but I was just happy that my daughter had taken such a wise course. Cadwallon would make a good husband. The prince stayed with us when the guests left. He was still as keen as ever to learn how to be a strategos but he spent every moment of the long dark evenings with my daughter in their quarters.

The days were becoming a little longer and Myrddyn brought Gawan to me. "Warlord, if we are to make your son into the wizard he wishes to be then we need to visit the cave."

I knew this had been coming. The cave was integral to Myrddyn's magic. His grandfather had first taken him there and he had lived there before seeking to serve me. Gawan had to experience the power of the cave. I shivered in anticipation. Would my mother come to speak with him too?

We left one early, chilly morning with snow flurries dancing around the forest. It would not lie so close to the sea but it made riding up the trails a magical experience. Gawan was as excited as I had ever seen. He knew of the power of the cave and he had heard, second-hand, of what had happened to us but this would be a unique occasion. He would be sleeping in the heart of the mystical mountain.

Leading a packhorse with food and kindling we rode in silence through the silent forest which was shrouded in mist. The mantle of snow lay like a cloak around the mountain's shoulders and, once more, the mountain seemed a living being and not an inanimate rock. We dismounted at the entrance to the cave and led our horses inside. They were reluctant to do so and we had to speak quietly to them and use our spirits to make them bend their will to ours.

Gawan gasped as Myrddyn lit the torch which illuminated the inside. The single torch threw shadows dancing around its walls making it seem even more alive. It contrasted with the witch's cave which had seemed dead and empty. We lit a circle of torches around the water and then Gawan and I began to build a fire with the kindling we had brought.

Night came quickly and we saw that outside the cave was now as black as the inside of the cave had been.

We ate a simple meal and laid out our cloaks. The torches and the fire kept out the cold and it felt almost cosy in the cave. Gawan was desperate to sleep so that he could dream but Myrddyn would not let him.

"First you need to drink this potion." He handed Gawan a flask.

"I never had to drink a potion, wizard."

"No, Warlord but your bloodline came directly from your mother. Hogan Lann did not always dream here. The potion merely opens the mind to the door which leads to the Otherworld. It will not harm him; I swear."

"I did not think it would. I was merely curious."

Gawan eagerly swallowed the potion and lay down on his cloak. "Do not try to dream. Just sleep. No matter what you see, you cannot be harmed. Your grandmother's spirit and your ancestors live here and will watch over you."

As he lay down I looked at Myrddyn. The wizard looked like a concerned father. This was a momentous occasion for the wizard. I doubted that he would have a son of his own and, perhaps, Gawan was as close as he would ever get to that state. When we heard Gawan's steady breathing then we knew he was asleep.

"What do you hope for, Myrddyn?"

For the first time since I had met him the wizard looked almost nervous. "I am hoping that he dreams my dream. I dream your dreams and my dreams. If your son dreams of mine as well as his own then it means that he will be a wizard. If not then he will just be a gifted healer."

"And is that a bad thing?"

"No, but Rheged and this land needs another Myrddyn, just as it needs another Warlord. You have been preparing your son to take over for some time. I need to do the same. Neither of us is getting any younger."

I was not surprised that he had divined my intention but I began to wonder what would be the effect of my son having that power too. I lay down on my wolf cloak, closed my eyes and prepared to enter the spirit world.

The wolves were coming for me. They circled in the woods around my city and they made no sound. They came closer and closer. My sentries on the wall saw nothing and when I spoke to one he had no eyes and was as a stone. The beasts began to feast on my horses and the stone sentries and I could do nothing. I was helpless and I found that I could not move. The leader of the pack had red glaring eyes and teeth dripping with the blood and the gore of the dead and he came steadily towards me. He did not rush but he slowly opened his mouth which became, in an instant, as big as the cave. Just before his teeth closed upon me there was a white light which made me cover my eyes and a scream which I suddenly realised came from within me. Then all was black and I saw my mother coming towards me and she was holding Gawan's hand. They both smiled at me and then at each other. Behind them, I saw Myrddyn and he was sleeping. I closed my eyes, for I was tired and I heard my mother's voice, "Trust your son he has the power. Have faith in your men for they fight for you. The end is coming. A new world is dawning." I opened my eyes to ask her a question and she began to fade from view. "You have done all that I have asked you to do and you are the saviour of Rheged. I am proud of you." Then she slipped away and all that was left was a thin grey cloud which disappeared as I looked. I heard a voice saying gently, "Warlord, awake."

I opened my eyes and there was a thin light from outside. The torches had almost burned themselves out and the fire was just red embers glowing against the glistening pool of Wyddfa. He helped me to my feet and we watched as Gawan kept dreaming. Myrddyn held his finger to his lips. Gawan began tossing and turning. He began to mouth unintelligible words. I wanted to wake him. Myrddyn shook his head and then reached down and stroked my son's head. He chanted in the same language which Gawan had used and the tossing and turning ceased and then Gawan lay still.

Myrddyn stood. "Your son will awaken soon." He examined my face carefully. As usual, I knew that he had dreamed my dream, or, at least, a part of it. He seemed satisfied and he began to pack the horses with the cloaks and the torches.

"I saw her."

I looked down. Gawan had awakened. "Your grandmother?"

"She was a lady in white and she knew me." He looked at me curiously, "She held my hand and we saw the wolves trying to eat you. She spoke to me and said you would be safe."

Myrddyn nodded and seemed satisfied. "Was there anything else which you saw?"

"I saw Cadwallon. He was older and a king. He slew King Edwin and then he too was killed by warriors."

At that sombre news, Myrddyn smiled. He saw my shocked expression. "I am not happy at Cadwallon's death but it will not happen until he becomes king. Nor will it happen while Edwin lives. I am happy because I dreamed that too and it means that Gawan will be a wizard. He too can talk to the dead."

"Don't I talk to the dead too?"

"No, they talk to you and that is the difference. Come we need to get back or they will worry about us." He stopped and looked at us both. "What Gawan saw may not come true but we cannot tell the prince. It would change him and King Cadwallon should be the warrior you make him into, Warlord. Your work is not finished."

"From what my mother said, I thought that it was. She said the end was coming. I thought that she meant the end of my life."

"There will be an end but we do not know yet what that will be. We just need to be prepared."

As we rode down the hill Gawan asked, "The wolves; I thought they were our friends for father is the Wolf Warrior."

"There are many kinds of wolves. I believe that these wolves are humans. I believe that they may be treacherous people who try to deceive our friends. These are dangerous times."

"I know. I worry that we have spread our best warriors too thinly. An attack on Caer Gybi now might be disastrous."

"Any attack now might be disastrous. Your son and I have much magic to perform and you have another army to build."

That evening, after the meal, I went to my Great Hall and sat at the oval table I used to speak with my captains. It was empty now for most were far away. My seat was marked by my wolf emblem and I sat there. I laid Saxon Slayer before me as I always did. There was an opening at the far end of the hall and through it, I could see Mona to the west. It was somehow reassuring to see it there when I spoke with my leaders.

"You sit alone Warlord."

I looked up and saw Prince Cadwallon there. "I like to come here sometimes to think." I spread my hand at my table. "This might be my greatest achievement."

"The table?"

"No, my prince, what it represents. Around this table, we are all equal. Any one of my commanders can give his opinion."

The prince smiled. "I have stood in this room and they normally do just as you wish, Warlord."

I laughed, "True but every man has the chance to give me his views and I listen." I looked at him, fixing him with my eye. "Have my decisions been poor ones?"

He blushed, "Forgive me, warlord, I meant no disrespect."

"Here in this room, you need not apologise. Tell me honestly what you think. Just answer the question. You are no longer a boy you are a man who has been blooded in war and now you are my son too."

"No, I do not think you have made poor decisions. *Wyrd* has intervened and you have had to change your plans." He looked around the table and moved his hand across the smooth surface.

"You have a place at this table now."

He looked up at me as though I had offered him a throne. "Me? Where would I sit?"

He was the young squire once more. I waved my hand around the table. "You can see where my leaders have either put their sign or their name. I have the wolf as does my son. There is a boar and a hawk. There is even a dragon."

"A dragon?"

"Aye, the red dragon of your father. As I recall there is an empty space next to it."

"Then I shall have mine in that place; the green dragon which will be my sign."

"A good choice."

"Indeed it is, Prince Cadwallon." We both looked up as Myrddyn and Gawan entered. "The dragon is the symbol of Wyddfa. Its colour can change. Might I suggest the colour should be black for you would be a Wolf Warrior would you not? Their sign is the black wolf."

"The Black Dragon," he mused. "Yes, that will be my sign. I will have a banner made." He looked wistfully at Saxon Slayer. "Would that I had a blade such as that one."

Myrddyn chuckled. "Swords such as that one do not arrive by happenstance. Lord Lann was chosen. A sword will choose you. That reminds me, I must examine the Roman Spatha we found in the witch's cave."

The prince became animated. "Could we do it now?"

"If the warlord is not busy..." He saw my questioning look. I had planned on enjoying some wine and a fire. "The four who discovered it must be there when it is examined."

I sighed; I did not want to disappoint the two young men. "Very well. But it had better be worth it." I realised that I sounded truculent but I didn't care.

Myrddyn's workshop was built into the rock wall of the mountain. He had chosen its position carefully and had had men working for many months until he was satisfied. Prince Cadwallon had never been inside and he walked almost reverently into it. There were baskets with herbs and bottles with liquids. There were powders and pastes and strange pieces of wood but what made you start were the lights which Myrddyn had in the workshop. There were torches and they burned not only brightly but also colourfully. It made it even more magical.

On the bench were the sword and the jet. "The coins?" I asked.

"Inconsequential. I have given them to Brother Oswald. We can melt them down and make our own."

I shook my head. For me, they had been valuable because they had been a link to our Roman past but to the wizard they were metal.

"Now the jet is valuable and we can use them to make protective amulets and necklaces. They are almost as good as the blue stone."

"You mean like the stone my mother and Nanna have on their necklaces?"

"Aye and like the one your father has on Saxon Slayer. Now the sword... I have cleaned it up as you can see."

The blade was polished. The part which had broken off was just the tip and the blacksmith could repair that. We leaned in to see the writing which was clearly seen on the blade. "As I am the only one who can read Latin well, I will read it."

He held the sword up. It make it possible for us to see the words as he read them. **"I WAS MADE FOR ULPIUS: GRANDSON OF THE WARRIOR MACRO: I FIGHT FOR ROME."**

Myrddyn almost caressed the sword. "There is a story behind this blade. Of that I am certain. I will have to dig out brother Osric's papers to see what I can discover."

The prince said, "Can I touch it?"

"Of course."

As soon as he held the blade I watched him shiver. He turned to me with an ecstatic look on his face. "It feels powerful. My fingers tingle."

I looked at Myrddyn who nodded. That was the sign that a sword belonged to you. The wizard carefully took it from the prince and said, "When it is repaired try it again but in daylight where you can see the mountain."

After the boys had gone he said, "The sword called to him. I felt it and I know Gawan did."

"But it is such an old sword."

"It is younger than yours, Warlord, and there is a connection to Rome and the men who defended this land. Your sword came from a place close to a Roman fort and this one was found within twenty miles of your home. They are connected. I have much to do before the spring."

"Why the spring?"

"Because that is when war will come."

The next morning we took the sword outside and Myrddyn handed it to the prince. The sun came out behind the mountain and sparkled on the shining blade.

"That is the sign, Prince Cadwallon. The sword is yours and the mountain approves."

And so Prince Cadwallon of Gwynedd wielded the sword from the stone, the sword of Rome and he used it until the day he died defending the free peoples of Britannia.

Chapter 16

I did not know how he knew but I trusted him. In typical wizard fashion Myrddyn could not tell me where the war would begin, just that it would. I worried that King Edwin would begin to claw back the land from Rheged. I had to trust my son, Hogan Lann. The north would have to rely on him. I could not be in two places at once.

I also knew that I had to do something to prepare and so I summoned my captains, Tuanthal, Daffydd and the garrison commander Llewellyn ap Gruffyd. The prince, Brother Oswald, Myrddyn and Gawan also attended.

"I need to know how many men we could muster if we had to fight."

Tuanthal had already been training his new riders and he looked glum. "There are but fifty I could take to war now. In another month there will be ten more who are ready and thirty others who would give the appearance of numbers."

"Thank you for your honesty. Daffydd?"

"We are more fortunate. With the men from Lord Raibeart and Lord Aelle added to the ones we had already recruited, we could have sixty. In a month they will be better riders."

"Llewellyn?"

"It depends how many men you wish to protect this castle. We have fifty men only here. There are despatch riders and others who work in the castle but we sent most of our men with Lord Hogan Lann."

I did not know if there was criticism in his words but if so it was deserved. We had cut our forces to the bone. "That would only give us ten foot soldiers."

Brother Oswald coughed. "Warlord, the fort at the Narrows has eighty men. You could take some from there."

"Excellent, that would give me another thirty."

Llewellyn asked, "And what of Caer Gybi?"

I shook my head. "We can reinforce the Narrows from here but Caer Gybi protects Mona. We have already taken the archers from the island; my brothers would need the men from Caer Gybi if a war began in the west."

It looked like an impossible situation. Myrddyn stood and studied the map. "I apologise Warlord for not being able to predict where war will begin but we can make plans. You have a mobile army of a hundred and sixty warriors. Captain Tuanthal has another forty who can make your army appear larger. If the war begins in the west then you can gather the men of Mona to aid you."

"And what if the north or the east?" The south was safer as we had allies there and we would have better warning of an attack. The north and the east were the frontiers.

"If it starts in the north then you use the men from Yr Wyddgrug and Caestre. If the east then the other way around. Both forts are well garrisoned."

He was right; we had deliberately been generous with the forces at both forts. Brother Oswald said, "And there is a garrison at the monastery fort of Ruthin. They could be used. It would give you another twenty men."

I felt better. Two hundred of my men were more than a match for a warband of Saxons. "Good. I want them all kept at battle readiness. Tuanthal, take twenty of your men and explain to the commanders of the forts what I expect. It will do them no harm to be more alert too."

Gawan asked, "And what about our ships?"

"That is an excellent thought. I will have Daffydd keep them close to Mona."

Brother Oswald's face told me the story in an instant, "I am sorry Warlord. I sent them on trading missions. Captain Daffydd is on his way to Byzantium." He must have seen my face clouding with anger for he added, hurriedly, "We cannot maintain an army without finance, Warlord, and that means trade."

He was right of course. We had the best army because we were rich and we were rich because of the trade and the peace. They need a good army. It was an inevitable circle. "You are right Brother Oswald but it might have been sensible to keep one ship close to home."

"You will have to use your brothers then, Warlord."

Both of my brothers kept a small ship each for protection and for trade. We only needed them to warn us of an approaching enemy. "You are right Myrddyn. Send a rider to ask my brothers to watch for enemies."

When they had all left me and I was alone with Myrddyn I told him of my fears. "This is my worst nightmare. It is my mother's warning. The wolves are coming and we are alone."

"We cannot know what is intended for us and what path we must follow but I have yet to dream your death."

"Perhaps it is not you who will dream my death. Have you thought of that?"

"I have and I have dismissed the idea as ridiculous. The only other one who could dream your death would be Gawan but you and I are bound by more than blood." He seemed supremely confident. "I will be dreaming of your death."

I almost laughed at the macabre nature of that statement. Myrddyn wanted to be the one to predict my death. I knew that he would not wish for my death but he craved the power of life and death. He was right. Our lives and our destinies were intertwined and depended upon each other.

Prince Cadwallon sought me out as I walked along the beach. "Warlord, I did not wish to bring this up at the meeting for I am new to this sort of thing but why do you worry about the east? My father and his men protect that part of the frontier."

"Your father is a bulwark against the Saxons but his eye is fixed on Mercia. There is a pass from Northumbria which does not touch Mercia. An enemy could strike at the gap between our fort and your father's. It was never a weakness when Aethelfrith was king for he held Caestre but now it is and King Edwin is just cunning enough to exploit that."

I looked northwards. I wondered how my son and my nephew were coping. Was it arrogance on my part which made me think that they might need me? It looked now as though I might need them. Myrddyn was correct, of course, we could never plan for every eventuality. I would have to deal with the problems when they came.

It was when the first of the spring flowers erupted into life that the rider galloped through the gates on his small hill pony. The commander of the guard brought him directly to me. The Prince, Gawan and Myrddyn were with me and we all knew that this could not be good news.

He was a stocky youth, no more than fifteen years old. "Warlord, I have news from King Cadfan. He is besieged by the men of Mercia and he begs you to come to his aid."

I looked at Myrddyn. "So war has come as you predicted. It is just from a different direction to the one I anticipated." I looked at the scout. "You have done well. Rest and then I will write a message for you to take back."

Saxon Slaughter

He shook his head vehemently, "No Warlord. I must return to my people. I will tell him that you are coming. I will be needed to defend my land and my king." With that, he sped from the hall and a few moments later we heard his hooves on the cobbles outside.

Myrddyn smiled, "He is keen."

"And he puts me to shame. My father and my family are in danger and I am not there."

"But we will be."

Captain Tuanthal and Captain Daffydd hurried into the hall. "We heard a messenger had arrived."

"He has. King Cadfan is under attack. Gather the men and send for the men from Ruthin." The men from the Narrows were already with us so we were ready to ride.

Tuanthal asked, "And the other two forts?"

"No, if this attack is at Wrecsam then it is imperative that the Clwyd Valley is protected. We shall have to use the forces available to us."

We were prepared. We had pack horses with spare weapons and the scouts were already champing at the bit. The young boys who were to begin their new role were keen to start their new task.

We left the main gate and headed along the coast road. The men from the monastery would join us at the Clwyd Valley. Hopefully, we would reach Yr Wyddgrug by dark. I wanted to spend the night there and see what intelligence they had for us. Our fort at Yr Wyddgrug had been the most exposed part of our defences in the time of King Iago and we had made it strong with a cleared forest of five hundred paces all around and double ditches. In the last six years, it had been a less dangerous place to live but the men who lived within had continued to improve the defences. We would sleep much easier within its walls.

I turned in my saddle to see the snake of men who followed me. There were just over two hundred of us and then the handful of boys who would act as scouts and slingers. It was not the largest force I had ever led nor was it the most experienced but it would have to do. At least we were just relieving King Cadfan. Hopefully, the Mercians would see our army arriving and assume we had greater numbers.

Prince Cadwallon was silent as we rode along. "Do not worry Prince Cadwallon. We will reach your father tomorrow and then he will be safe; as will your family."

"It is not that Warlord there is a thought at the back of my mind and it is trying to tell me something but I cannot reach it."

Gawan and Myrddyn both became interested. "That is how a wizard works."

I scoffed, "Can it be that important?"

"You speak of magic, Warlord and do not know the magic that exists in all men's minds; if they choose to use it. The prince knows something which the spirit world thinks is important." He turned his attention to the prince."Let us try a game that Gawan and I play."He pointed to the sky and a particularly fluffy cloud. "Do you see that cloud?" He nodded, "What is it?"

"A cloud."

"Good but what does it look like? Say whatever is in your mind."

"I feel embarrassed."

"There are just the three of us. I know you Prince Cadwallon and we will not mock whatever you say."

He sighed, "It looks like a wood with trees in the middle and bushes on the outside."

"What else?"

He suddenly stiffened, "I can see warriors."

"Good and anything..."

"The thought has come into my head. That messenger, from my father; why did he neither address nor recognise me? I have only been gone for a couple of years. He should have known me and my father would have sent a message with someone we knew."

I saw it all clearly. It was a trap. I knew not whether Wrecsam had been attacked by the Mercians or not but this was a trap for me and my men. "What do we do wizard?"

He looked around. We were deep in the valley and halfway between our two forts. "I would suggest, Warlord, putting some of Tuanthal's men on the ridges. I do not think that we are in danger yet for Yr Wyddgrug would have stopped a large band coming down the valley."

"Unless the fort was taken."

"In which eventuality then we would be in grave danger for that is the strongest border fort we possess."

Every warrior was warned and we rode the last few miles in anticipation of an ambush. It never came but I did not regret the vigilance. This was a typical King Edwin trick. I was beginning to see his hand in the twists and turns of his convoluted plots.

Saxon Slaughter

We were all relieved to see the walls of the fort still intact and lit by the rays of the setting sun. My banner still flew from its walls. The scouts had warned the garrison of our arrival and they were waiting for us.

As soon as we entered I leapt from my horse and sought out Gruffyd the commander of the fort. "Have you seen enemies in the past week?"

"There have been scouts in the woods; my men found their signs but they saw nothing."

"Have you heard of any problems at Wrecsam?"

He rubbed his beard. "It is strange but we usually have a rider once every couple of days but there have been none for seven days. I thought perhaps they were busy with the Mercians."

I felt my scalp being to tingle and I rubbed my head. "Did a rider not come through last night or this morning; A youth riding a pony?"

"No, but a single rider can avoid the valley and ride along the other side of the ridge. We patrol it during daylight hours but not the night."

"Ask your patrols to tell you if they saw such a rider. It would have been a few hours ago and, Captain Gruffyd, we are on a war footing."

My men needed no explanation. He merely nodded and strode off. "It seems, Prince Cadwallon that you too have some of the sixth sense which Myrddyn and my son possess. We now have to divine what sort of problem we face."

As we ate a hearty meal of game hunted from around the fort we heard the reports of the patrols. It turned out that they had detected someone riding along the ridge but they had not seen him. His hoof prints clearly showed his outward and homeward journey.

"That alone shows that he was a spy. What we have to discern is his purpose."

Gawan looked puzzled. "Surely it was to ambush us as we raced to the king's rescue?"

"Not necessarily. It could be a ploy to pull us away from our fort and this valley; to isolate Caestre."

"If the Warlord had brought every man he could then the Saxons, or the Hibernians would now be in our castles."

"But the spy spoke the language of my people." The prince looked outraged.

Gawan smiled, "Which makes him either a traitor or someone who can pretend to be what he is not."

I nodded to the prince. "These are all valuable lessons Prince Cadwallon. " I now knew that I had to be on my guard. "Tomorrow we will proceed cautiously and assume that Wrecsam is under attack. I will just take the warriors I brought with me and leave this fort fully manned. I want riders sending to the other forts warning them that they may soon be under attack."

Gruffyd did not seem convinced. "But if it is a large warband then you will be walking into a trap."

"We do not have far to go. We can either send for help or retreat but I will not jeopardise the valley and our heartland until I know what we face." I was aware of how harsh my voice sounded. This was not the way I normally spoke but I only had two of my regular captains and there was no time for debate.

"Daffydd, make sure you have plenty of arrows and, Tuanthal, I want each of your men armed with three javelins. Have two of the scouts bring spare horses with more. We have one advantage and that is that we can hurt them before they close with us and we can run."

Tuanthal shook his head. "We have sixty warriors who will be on foot."

"I know and I will be with them. You and the prince can command the horsemen."

"Are you sure that is wise? It seems risky to me."

"It is but I need a shield wall that they can attack so that you can thin them out. I want them to bleed on our swords and shields. Besides," I added with a wry smile, "they want me so they may well ignore the rest of you."

"And what of us, father?"

"You and Myrddyn can stay here in the fort. There is nothing that you can do in a shield wall."

Gawan looked almost angry. "I may not be able to hold a shield but I can carry your banner and I can wield a sword."

"And I still have a few tricks up my sleeve. We will be with you."

I nodded. I had expected them to make some objection and both could handle a sword. I knew that I would need Myrddyn's eyes and his mind. I took comfort from the fact that my son would be behind me. If we died, then we died together.

The night seemed short after we had made our plans but we were ready. The scouts would ride before us and we would have a screen of horsemen protecting the archers and the shield wall.

Chapter 17

As we left, just before dawn, I said to Gruffyd, "We do not go to our death but this is inevitable. Guard our retreat!"

"I will, Warlord, you have my word." And that was good enough. I knew that they would lay down their lives to enable the survivors to be rescued.

We moved across the col at the head of the valley and the ground suddenly swept west. The land seemed gentler. There were few farms here but sheep grazed the cleared areas whilst few cattle could be seen in the distance. It was hard to see where they would ambush us. I began to doubt myself. Perhaps they had lured us away from the Clwyd Valley and I was doing just what they had predicted I would do.

"Do not doubt yourself, Warlord. If they have deceived us there are enough men in the forts to hold them until we return. We need to see King Cadfan to confirm that he is not under attack."

Poor Prince Cadwallon was on the horns of a dilemma. He felt he was letting me down and yet he still worried about his father. He was learning valuable lessons for the day he became king.

Suddenly a scout, accompanied by one of Tuanthal's warriors galloped up to us. "My lord this scout has ridden to Wrecsam. There is a large army surrounding it"

In a way I was relieved. My forts would be safe and the spy had spoken a partial truth.

"My lord, he also says that there is a warband coming from the north to aid them."

"How many warriors?"

"Two hundred or more."

"Prince Cadwallon, ride to Captain Tuanthal. We will destroy this warband before going to the aid of your father."

As he rode away Gawan said, "This could be the ambush."

I smiled, "You are learning. It is the ambush." I waved my hand around the landscape. "This is not ambush country. He is luring us with his own warband and then he will attack us from," I looked around and saw a low ridge to the north-west, "that direction."

"Then why go there? Why not retreat back to Yr Wyddgrug or Wrecsam?"

"If we go to Wrecsam and manage to enter we are trapped. If we return to Yr Wyddgrug then Wrecsam will fall. Our only hope is to make them ambush knowing that they will."

"Your father is right Gawan. This shield wall of sixty-three men will have to hold while our men weaken them."

We soon saw the warband. They were not in any order; they were just hurrying along the road towards Wrecsam. It looked to me as though there were less than two hundred but it made little difference. As soon as they saw my horsemen they went into a shield wall. Normally that would deter horsemen but mine had archers close by.

"Lock shields!"

As a precaution for the ambush which was coming, I prepared my men to receive warriors armed much as they were. Few of my men had mail but each one had a spear, a shield and a good sword. All wore a leather jerkin studded with metal strips. The Saxons would get a surprise.

I saw Daffydd's men dismount and the scouts held their horses. The rain of arrows was constant until each archer had loosed twenty arrows. Tuanthal and his men charged in and hurled the first of their javelins. Following the arrow storm, many of the Saxons broke ranks and tried to flee. It was what my horsemen had been waiting for and they hunted them down.

I heard a cry from behind me and saw that the trap had been sprung. Two hundred Saxons were moving down the slope in a wedge formation. "Turn and face." I turned to Gawan. "Keep the banner flying. It will spur on our men and dishearten the enemy." I slid my dagger into my left hand and adjusted my helmet so that it was comfortable. The wedge was making steady progress. "Myrddyn, keep your eye on Tuanthal." I could rely on Tuanthal not to abandon me but he would ensure that the first warband could do no more damage. We had to buy him the time. My men thrust their spears before them and we presented a wall of steel.

"Warlord, look at the banner. It is Aethelfrith!"

I had been wrong. It was not Edwin. It was the man I had maimed. His thirst for revenge must have been strong. I could see him as he limped down the hill. His hatred of me worked in our favour for his men came at his pace and that meant my horsemen would have more time to come to my aid. *Wyrd*!

"Keep your shields together and don't let the bastards push us down this slope!" They all cheered. Most of them had never fought alongside my wizard or me and I think they felt it an honour to do so. I looked at

Saxon Slaughter

the faces of those around me and they were smiling and appeared eager to come to grips.

"With your son and the Wolf Banner, we will destroy these pirates!"

The greybeard who spoke those words had scarred arms and I saw the many warrior bands on his sword. These were the kind of men you needed to be alongside you. We might be outnumbered but we had spirit.

"Tuanthal has rallied his men and Daffydd is mounting his archers."

Myrddyn's voice meant that we had some hope. Aethelfrith halted his men just thirty paces from us. It was a strange thing to do but I think he thought they were going to slaughter us and he wanted to gloat.

"I told you that I would return and I have. We will kill you and feast on your heart. When you are dead and the men of Gwynedd are destroyed I will make your women my playthings."

The greybeard mumbled, "If he thinks our women are playthings he is in for a shock!" My men laughed. They were in good spirits

I too laughed. Aethelfrith and his threats were pitiful. "My son and I could kill you and your oathsworn with no more trouble than swatting a fly. Do your worst but this day you die!"

My men roared, "Wolf Warrior!" as Gawan swung my banner above our heads.

He roared his war cry and he launched himself at my thin line of warriors. He was in the second rank of mailed men and his injury made him wince. I brought Saxon Slayer down overhand at the lead warrior, who was much shorter than I was. His sword struck thin air as I split his helmet and head in two. When Aethelfrith's men closed with mine they were met by spears and they could not bring their weapons to bear. I felt Gawan's sword slice down at the warrior to my right and, as he fell, I stepped into the gap and faced a snarling Aethelfrith. I stabbed forwards and he flinched as his shield barely moved my sword. At the same time, I stamped forwards as I punched him in the face with my shield. Their wedge was no longer a wedge and their best warriors were falling. I found some space and I swung the sword at Aethelfrith's head. It caught the side of his helmet with such force that the straps broke and it flew off into the crowd of warriors behind him.

"I have killed many kings with this and today I will kill one who was a king." I swung my sword again and he tried to parry it. Sparks flew as the blades met but he recoiled. His weak leg gave a little and I stabbed down into his chest. Blood spurted and he dropped his sword.

"My sons will avenge me." There may have been more he intended to say but that was all he managed and Aethelfrith the King of Bernicia died.

His men were oathsworn and they hurled themselves at us to avenge their lord. Our spears began to be whittled down and then I heard the sound of wind as sixty arrows dropped from the sky onto the Saxons waiting to get at us. Then the sound of hooves drumming along the ground marked the arrival of my cavalry. Tuanthal led half around their right flank and Prince Cadwallon the other half around their left. This was the first time the prince had led warriors and, as the shield wall collapsed, I was able to see what a great warrior he would become. He laid about himself with his sword and none could withstand him. He and a phalanx of horsemen drove a wedge into the Saxon lines.

"Shield wall, push!" Our locked shields enabled us to push the Saxons into the blades and arrows of the horsemen. They died to a man; the loyal oathsworn of King Aethelfrith of Bernicia died protecting his body.

There were many wounded amongst our men but not as many dead as I had feared. Daffydd had lost none and Tuanthal only three. I had suffered fifteen dead. I mounted one of the spare horses and surveyed the field from its back. As I climbed onto the back of the small pony I winced for my wound ached. I had not fought since it had healed and my body was complaining. I was just happy that the fighting might be over for the day. The ambush had failed but King Cadfan was still besieged. I made my decision and rode back to Myrddyn.

"You stay here with the warriors and the wounded. I will ride with the archers and the horsemen to Wrecsam."

He nodded and picked up three spare javelins which were close to the pack horses. He handed them to me. "Be careful Warlord. The trap may not just have been the work of Aethelfrith. Cearl may be a party to it."

"I will be cautious."

I turned the horse's head around and Gawan said, "And what of me?"

I lifted my helmet from my head, "You can help Myrddyn."

He held the wolf banner up. "And this? What of your standard?"

"I ride on a horse. You cannot defend yourself on a horse if you hold the standard."

In answer he handed the banner to Myrddyn and grabbed the reins of one of the other spare horses; I saw his face show the pain he endured but he hauled himself up into the saddle and held his left hand out for the banner. "I can ride and I can hold the banner. That is enough."

Saxon Slaughter

I opened my mouth to speak and Myrddyn said, "He is your son, Warlord, would you expect anything less?"

"You are right. Come on then you mad men, let us ride to glory."

The men of the shield wall cheered as we trotted off. Their cries of "Wolf Warrior" still rang in my ears. The dead and dying littered the field and my warriors were walking across it despatching the Saxon wounded. Tuanthal pointed to the northwest, "My lord, look there."

I turned and saw the remaining Saxons fleeing towards the coast where, presumably, they had their ships. They would return from whence they came but they had a price to pay yet. I would hunt them down and punish them for this raid.

My horse was little more than a hill pony, as were most of Tuanthal's mounts. This would not allow me to charge and fight on horseback; it could not carry my weight. The beast was to carry me close to their walls so that I could view the town. The scouts we had sent out met us a mile from the besieged burgh.

"Warlord, there are many Saxons around the walls and they are battering at them with their axes."

"But the town still holds?"

"Yes my lord. We saw the king on the fighting platform."

"And do they have warriors watching this way?"

"No, my lord. They are all fighting at the walls. Their king is on the far side leading the men there."

I waved my two captains to me. "It seems that we still have a chance; despite our small numbers." I looked at the horsemen and the archers. We had about a hundred and fifty men. Not a huge number but I wondered what the Saxons would see. If we appeared as a line then they might assume that I had brought the full weight of my army against them. If their king had been with the men we would be facing it might be different but it was worth the gamble. I hoped, at the very least to get myself into the town.

"We will ride and form a long line on the ridge above the town. Daffydd, you place your men on the flanks. We ride as though we are considering charging. I want the men to make as much noise as we can. As soon as we begin to move then place your archers behind the horsemen. We will charge and loose javelins and that will give Daffydd the time to dismount and harass them with arrows. If we can I want the archers and myself to get into the town. Tuanthal, you are to stay outside the walls. Collect Myrddyn and the others and continue to wage a war at distance. I want them weakened. If you need to, then return to our fort and bring some of those warriors. We know that these are the only enemies close to the Clwyd Valley."

Tuanthal had been with me a long time and he too was showing the flecks of grey in his beard but when he grinned, as he did now, he was the young boy I had first taken to war from the Castle Perilous. "At last I get to tell the wizard what to do!"

We all laughed and Gawan shook his head, "Good luck with that one then."

The ridge was a low one and was a mile from the town. It would help us to gain speed when we trotted down the slope.

I waited until the men were in line. I looked at Gawan. "How is the hand?"

"Painful but it will not stop me. You can rely on me." He looked determined. I peered along the line of warriors; Tuanthal was on the right-hand end of the line and Prince Cadwallon on the left, his dragon banner marking him for our enemies.

"I know." I turned along the line, "Wolf Warriors!"

A cheer erupted and they all roared back at me. I saw a few of the faces at the rear of the Saxon attack turn to look at us. Beyond them, I could see that the Mercians had begun to fire the walls. We had no time to lose. "Forward!"

We trotted down the line and I saw the Mercian leader trying to reorganise his men. We were hardly going at more than a fast walk but it must have appeared quicker to those about to receive us. Their numbers were hard to estimate but they must have outnumbered us. Our hope was to carve a hole in their middle and weaken them.

I steadied myself and readied my javelin. It was many years since I had thrown one from the back of a horse. I hoped I would not make a complete fool of myself; I had seen men fall from their horses when they had attempted to throw one. I laughed when I realised that I would not have far to fall. I heard a cheer as Tuanthal's men cheered my laughter. They thought it meant I did not fear the Saxons.

I threw it high knowing that a plunging javelin was harder to avoid and it was an easier throw. As their shields came up we hurled our second one. Tuanthal shouted, "Fall back!"

I dutifully turned along with the other warriors. I noticed that four of Tuanthal's men were within arm's length of me and my son. My captain of horsemen was protecting his Warlord and standard-bearer! I saw

Prince Cadwallon fighting off those Mercians who tried to kill the Prince of Gwynedd. He rode his own horse which was bigger than ours and they stood no chance. He looked imperious as he slew all around him.

The Saxons, seeing how few we were, ran after us. It was a mistake for, as we rode away from them, our archers loosed a flight of arrows high into the air. We wheeled left and right to ride behind them and they loosed another four flights by which time we had ridden around them and were ready to advance once more.

"Forward!"

As we rode towards the enemy again I saw that the ground was littered with their dead. I turned to Gawan, "How does your hand feel?"

"Do not worry, Warlord. Your banner will stand by you."

The Saxons were now totally disorganised. Daffydd and his men had moved forwards to close with the leaderless Saxons. We all threw our last javelins and I looked towards the gate to see if I had a clear passage through to the town. It was a mistake. One warrior, braver than the rest, ran at me and hurled his spear at me. It was not the best thrown spear but it plunged into the throat of my small horse and he tumbled to his death. It was many years since I had fallen from a horse but I remembered what to do. I went with the fall and rolled. When I had been younger it was easier. My age told and I hit the ground hard and was winded. I lay there on the ground staring at the sky.

I heard a yell and saw three Saxons racing to finish off the Warlord. I tried to rise but my mail was heavy. The spear which was intended to stick me like a pig came towards my face. I grabbed the head of the spear and pulled the warrior towards my mailed fist. I heard his nose crack. I heard metal on metal and felt a sharp pain in my leg. I saw a sword held by a triumphant Saxon and it was covered in my blood. Before either he or his companion could finish me off my banner appeared before my face and the pointed end went into my would-be killer's eye. I whipped my shield around just in time to block the sword which swung from the sky.

Gawan wheeled around and leapt from his horse. He planted the standard next to me and drew his own sword. I drew Saxon Slayer and we grinned at each other.

The Saxons had seen me fall and began to flood towards us. There were less than a hundred of them remaining but my son and I would not be able to fight them all. Myrddyn had been wrong; he had not dreamed of my death but it would be a death that would be remembered. The Warlord and his son fighting a warband!

Luckily for us, they came at us one by one. I was winded and I was wounded but I was still the Wolf Warrior. I did not wait for the first spear to stick me; I knocked it aside and gutted the warrior. Gawan took the head from another who tried to kill me with his axe. I heard Tuanthal shouting something from behind me but I dared not look. Then I saw them thirty paces away, being skewered by Daffydd's arrows and I heard the sound of hooves. I began to feel a little weak and I felt the warm blood slide down my leg from the wounded thigh. My death would not be long in coming.

A huge warrior with mail and a full face mask loomed before me. He swung his two handed axe. I could barely move my left arm and I was slow to bring up my shield. Suddenly my wolf standard appeared before me and deflected the axe. Before the warrior could swing again I thrust forwards and Saxon Slayer went beneath his helmet and into his throat. He was a brave warrior and, as he died, he pulled on Saxon Slayer, ripping his dying hands to shreds. I fell with him and landed on his body.

I heard Gawan shout, "Move father!"

I rolled to my right and a sword embedded itself in the dead Saxon's body. I swung my sword blindly and was rewarded when it struck the bone of the warrior's leg. He collapsed in a heap and bled his life away. Gawan held out his mangled hand for me to help raise me. When it touched my thigh and came away bloody he stepped before me. "You are wounded."

"Aye, and I have a shield. Get behind me." He shook his head and stood defiantly.

I could see that there were still forty warriors before us; more than enough to kill us. And then I heard a Roman horn and the northern gate opened. The men of Wrecsam raced towards the Mercians as Tuanthal and his horsemen fell amongst them. They were slaughtered to a man. The men of Wrecsam were wreaking revenge on those who had attacked them and my horsemen were taking out their anger on those who had felled their leader. I have never seen my horsemen be so ferocious and so merciless. Four of them leapt from their horses and helped Gawan to support me.

I turned to speak with Gawan and it was as though I was falling into a dark black hole. My leg did not seem to want to support me and crumpled.

Chapter 18

I awoke to the sight of Gawan and Myrddyn standing over me and both looking concerned. "Did you dream this wizard?" I noticed that my voice sounded sleepy.

"No Warlord, and I have chastised myself many times for not being here with you when you needed me."

"My son did more than well."

"I know. "

"How long have I been here?"

"The battle was yesterday. I arrived last night and it is now morning."

"Have we won?" They both exchanged a look. I could see that they were hiding something from me. Whatever they had given to me for the pain had worked but it had also made me irritable. "I am still the Warlord, tell me!"

Myrddyn nodded at Gawan who began to speak. "The Mercians are still camped at the southern end of the stronghold." He took a deep breath. They have been chanting that you are dead." He paused.

"And the rest?"

"King Cadfan has been badly wounded. We are not certain if he will live. The Mercians will not leave for they think we shall soon be leaderless."

I closed my eyes. I knew what had to be done. I opened them and saw my mail. "Gawan bring me my mail. I will need my standard too."

Myrddyn shook his head and tried to restrain me. "You have had a bad wound. I have had to put in twenty stitches. I do not want them bursting and you bleeding to death."

I scanned the room and saw one of Tuanthal's men holding a torch. "Warrior, bring that torch over here." My men were used to obeying me and he did so but he looked worried. "Cauterise the wound." He shook his head. "That is an order. You are oathsworn." He steeled himself and took a step toward me.

Myrddyn grabbed the torch from his hand. "This is nonsense but if you insist then at least let your healer do it. Gawan lift up your father's undershirt. Guard, grab his arms and stop him from moving."

As Gawan lifted my shirt I saw the angry red line running from my hip down my thigh. It almost reached my knee. It was an impressive wound.

The guard's strong hands gripped my arms and Myrddyn plunged the torch into the wound. There was the usual smell of burning hair and burning flesh but the pain was not as bad as I had experienced before. Myrddyn saw my surprised look and said, "I gave you a potion. It would knock out a horse. Next time I double the dose for you."

Then the pain hit. Waves shot up my side and made me close my eyes and clench my teeth. I gripped the table before me as though I was hanging onto life itself.

"There, are you satisfied now?"

"Put on my mail. We will go and speak with Cearl. Tell the prince I will need him too."

As the mail was lifted over my head I noticed the strong smell of sweat, horse and blood. I needed to have my mail cleaned when all this was over. I strapped my sword on and said to the guard, "Carry my helmet for me. Gawan, my wolf cloak."

I knew that I had to persuade the Mercians that, not only was it me but I was fit and ready to fight; regardless of how I felt.

Gawan walked next to me and I was grateful for his support. My legs did not want to walk. He carried my wolf banner and my shield. When we left the Great Hall we were seen by the men on the walls. They let out a huge cheer. I saw Daffydd on the walls with his archers and he smiled and waved; the relief was clear even from that distance.

"Where is Tuanthal?"

"He is outside the town. He has positioned himself to the north so that he can swoop down on the Mercians should they try anything. We have more men coming from the Clwyd valley; they should be here by noon." I hoped that by noon the Mercians would be gone.

Prince Cadwallon appeared at my side. He looked ashen. "How is your father?"

"He is gravely wounded."

"Myrddyn, go to him."

"When you have spoken with the Mercians then I will go. He has healers. If you are going to do this then let me add a little magic of my own." I did not know what he was up to but I knew that it would be clever. I nodded my agreement. "Prince, if you would wait with the Warlord I will see what I can do." He saw my look, "Let us try a trick like at Penrhyd eh?"

We walked over to the ladder leading to the wooden gatehouse. I say we walked but I limped. The gatehouse still smouldered from where they had tried to fire it. King Cadfan knew better than to have a wooden wall which did not have plenty of water close to hand.

Myrddyn stepped to the top of the tower and nodded to the warrior who held the Roman horn. He sounded a blast on it. Then Myrddyn began to speak. I had learned, over the years that being a wizard needed a lot of acting skills and a good voice. Myrddyn had both. He began to speak and his voice carried across the silent fields to the waiting Mercians.

"Mercians, King Cearl, I am Myrddyn the wizard." He then threw a handful of dust at the torch which still burned at the corner of the tower. It blazed purple, yellow and green and the flames leapt into the air. I heard the gasp from the warriors. I had seen him do that before. It was more effective at night time but, as a trick, it always worked.

I heard an indistinct voice. Then Myrddyn shouted. "Advance, bring just your guards and I swear that you will not be harmed." He glanced down at me and waved for me to ascend halfway up the ladder. Each movement sent rivers of pain running through my body. I gritted my teeth to get halfway and I was relieved when I could stop.

I heard King Cearl. I had never met him but I assumed it must be he. He spoke in Saxon.

"You may be the wizard but the King of Gwynedd and Lord Lann of Rheged are dead. I claim the field and all the lands of those two warriors."

Myrddyn laughed. "You have a handful of warriors and you would walk into this land and take it. There are many warriors just waiting for my command to sweep down on you and end your insolence."

It was the king's turn to laugh and I heard him say, "Then send the handful of men on ponies. Your equites are many miles hence. Do not try to deceive me, wizard. I am not a fool to be taken in by your little tricks."

"And I say that the warlord is not dead."

"Then you lie. My men saw him cut down and be carried from the field. The warrior who thrust his sword into him was one of my greatest champions. The Warlord is dead!" All the Mercians cheered his words.

"Is he?" I could see Myrddyn clearly and he put his hands before him and closed his eyes. He began to chant; the language was neither Saxon nor the language of Britannia but a mixture of Latin and Arabic. I was impressed. He had learned much in Constantinopolis. I knew it meant nothing but they did not. Once again he threw some dust into the torch and then said, "Warlord, I summon you."

I did not need a gesture to tell me what to do and I stepped up the stairs followed by Gawan and the sentry with my helmet. It was my turn to act. I put the pain from my mind and I peered over the wall. King Cearl and twenty oathsworn stood a hundred paces from the walls. Behind him, I could see the massed Mercian army. Had I had all my army we could have swept them from the field but my handful of men could do little damage to such a mighty host.

"I am the Warlord and I am not, as you can see, dead." I saw his men recoil. They had been told I was killed and here I was as large as life. Even the king looked taken aback.

"This does not change anything. Although I am not surprised that Myrddyn is a Necromancer also and has raised the dead. King Cadfan is dead and Gwynedd is mine."

I waved for Cadwallon and he stood there on the other side of Myrddyn holding his banner. "This is Prince Cadwallon. His father lives but, even if he were dead then his son would lead the armies would he not?"

King Cearl was taken aback. "I heard that Aethelfrith had killed him and your son."

"Do not believe snakes, they lie but that one will lie no more for he died at my hand. Here is the Prince of Gwynedd and here is my son Gawan."

King Cearl's shoulders sagged. He was beaten. Two of the warriors stepped forwards. The taller one shouted defiantly, "No matter what the king does, I swear that we will have vengeance for the death of our father."

That was the first time I saw Oswiu and Oswald although they would both become thorns in the side of Rheged.

"Your father had no honour I hope you have more." I slid Saxon Slayer out and held it aloft. "King Cearl, if you withdraw and agree not to attack this land I will not invade and destroy Mercia. This I swear by Saxon Slayer."

The two brothers began to argue with the king but I could see his dilemma. His plans, cunningly wrought, had failed and his ally, Aethelfrith was dead. By harbouring his sons he would now be the enemy of Edwin and he could not afford to fight Edwin and me. He silenced the two brothers with a wave of his hand.

"I will take you at your word but if any more Mercian land is taken then I swear I will not rest until Wyddfa belongs to me."

As they began to leave the field Myrddyn said quietly, "A bold threat to make when so close to the mountain. And now, Warlord, let us get you to bed so that I can look after the king."

I was feeling light-headed and I allowed Gawan to lead me back to my quarters. The warriors on the walls banged their shields in time as we walked across the courtyard. Myrddyn had done it again. I watched his back as he headed to the king's quarters. This would become another legend of the Warlord and Myrddyn; how the Warlord had been brought back from the dead. Even the warriors who were in the stronghold would begin to believe that story in time. Despite what the followers of the White Christ said people liked to believe in magic. I had to confess that it had not harmed my reputation either. I allowed my men to put me to bed, without the armour and as I closed my eyes I saw Gawan giving instructions to the guard on the door. I would not be disturbed.

I ached when I awoke and felt as though I had fallen down a mountain. I looked down at my body and saw the old scars, new scars and the black, almost green bruises from my fall. I was becoming too old to take this kind of punishment. I dressed, albeit awkwardly and surprised the guard at the door. "I am ready for food!"

He smiled at me; a mixture of relief that I was hungry and joy that I was still alive.

"I was ordered to bring you to the Great Hall. The others are there already."

When I entered the hall was full of the leaders of the men who had fought. They all stood when I entered and applauded. Gawan and Prince Cadwallon came over to me to help me to a chair.

"I am not an invalid. I can still walk but I limp a little." I smiled. Despite my words, I was grateful for their support. I had not eaten for more than a day and I had lost much blood.

When I was seated I was brought beer, bread, cheese and cold meats. I was surprised that they had such supplies in Wrecsam. The king had shown great foresight.

I listened to the conversation between Tuanthal, Daffydd and the other leaders. They were all in high spirits. I suspect they had thought we would be defeated and the unlikely outcome would be the topic of conversation for a long time to come. I noticed that neither the king nor the queen was present and I turned to Prince Cadwallon. "How is your father?"

"Myrddyn is still with him. He will live but he was badly wounded."

I could hear, in his voice, how upset he was. I rose. "Take me to him."

"No Warlord, you are recovering yourself."

"I swore an oath to protect your father when he sought my help years ago. I would not let him down now, besides I have supped and I have eaten. I feel better." It was a lie, of course, I felt dreadful. I was playing a part that they all expected. I was the one like the oak tree. So long as I was invincible then Rheged would survive. The fact that I had come so close to death and recovered would merely make me seem more resilient.

The queen was red-faced and tearful. Myrddyn was examining the wound and the king was lying with his eyes closed. The queen said, "Oh, Warlord! Thank you for coming to our aid."

I took her hand. "I will always come to your aid."

King Cadfan's eyes flickered open and he smiled, a little wanly it must be said. "I thank you too Warlord and thank you for making my son the warrior he is. My people on the walls said he fought like ten men and slaughtered the Saxons."

"He is a powerful warrior and you can be proud of him." He gestured to the bed and I sat down. I looked at Myrddyn, "Well wizard, will he live?"

Gawan was shocked, "Father you cannot ask that!"

King Cadfan smiled, "He is right to do so and I would know that answer too."

Myrddyn was not put out by either response. "You will live your majesty but you will never use your left arm again and your leg may have to be amputated at some point. You will be crippled for the rest of your life."

He closed his eyes briefly and then when he opened them he took his wife's hand. "But I will live and that is something." He looked at Prince Cadwallon. "Son, I would ask a favour of you."

The prince was almost tearful. He had grown up in the past few years but it was still a short time since he had been but a boy. "Anything father, anything."

"I would that you would take over the mantle of king. I will retire and you shall rule as King Cadwallon."

It did not shock me; I knew the king better than anyone but it was still slightly unexpected.

The prince looked at me and then Myrddyn. Myrddyn nodded and I said, as I bowed, "Your majesty I swear I will protect you and this land as I tried to do for your father. I think you will be a good king."

Saxon Slaughter

Gawan and Myrddyn both bowed and, after what seemed an age, King Cadwallon also nodded and said, "I accept."

We left eight days later after the coronation and after the walls and defences had been repaired. My daughter had arrived to be with her husband and she was overwhelmed with her new title. She was now a Queen. Myfanwy agreed to stay with her for a while and help her in any way she could. Our reunion was brief but loving. We had both nearly lost each other and, when she returned to our home we had much to make up.

We travelled back to my home, a little more slowly than we had arrived. The bodies of the dead Saxons still lay where they had fallen but they were now picked clean of flesh by the carrion birds. We had gained much metal and lost fewer men than we usually did but it had been a costly battle for us. We had lost a king and I knew that I would never be able to fight as I had that day before Wrecsam. The next time I fought I would die; even if Myrddyn had not dreamed of my death. I knew it.

I turned to Gawan and Myrddyn as we dropped down the Clwyd valley under the shadow of Wyddfa. "When I am a little better I would go to the cave."

"Why father?" There was fear in Gawan's voice.

"Because I need to."

"I think you are right to do so and I wish to communicate with the spirits too. I did not see as much as I should have and I believe that the spirit of the witch is on Mona. There is evil in our land and I fear it will destroy Rheged unless we can find it and destroy it."

I smiled at Gawan, "And remember, my son, our family is sworn to protect Rheged, even if it cost us our lives."

The End

Glossary

Name-Explanation
Aidan- one of Lann's captains
Aedh-Despatch rider and scout
Aelfere-Northallerton
Aelle-Monca's son and Lann's stepbrother
Aethelfrith-King of Bernicia and Aethelric's overlord
Alavna-Maryport
Artorius-King Arthur
Banna-Birdoswald
Belatu-Cadros -God of war
Belerion-Land's End (Cornwall)
Bors- son of Mungo
Byrnie – mail shirt
Caedwalestate-Cadishead near Salford
Caergybi-Holyhead
Cadfan- King of Gwynedd
Cadwallon ap Cadfan- Prince of Gwynedd
Civitas Carvetiorum-Carlisle
Constantinopolis-Constantinople (modern Istanbul)
Cymri-Wales
Cynfarch Oer-Descendant of Coel Hen (King Cole)
Daffydd ap Gwynfor-Lann's chief sea captain
Daffydd ap Miach-Miach's son
Dai ap Gruffyd-Prince Cadfan's squire
Delbchaem Lann-Lann's daughter
Din Guardi-Bamburgh Castle
Dunum-River Tees
Dux Britannica-The Roman British leader after the Romans left (King Arthur)
Erecura-Goddess of the earth
Einar- A Dane serving the Warlord
Fanum Cocidii-Bewcastle
Felan-Irish pirate
Freja-Saxon captive and Aelle's wife
Gareth-Harbour master Caergybi

Saxon Slaughter

Garth-Lann's lieutenant
Gawan Lann-Lann's son
Glanibanta- Ambleside
Gwynfor-Headman at Caergybi
Gwyr-The land close to Swansea
Halvelyn- Helvellyn
Haordine-Hawarden Cheshire
Hen Ogledd-Northern England and Southern Scotland
Hogan Lann-Lann's son
Icaunus-River god
King Cadfan Ap Iago-King of Gwynedd
King Ywain Rheged-Eldest son of King Urien
Lann-[1] Warlord of Rheged and Dux Britannica
Loge-God of trickery
Loidis-Leeds
Maeresea-River Mersey
Mare Nostrum-Mediterranean Sea
Metcauld- Lindisfarne)
Mungo-Leader of the men of Strathclyde
Myfanwy-Lann's wife
Myrddyn-Welsh wizard fighting for Rheged
Nanna Lann-Lann's daughter
Nithing-A man without honour
Nodens-God of hunting
Oswald-Priest
Penrhyd- Penrith, Cumbria
Penrhyn Llŷn- Llŷn Peninsula
pharos- lighthouse
Pol-Equite and Hogan Lann's standard-bearer
Prestune-Preston Lancashire
Prince Pasgen-Youngest son of Urien
Raibeart-Lann's brother
Riemmelth- Prince Pasgen's daughter
Roman Bridge-Piercebridge (Durham)
Roman Soldiers- the mountains around Scafell Pike
Scillonia Insula-Scilly Isles
Solar-West facing room in a castle

---

[1] Lann means sword in Celtic

Sucellos-God of love and time
Tatenhale-Tattenhall near Chester
The Narrows-The Menaii Straits
Treffynnon-Holywell (North Wales)
Tuanthal-Leader of Lann's horse warriors
Vectis-Isle of Wight
Vindonnus-God of hunting
Wachanglen-Wakefield
Wrecsam- Wrexham
wapentake- Muster of an army
Wide Water-Windermere
Wyddfa-Snowdon
Wyrd-Fate
Y Fflint-Flint (North Wales)
Ynys Enlli-Bardsey Island
Yr Wyddgrug-Mold (North Wales)

Historical note

I mainly used four books to research the material. The first was the excellent Michael Wood's book "*In Search of the Dark Ages*" and the second was "*The Middle Ages*" Edited by Robert Fossier. The third was the Osprey Book- "*Saxon, Viking and Norman*" by Terence Wise. I also used Brian Sykes' book, "*Blood of the Isles*" for reference. In addition, I searched online for more obscure information. All the place names are accurate, as far as I know, and I have researched the names of the characters to reflect the period. My apologies if I have made a mistake.

There is evidence that the Saxons withdrew from Rheged in the early years of the seventh century and never dominated that land again. It seems that warriors from Wales reclaimed that land. I have used Lord Lann as that instrument. King Edwin did usurp Aethelfrith. Edwin was allied to both Mercia and East Anglia.

There is a cave in North Yorkshire called Mother Shipton's cave. It has a petrifying well within. Objects left there become covered, over time, with a stone exterior. In the seventeenth century, a witch was reputed to live there. I created an earlier witch to allow the Roman sword to be discovered and to create a link with my earlier Roman series.

The Saxons and Britons all valued swords and cherished them. They were passed from father to son. The use of rings on the hilts of great swords was a common practice and showed the prowess of the warrior in battle. I do not subscribe to Brian Sykes' theory that the Saxons merely assimilated into the existing people. One only has to look at the place names and listen to the language of the north and northwestern part of England. You can still hear anomalies. Perhaps that is because I come from the north but all of my reading leads me to believe that the Anglo-Saxons were intent upon conquest. The Norse invaders were different and they did assimilate but the Saxons were fighting for their lives and it did not pay to be kind. The people of Rheged were the last survivors of Roman Britain and I have given them all of the characteristics they would have had. They were educated and ingenious. The Dark Ages was the time when much knowledge was lost and would not reappear until Constantinople fell. This period was also the time when the old ways changed and Britain became Christian but I have not used this as a source of conflict but rather growth.

King Cadfan was succeeded by his son when he was still alive and he retired to a quiet life. I have used this battle with the Mercians as the reason for that retirement. It was also about this time that Aethelfrith was killed in battle. His sons, Oswiu and Oswald became famous and outshone their father and Edwin. King Cadwallon became the last great British leader until modern times. Alfred ruled the Saxons but no one held such sway over the country from Scotland to Cornwall in the same way that King Cadwallon did. Of course, I have him aided by Lord Lann the Warlord.

The Warlord and King Cadwallon will return and they will meet the Saxons once more on the field of battle.

Griff Hosker
February 2014

Saxon Slaughter

Other Books by Griff Hosker

If you enjoyed reading this book, then why not read another one by the author?

Ancient History

The Sword of Cartimandua Series
(Germania and Britannia 50 A.D. – 128 A.D.)
Ulpius Felix- Roman Warrior (prequel)
The Sword of Cartimandua
The Horse Warriors
Invasion Caledonia
Roman Retreat
Revolt of the Red Witch
Druid's Gold
Trajan's Hunters
The Last Frontier
Hero of Rome
Roman Hawk
Roman Treachery
Roman Wall
Roman Courage

The Wolf Warrior series
(Britain in the late 6th Century)
Saxon Dawn
Saxon Revenge
Saxon England
Saxon Blood
Saxon Slayer
Saxon Slaughter
Saxon Bane
Saxon Fall: Rise of the Warlord
Saxon Throne
Saxon Sword

Medieval History

The Dragon Heart Series
Viking Slave
Viking Warrior
Viking Jarl
Viking Kingdom
Viking Wolf
Viking War
Viking Sword
Viking Wrath
Viking Raid
Viking Legend
Viking Vengeance
Viking Dragon
Viking Treasure
Viking Enemy
Viking Witch
Viking Blood
Viking Weregeld
Viking Storm
Viking Warband
Viking Shadow
Viking Legacy
Viking Clan
Viking Bravery

The Norman Genesis Series
Hrolf the Viking
Horseman
The Battle for a Home
Revenge of the Franks
The Land of the Northmen
Ragnvald Hrolfsson
Brothers in Blood
Lord of Rouen
Drekar in the Seine
Duke of Normandy
The Duke and the King

Saxon Slaughter

Danelaw
(England and Denmark in the 11th Century)
Dragon Sword
Oathsword

New World Series
Blood on the Blade
Across the Seas
The Savage Wilderness
The Bear and the Wolf
Erik The Navigator
Erik's Clan

The Vengeance Trail

The Reconquista Chronicles
Castilian Knight
El Campeador
The Lord of Valencia

The Aelfraed Series
(Britain and Byzantium 1050 A.D. - 1085 A.D.)
Housecarl
Outlaw
Varangian

The Anarchy Series England 1120-1180
English Knight
Knight of the Empress
Northern Knight
Baron of the North
Earl
King Henry's Champion
The King is Dead
Warlord of the North
Enemy at the Gate
The Fallen Crown

Saxon Slaughter

Warlord's War
Kingmaker
Henry II
Crusader
The Welsh Marches
Irish War
Poisonous Plots
The Princes' Revolt
Earl Marshal
The Perfect Knight

Border Knight
1182-1300
Sword for Hire
Return of the Knight
Baron's War
Magna Carta
Welsh Wars
Henry III
The Bloody Border
Baron's Crusade
Sentinel of the North
War in the West
Debt of Honour
The Blood of the Warlord

Sir John Hawkwood Series
France and Italy 1339- 1387
Crécy: The Age of the Archer
Man At Arms
The White Company
Leader of Men

Lord Edward's Archer
Lord Edward's Archer
King in Waiting
An Archer's Crusade
Targets of Treachery
The Great Cause

Saxon Slaughter

Struggle for a Crown
1360- 1485
Blood on the Crown
To Murder a King
The Throne
King Henry IV
The Road to Agincourt
St Crispin's Day
The Battle for France
The Last Knight
Queen's Knight

Tales from the Sword I
(Short stories from the Medieval period)

Tudor Warrior series
England and Scotland in the late 14th and early 15th century
Tudor Warrior

Conquistador
England and America in the 16th Century
Conquistador

Modern History

The Napoleonic Horseman Series
Chasseur à Cheval
Napoleon's Guard
British Light Dragoon
Soldier Spy
1808: The Road to Coruña
Talavera
The Lines of Torres Vedras
Bloody Badajoz
The Road to France
Waterloo

The Lucky Jack American Civil War series

Saxon Slaughter

Rebel Raiders
Confederate Rangers
The Road to Gettysburg

Soldier of the Queen series
Soldier of the Queen

The British Ace Series
1914
1915 Fokker Scourge
1916 Angels over the Somme
1917 Eagles Fall
1918 We will remember them
From Arctic Snow to Desert Sand
Wings over Persia

Combined Operations series
1940-1945
Commando
Raider
Behind Enemy Lines
Dieppe
Toehold in Europe
Sword Beach
Breakout
The Battle for Antwerp
King Tiger
Beyond the Rhine
Korea
Korean Winter

Tales from the Sword II
(Short stories from the Modern period)

Other Books
Great Granny's Ghost (Aimed at 9-14-year-old young people)

For more information on all of the books then please visit the author's website at www.griffhosker.com where there is a link to contact him or visit his Facebook page: GriffHosker at Sword Books

Milton Keynes UK
Ingram Content Group UK Ltd.
UKHW020723021024
1958UKWH00081B/2010

9 781724 460257